# Murder

### at

## Ebbets Field

# Murder
## at
# Ebbets Field

## TROY SOOS

KENSINGTON BOOKS

KENSINGTON BOOKS are published by

Kensington Publishing Corp.
850 Third Avenue
New York, NY 10022

Library of Congress Card Catalog Number: 94-073288
ISBN 0-8217-4889-0

First Printing: April, 1995

Printed in the United States of America

# Murder

at

## Ebbets Field

# Chapter One

**A**ncient hostilities, rooted in tradition and nurtured by each generation, were once again about to explode into open warfare. And I was in foreign territory, about to serve as one of the combatants.

I gave my uniform one last check. It was clean and pressed and needed no adjustment, but I rebuckled my belt a notch tighter anyway. The biting grip around my gut made me feel meaner, more primed for battle. Ready now, I hopped out of the visitors' dugout and onto the turf of Ebbets Field.

"Go back to the Polo Grounds, ya jerk ya!" greeted my entrance.

I immediately told myself to ignore the hoarse yell and tried not to flinch any acknowledgment that I'd heard. I knew it wasn't aimed at me personally. One of the few advantages of being an underutilized utility infielder was that hecklers cast most of their invective at the stars. They rarely squandered it on Mickey Rawlings.

That Dodger fan behind the dugout probably didn't even know my name. It was my uniform that incited him. The road gray of the flannels identified me as a visiting player—the enemy. And the black interlocking *NY* on my left sleeve branded me a mortal enemy—a New York Giant.

This was my first experience with a baseball rivalry so fierce. Two years ago, when I played for the Boston Red Sox, our matches against the Yankees were often more brawls than games, but I don't think it was really a "rivalry" since everybody hated the Yankees. Whatever it was, it was kids' stuff compared to the blood feud that existed between the Giants and the Dodgers.

Although it was still an hour until game time, both decks of the intimate ballpark were more than half-filled; today was sure to be a sellout, and soon there would be 20,000 Brooklyn rooters crammed into the park. The boisterous Saturday crowd seemed to hover over me, pressing against my back. The seats were so close to the playing field that a fan who tired of hurling jeers could almost reach out and throw a punch—not an uncommon means of expression here in the wilds of Flatbush.

I quickly walked toward second base, stepping past the row of bats on the ground in front of the dugout. The infield grass, what was left of it, crunched underfoot. New York had been in a scalding dry spell for two weeks, and despite the best efforts of the groundskeepers, the turf was now little more than scanty yellow thatch.

While my teammates exchanged warm-up tosses in left field, I inspected the basepaths. I wanted to see how a ball would play on this ground—how high it would bounce, where it would roll. As I walked, my spikes clacked without making a dent. The sun had baked the clay of the basepaths to rock and left the burnt brown surface cracked and peeling. With the hard earth and sparse grass, ground balls would shoot across this infield. To have a chance at fielding them,

I'd have to play deep, all the way back on the edge of the outfield grass.

I didn't get into many games, but I prepared for each one as if I was a starter. A utility player's career depended on attention to details and doing the little things right. I wasn't a slugger who could win a game with one swing of the bat, but I'd be the one to lay down a sacrifice bunt to move the winning run into scoring position. And if we needed a base runner, and the pitcher threw me one inside, well, I'd manage to take it on the hip while pretending to twist out of the way.

A sudden roar of taunting jeers from behind the third base dugout told me another Giant had emerged. And the vigor of the cussing told me it had to be John McGraw. The Giants' manager was a lightning rod for abuse at every park in the National League, but he was especially hated here in Ebbets Field.

McGraw, impervious to the badgering, calmly strode to the bullpen along the left field foul line where Christy Mathewson was pitching to Chief Meyers. McGraw carried himself as if he fully believed himself to be the *"Little Napoleon"* the sportswriters had dubbed him.

"Yer headin' for the cellar, McGraw!" a voice screeched from the bleachers.

I looked above the left field wall and quickly reassured myself that we were *not* heading for the cellar, though we had been slipping lately. The flags of all eight National League teams flew above the outfield wall, arranged from left field to right according to their order in the standings. The one next to the left field foul pole was the black and orange banner of the New York Giants. We were going into the first day of August in first place, three games ahead of the Chicago Cubs. If we could hold the lead, the Giants would win the 1914 pennant, their fourth in a row. And I would be going to my first World Series. To play in a World Series, even in only one inning of one game, was my greatest ambition. That and to someday bat over .250.

The Dodgers' blue and white flag was above the right field wall. All the way in right. They were in last place, out of competition for the league championship. The Dodger fans were cramming this ballpark not to cheer their team on to a pennant, but to demand that they do the second best thing: kill the Giants' chances.

A loud plocking sound reverberated below the Brooklyn flag. The noisemaker was Casey Stengel, the Dodgers' star right fielder. Wearing dark glasses to fend off the intense sun, he was throwing a baseball at the concrete wall and fielding the rebounds. Not an easy task because the wall had a fold that ran along its middle. The right field fence was constructed in a way that gave it a buckled look, with a bottom half that sloped back and an upper section that rose vertically. The only thing odder than the shape of the fence was the advertising that covered it. Stengel was throwing at a billboard that bragged:

> *Casey Stengel Caught 400 Flies Last Season*
> *Tanglefoot Fly Paper Caught 10 Million*

I thought maybe he didn't like the comparison. Myself, I'd have been flattered.

• • •

After batting practice, McGraw sat in the middle of the dugout bench, penciling in the lineup card. I sat a few feet away from him, peering from the corner of my eye to see if I'd be on it.

"Mr. McGraw!" A husky ruddy-faced man of about thirty-five stood in front of the bench. He was casually dressed in a light blue soft-collar shirt and tan trousers that hung from burgundy suspenders. The straw boater he wore was tilted so far back that it made his head look like a big sunflower. "A word if you please," he asked.

McGraw's pencil stopped. "What?" The tone suggested he didn't please.

"Allow me to introduce myself, Mr. McGraw. I'm Elmer Garvin." He stuck out his hand. McGraw dismissed it with a glare. Garvin quickly slipped his hands in his pockets and coins began to jingle. "I'm a director with the Vitagraph Motion Picture Company—" I paid close attention now. Baseball was my life, but the movies were my passion.

"What's that got to do with me?" McGraw grunted.

The pocket change rattled louder and Garvin's face grew redder. "We're making a baseball picture, Mr. McGraw. With Miss Florence Hampton." He jerked his left hand out of his pants long enough to point to a box seat on the home plate side of the Dodger dugout. There, wearing a broad-brimmed pink bonnet, was a lady I'd seen many times before, in a dozen Vitagraph productions and on the covers of *Photoplay* and *Moving Picture World* magazines. The details of her face weren't clear from this distance, but I could see a toothy white smile that shone out from the shadow of her bonnet. On the field in front of her, two men were carefully placing a wooden box on top of a hefty tripod. While I watched the camera being set up, I heard Garvin say, "We'd like to use one of your players for a few shots—give the picture some realism, you see—" At this, I turned back to Garvin and McGraw.

"My players got a game to win. We ain't in the picture business."

Garvin's voice became higher and his hands worked his pockets so vigorously I thought he'd tear a hole through them. "The Dodgers are letting us have Casey Stengel," he said plaintively.

"The *Dodgers* ain't in a pennant race."

Garvin pulled both hands from his pockets and flailed them about in the air, pleading incoherently. I felt sorry for him. McGraw wasn't exactly known for cooperation. There had been no World Series in 1904 because McGraw had refused to play an American League team—"minor leaguers" he'd called them.

A tall elderly gentleman approached from behind the director. He was overdressed for ninety-degree heat but appeared entirely comfortable in a charcoal gray tweed suit. Most men in the stands had removed their coats and some had undone their collars; this one not only wore a high tight collar but a navy cravat was around his throat, a pin-striped vest covered his lean torso, and spotless white spats topped his high-button shoes. "Mr. Garvin, perhaps I can be of some service," he said. "Mr. McGraw and I are fellow Lambs, you know." He spoke with a foreign-sounding accent—and it wasn't Brooklyn. It was stilted and proper. English, maybe, but not exactly English.

Garvin stepped back and spread his hands as if to say, "He's all yours."

His reinforcement stepped forward and lifted his black Homburg enough to expose a fringe of snowy hair. "Arthur V. Carlyle, Mr. McGraw. Perhaps you'll recall that we've met at the Club."

McGraw said with little enthusiasm, "Yes, how are you, Mr. Carlyle?"

"Very well, I thank you." Carlyle made a slight bow. "Did Mr. Garvin here explain to you about this baseball picture he's filming?" McGraw nodded. "Well, to be frank, he's in need of some assistance. He needs something special for the picture, something that will make it more than just another flicker."

Garvin gave Carlyle a look that showed he didn't think it would be "just another flicker" with or without McGraw's help.

Carlyle went on soft-soaping McGraw. "If you would be so kind as to allow one of your players to be filmed, it will give the picture much greater realism—and stature, of course. Please, Mr. McGraw. For a fellow Lamb."

McGraw paused. I wasn't sure what a Lamb was—and it didn't seem a description that could ever apply to McGraw— but this appeal to Lamb loyalty appeared to be working. "All right. You can use one player," he conceded. *"After* the game."

Garvin piped up, "How about Christy Mathewson?"

McGraw shot back, "How about Mickey Rawlings?"

"Who's Mickey Rawlings?" Garvin asked. I was thinking nearly the same thing: Who, me?

McGraw jerked his thumb at me. *"This* is Rawlings." Garvin looked unimpressed.

Carlyle said, "Thank you, Mr. McGraw. We do appreciate it." Then he turned to me. "Mr. Rawlings, would you be so good as to join us after the game?"

I gulped and nodded.

Carlyle touched Garvin's elbow and led him away. I heard Garvin mumble, "Who the hell is Mickey *Rawlings?"* and Carlyle respond, "They're only baseball players, Mr. Garvin. I expect one is the same as another."

McGraw finished the lineup card and I wasn't on it. It

didn't seem quite so disappointing this time. I was going to be in a movie!

• • •

The game started with Brooklyn's Sloppy Sutherland facing the top of our batting order. Sutherland was short for a pitcher, about five foot eight, and his build was slight. In fact, he was about my size, but he had a whipping right arm that had won twenty games for the Dodgers in his rookie season. Now in his second year, he already had seventeen wins with two months left to play. He quickly showed himself ready to garner number eighteen, striking out the side on an economical ten pitches.

In contrast, fifteen-year veteran Christy Mathewson struggled from the beginning. By the fourth inning, it was clear that his trademark fadeaway pitch wasn't fading sufficiently far away from the Dodger bats. To the vocal delight of the Brooklyn partisans, they pounded him for six runs, with Stengel driving in three of them on a pair of doubles. The mood in our dugout grew grim. For the league champions to lose to the cellar dwellers was bad enough, but for that team to be the Dodgers and for us to lose on their home ground was humiliating.

As the game progressed, I divided my attention between the movie crew and the ballfield. The cameraman cranked away at the action on the field; Garvin stood near him, waving his arms as if directing the game. Between innings, the camera was swung toward the stands to film crowd scenes. The hams in the crowd obliged, standing and waving whenever it was aimed in their direction.

In the top of the sixth inning, McGraw barked at me,

"Rawlings! You're up for Matty." With the game a lost cause, it made sense to rest Mathewson for the pennant stretch.

I picked up my lightest bat, one that would give me a quick swing. As I walked to the plate, I glanced at the infielders. I noticed the second baseman move in a few steps. Normally it would be a wise move since I wasn't a power hitter. But with the ground rock-hard, he had just made a mistake.

Stepping into the batter's box, I quickly went through my standard ritual: a scrape of the ground with my right shoe, two half-swings with the bat, and then the involuntary part— the nervous flip of a stomach that tended to be overly impressed by big-league pitchers.

Sutherland loaded the horsehide with talcum powder from his hip pocket. A talcum ball, a more hygienic version of a spitball, was the only pitch he threw. Like a spitter, it would squirt out of his fingers as hard as a fastball but with no spin. It was an unpredictable pitch, as likely to veer at my head as to bounce on the plate.

Sutherland's first pitch didn't go to either of these extremes; he put it waist-high on the outside corner, right where I wanted it. With an inside-out swing, I slapped down at the ball, driving a bouncer toward second. A routine groundout, nine times out of ten, but the second baseman hardly had a chance to react before the ball scooted past him to right field.

A fine piece of hitting, I complimented myself as I arrived at first base. If the cameraman caught it, maybe it would be used in the picture. I looked back next to the Dodger dugout. To my horror, blue-suited stadium police were removing the camera from the field and escorting the Vitagraph crew out of the park. *What about my movie?*

Florence Hampton was the only one of the movie people

who remained. Of course, since she owned a share of the Dodger team, she couldn't be kicked out.

I didn't get beyond first base as Sutherland retired the rest of the side. When Rube Marquard took Mathewson's place on the mound, I was out of the game, my work done. Back on the bench, I stared wistfully at Miss Hampton. She showed no embarrassment at the eviction of her coworkers. Instead, she threw herself into cheering her team, waving a Dodger pennant and yelling encouragement to the Brooklyn hitters.

The Dodgers added two more runs to none for the Giants by the time Sutherland struck out Chief Meyers to end the game. Before the umpire lowered his arm from the strike call, I was off the bench and on my way to the railing in front of Florence Hampton.

She rose to her feet, displaying a tall shapely figure well-defined by a ruffled white shirtwaist and an ankle-length pink skirt. A broad scarlet sash was tied around her narrow waist, giving her something of an old-fashioned but very appealing hourglass form. Long locks of strawberry blond hair that had escaped from her bonnet hung down along her cheeks in loose curls; they framed a face that featured large bright blue eyes, high cheekbones, and a slim nose with a slight upturn at the end.

"You must be Mr. Rawlings," she said. "Thank you for agreeing to help us with our picture."

"Am I still going to be in a movie?" I blurted. "The camera's gone."

She flashed a warm smile. "Yes, you'll still be in the picture." I noticed she was holding a white-gloved hand over the rail. It was palm down, with her fingers bent. I wasn't sure if I was supposed to shake it or kiss it.

Remembering my manners, I said, "It's nice to meet you,

Miss Hampton." I took her hand lightly and shook it sideways.

By now, Casey Stengel had trotted in from right field. Instead of shaking her hand, he doffed his cap and made a deep bow, proclaiming, "Charles Dillon Stengel, at your service."

Florence Hampton laughed. It was an easy honest laugh that lit up her eyes and rocked her shoulders.

Stengel looked delighted at her reaction, his face contorting into a massive grin.

Miss Hampton said, "We've had to make a small change in plans. Mr. Ebbets decided he doesn't want us filming in his ballpark, so we're going to finish the picture at the studio. That's only fifteen minutes from here by automobile. If you pick up whatever you need in the clubhouse, I'll drive you boys there."

"Yes ma'am," I said, and took off for the locker room. Stengel sprang away, too.

She yelled after us, "I'll meet you outside the right field gate. And don't change clothes. Keep your uniforms on!"

Trotting to the clubhouse, I remembered hearing rumors that she often asked ball players to do just the opposite.

# Chapter Two

I pushed my way out of Ebbets Field through a door in the bent right field wall. I was still dressed for the game but not comfortable about it. Bedford Avenue was not the place to be wearing a Giants uniform.

At least there weren't many people on the street. Charlie Ebbets had built his ballpark on a filled-in swamp known as Pigtown in a desolate area of Flatbush near Crown Heights. The neighborhood hadn't changed much since he opened the park in the spring of 1913. A small cluster of shanties across the street was the only nearby habitation. Four scruffy goats nibbling at a pile of garbage next to the shacks were the only visible inhabitants.

Casey Stengel soon joined me; he popped out of the gate whistling with great gusto but no melody. Like me, he had his gear in one hand and folded street clothes in the other. I thought if we were making a comedy, Stengel would be sure to steal the picture. He wouldn't need the baggy pants of Charlie Chaplin or the roly-poly build of Fatty Arbuckle. Nature had given him an audacious nose and jumbo ears that were guaranteed to generate laughs.

"Good game," I said.

"Well, I never really had a problem with Mathewson. See, that fadeaway pitch he throws, well there was this fellah in Kansas City—Piano Legs Donlin I think his name was—and he threw the exact same thing, except I think he had a different name for it. But the way I figure, it's nothing more than a curve ball that takes a wrong turn. Now me being left-handed, when a righty like Matty throws that fadeaway it breaks away from me the same as if a lefty threw me a regular curveball—"

With a screech of tires, a shiny blue Pierce-Arrow touring car swung around the corner from Montgomery Street. As it raced toward us, I saw Florence Hampton in the driver's seat. She pulled over in front of us, stopping the car so sharply that she almost stalled the engine.

Stengel hopped into the front seat, still talking, something about a pitcher in Memphis I think. I hoisted myself from the running board onto the back seat, laying my clothes on the soft white leather upholstery and my equipment bag on the floor. Unlike Stengel, I had kept my cleats on. I twisted my feet sideways so as not to damage the thick carpeting on the floor.

Miss Hampton hastily looped a red silk scarf over her bonnet and knotted it under her chin. In the sunlight, she looked younger than she did on screen, probably not more than thirty.

"We're off!" she yelled as she deftly threw the car into gear. Picking up speed, she made a hard right onto Sullivan Place. The main entrance of the ballpark was coming up on our right, and people were still flowing out of it. Stengel sat up and turned a little so the large blue *B* on his left breast could be seen. Then he took his cap off and waved it at the fans. A few cries of "Casey!" went up from the crowd. I quickly removed my own cap and tucked the red bill into the crease of the seat. Then I folded my arms across my chest and laid my hand over the *NY* on my left sleeve.

Florence Hampton slowed down in the heavy traffic, driving cautiously now. Without once using her horn, she carefully negotiated the car ahead, patiently giving right-of-way to pedestrians and horses.

Until we got to the tracks, the crisscross of trolley tracks that gave the Brooklyn team its original name of Trolley Dodgers, where she suddenly turned into a race car driver, zipping along with a speed and daring that Barney Oldfield would envy. She seemed to view the trains as jousting competitors, and she challenged them to beat her to the crossings. Conductors rang warning bells at her; she squeezed blasts on her horn in reply as she raced ahead. Each time she won, a smile of victory flashed across her face. Fortunately, she didn't lose.

After the trolley maze, she turned south on Ocean Avenue and sped along as fast as the bumpy road and the wind resistance from Stengel's ears would allow.

We passed neat frame houses with striped awnings over their front doors and closed shutters to keep out the heat. Evenly spaced maple and poplar trees lined the road. The journey started to seem an idyllic summer automobile outing, and I was lulled into a warm tranquil state.

Then it struck me how peculiar this situation really was. I'm a utility baseball player on my way to be filmed for a moving picture. I'm going to be in it with Casey Stengel, one of baseball's biggest stars. And I'm being chauffeured by Miss Florence Hampton, who before today had seemed so ethereal, so unreal—a radiant image on a movie screen.

There was almost a daily mention of Florence Hampton in the newspapers and every month an item in the movie magazines. From these I knew something of her past. As a Ziegfeld Follies chorus girl she'd married showman William Daley and then had gone on to success on the stage and in the movies. Earlier this year, she'd inherited Daley's share in the Dodgers when her husband died. And there was more: some of the less reputable papers hinted at scandal—that the young widow had a fondness for wild parties and young ball players.

• • •

As we approached the intersection of Locust and East 15th Streets, I spotted a towering smoke stack with *Vitagraph Co.* painted down its side. It was at the corner of a massive factory complex that occupied an entire block.

Florence Hampton turned into an open gate, and we entered a courtyard surrounded by three-story buildings of yellow brick.

The yard was filled with an odd assortment of vehicles parked about haphazardly—a fire engine, a stagecoach, a milk truck, and enough tin lizzies to start a taxi company.

She killed the engine and we eased out of the car. As she undid her scarf, I asked, "Is all this for making movies?"

"Oh yes. There's a lot that goes into making movies nowadays." She removed her hat and shook her hair. "Vitagraph has hundreds of people working here."

The largest two buildings were at the east and west ends of the yard; except for their sloped glass roofs, they looked like enormous warehouses. "What are the buildings with all the glass?" I asked.

"That's where we shoot the pictures. The glass is to let the light in. We have two companies here." She pointed to the east building. "That's Studio A, where they make the *prestige* pictures—costume dramas, really." She laughed and started toward the west building. "This is Studio B. We do the low-brow pictures—comedies, westerns, the things people really like. We're the *fun* company."

Stengel looked like a kid seeing his first circus. He had a dazed grin on his face, but no word came out of his mouth.

When Miss Hampton opened the door of the "fun" studio, a splash of scalding air smacked me in the face. The glass roof let in plenty of light, but it also made the building a hothouse.

The cavernous interior was laid out more like a factory than a studio. Along one wall was a row of open-fronted movie sets partitioned by flimsy pasteboard walls. A row of cameras, looking like a cinematic firing squad, was in front of the sets, with one camera aimed at each scene. The rest of the building was a clutter of light stands, white reflector sheets, odd props, and building supplies. The room echoed with the din of production: directors bellowing through small hand-held megaphones, a piano and a violin playing two different tunes on two different sets, carpenters hammering at partially constructed walls.

Treading our way over ropes and cables, I looked into the first set where four men dressed as Confederate officers huddled in what was supposed to be a tent. There was a Western barroom, a bakery with a stack of pies, a jailhouse cell—

Suddenly my right foot snagged, and I started to fall. Trying to catch myself, I grabbed hold of a spotlight—a *hot* spotlight. I burned my hand and quickly let go, falling to the floor. The light stand wobbled teasingly. Then it tumbled after me, shattering with an explosion and a puff of acrid smoke.

All sounds in the studio ceased. The silence was absolute

until a workman in coveralls broke it. "Why don't ya watch where yer walkin'! Ya stupid . . ."

Stengel reached for my collar and helped pull me back up. "You trying to get us kicked out of here?" he muttered.

Florence Hampton yelled back at the workman, "If you didn't leave those wires all over the floor, people wouldn't trip on them."

The man grumbled, "Yeah, well, he's crazy for walkin' around in here with those shoes, anyway. He puts one of them spikes through a wire, he's going up the same as that Klieg light." I quickly pulled off my cleats.

Miss Hampton gently laid her hand on my forearm. "Don't worry," she told me. "It happens all the time. I'm surprised we don't have more accidents. Did you hurt yourself?"

I said no, which was nearly true.

From the farthest end of the building Elmer Garvin called, "Down here, Miss Hampton!" Through his horn he bellowed, "All right! Everybody back to work!"

We walked over to him, I in my stocking feet.

"We just got it ready," Garvin said proudly, pointing to the set.

I couldn't see any reason for his pride. A glove and a few bats were the only props. What was supposed to be a baseball diamond was crudely painted in bold purple on a pale yellow canvas backdrop. I knew the camera couldn't pick up the hideous color scheme, but I didn't at all like the idea of a yellow and purple baseball field.

"Now don't touch anything," Garvin said. "The paint's still wet." He directed the warning at me for some reason. Then he called a gangly boy, who took our gear and clothes to the dressing room.

Garvin gently pushed Stengel and me until we were

standing where he wanted. He took a close look at my head and scowled. "Blond hair doesn't film good," he said. "Put your caps on."

"Light brown," I muttered, as we complied.

Garvin then seated himself on a stool next to the camera. "We don't have much time," he announced to the crew. "So let's get this going." Although we were within easy hearing distance, he put a megaphone to his mouth and barked at Casey and me, "Okay, here's the story. You two are both wooing Miss Hampton. She can't choose between you. So you argue and try to settle it between yourselves. Now, let's see you argue."

Casey started gesturing wildly with his hands. I pantomimed yelling with exaggerated mouth motions.

"What the hell is that?" Garvin squawked.

"Arguing?" I suggested.

Garvin stood up and shook his head. "You look like a couple of monkeys. You look like you're *trying* to act. That's no good. Let me see . . ." His pocket change started to rattle. "I've got it! Who's the better team: the Dodgers or the Giants?"

"The Giants," I said quickly.

"The Dodgers," snapped Casey. A chorus behind the camera echoed, "The Dodgers!" The crew broke into laughter.

Garvin's face reddened. "Very funny!" he barked. "Now *quiet* while I try to teach these two how to act." He turned back to us, "Just argue about who's got the better team. And do it out loud. Nobody's gonna know what you're really saying. Start camera!"

Stengel and I started to argue heatedly while the cameraman crouched behind his machine, turning the crank and recording our argument on celluloid.

"Stop camera! That was good. Now you're going to decide who gets her."

"How?" Stengel asked.

Garvin dug into his pocket and flicked a dollar at him. "Flip a coin," he said.

I suggested, "How about with a bat? You know, like to see who gets first pick when you choose up sides."

"Fine," Garvin agreed. "A bat would be better. Start camera! Go ahead, boys."

I picked up a bat and tossed it in the air. As it came down, Stengel caught it at the label, and we went into the old routine as easily as if we were kids back on a sandlot. We alternated his fists and mine as we put them on top of each other climbing to the knob of the bat. Acting suddenly seemed easy.

"Wonderful! I love it!" yelled Garvin.

I got a fist almost to the top of the bat, then Casey capped his palm over the knob. Damn! This was just make believe, but I wanted to win.

"Stop camera! Very good, boys. Now step back a little."

Stengel and I shuffled back to the painted canvas. Garvin turned to his left. "Are you ready, Miss Hampton?" She was out of my sight, behind one of the side walls, but she must have indicated yes because Garvin said, "Start camera!"

She came into view, walking slowly across the front of the set. With one hand she twirled a parasol; with the other she held the arm of Tom Kelly, her usual leading man. I was jealous. And when I saw how Kelly was dressed, I was shocked.

Garvin barked, "Okay, boys. You've both lost her. Try to look surprised."

No problem there. Kelly was wearing a chest protector over a dark suit and he carried a mask. We lost out to an

.

*umpire?* My mouth gaped in disbelief. Who the hell is going to believe she'd pick an umpire over a ball player? Hell, I'd rather lose her to Stengel than to an umpire.

"Stop camera! Perfect! That's it for today!" Miss Hampton immediately removed her hand from Kelly's arm. I remained immobile, staring at her.

My mouth was still open when it was suddenly filled and everything went white. I clawed at my eyes, scooping out white goo. I spit the same stuff out of my mouth.

When my eyes cleared, I saw in front of me a wiry young lady dressed in brown jodhpurs, knee-high boots, and a man's khaki shirt with the sleeves rolled up. Her chestnut hair was pulled back in a long thick braid. She was serial star Marguerite Turner. Two nights ago I had seen her in episode six of *Dangers of the Dark Continent.* I deduced from her clothes that she was probably filming the next installment in the series. In her right hand she held an empty pie tin. I was now wearing its contents.

"Oops," she said innocently. "Sorry, but when I saw the Giants uniform it just slipped." Her voice was low and a little husky.

She looked at me with dark, heavy-lidded eyes that seemed to pop out of her head. On her tawny round face was a smirking half-smile that could be taken as either annoying or endearing. I must have found it to be the latter because I suddenly didn't mind having lost Florence Hampton to an umpire.

Then I noticed the crowd was laughing and I felt myself blushing through the meringue that caked my face.

Lights started to click off and the crew dispersed. Turner still stood in front of me, her smile turned quizzical. I was probably supposed to say something, but all I could think of was that my acting debut was far from what I'd hoped it would be.

One of the Civil War generals came over, his white goatee bobbing. "Well, Mr. Rawlings, I see Miss Turner has initiated you into our little family." It was Arthur V. Carlyle. I hadn't recognized him at the ballpark, but now I remembered him as one of Vitagraph's stock character actors. He usually played proper butlers or kindly grandfathers. "I'm one of the few who hasn't been subjected to Miss Turner's little joke," he said. He looked at her with stern eyes. "Of course, if she ever tried it, I would put her over my knee."

Marguerite Turner shrugged and walked away. Carlyle said to Stengel and me, "I'll show you to the gentlemen's dressing room. You can clean up and change your clothes there."

• • •

In a cluttered room that was more of a storage space than a dressing area, Casey and I stripped out of our uniforms and Arthur Carlyle and the other actors out of their costumes. We were all crowded together before a long low table that held a hodgepodge of mirrors, hair brushes, and makeup boxes.

While I wiped my face with a towel, Carlyle stood on my left, carefully peeling off his fake beard. He put it away in a makeup kit the size of a mechanic's toolbox.

It reminded me of when I used to play semi-pro ball for factory teams. I'd be given my own toolbox and a set of work clothes, but my real purpose was to play baseball on the company team. I was never really a carpenter or a pipe-fitter, just a ball player in disguise—an imposter. The same as I'd been on the movie set. I wasn't an actor. I was a baseball player.

Yeah . . . a baseball player. And that's a wonderful thing to be.

Feeling better now, I decided I was going to leave this place with my dignity intact and looking good. I donned one of my more fashionable outfits: a blue candy-striped blazer, cream-colored trousers, and a scarlet silk necktie speckled with fine white polka dots. I took extra care to make sure everything was right, retying the four-in-hand three times until I was satisfied with the knot and buffing my brown patent leather shoes with a handkerchief.

Stengel patiently waited for me to finish my primping, then we left the dressing room together.

Marguerite Turner was waiting outside the door. She had changed into a pale yellow frock with a low-cut square neckline. The dress looked a size too large and hung lopsided from her shoulders. Her half-smile was gone and she looked contrite. She said, "I'm sorry about the pie, Mr. Rawlings. I really didn't mean to embarrass you."

"You didn't," I lied. "I was just a little surprised is all."

Stengel snorted.

"We have a party on Saturday nights," she went on. "To celebrate the end of the work week. I'd be very happy if you would join us." She appeared to notice Casey for the first time and added, "Of course you're invited too, Mr. Stengel."

He answered before I could put my mouth in gear. "Thank you, but I'm afraid I have another engagement this evening. See, there's a few other fellahs and me who get together for a friendly little game of poker. And Saturday being our regular game night—"

"I'd be happy to go the party," I said.

*Chapter Three*

**W**hile digging a tiny fork into a colossal oyster, my perspective on the day suddenly reversed. Never mind our loss to the Dodgers or my mishaps in the Vitagraph studio. The day was actually quite a success. I'd had a single in one at bat, bringing me closer to the .250 mark. I'd made a movie. And now what was starting to seem the highlight of the day: I was on a Saturday night date. Well, maybe not a date exactly, but I *was* having dinner with a young lady. As well as with fifty or sixty other guests of the Vitagraph Company.

We were in the dining hall of the Sea Dip Hotel on Coney Island. The hotel was right on the ocean, and the open windows of the room let through a cross-breeze that carried the sharp scent of salt air and the faint odor of decomposing sea creatures. The smell wasn't all that appealing, but the cooling draft made it possible to sit still without working up a sweat.

"Oysters and champagne make the best meal in the world, don't you think?" Marguerite Turner said.

"I haven't had the two together before," I answered. Actually, I'd never had champagne at all and still hadn't touched the full glass in front of me. Not all forms of alcohol agreed with me, and I wasn't sure if this was the time to experiment with a new one. I did like beer though, and the bubbles that percolated in the hollow-stemmed glass made me think champagne might be similar.

I hadn't really been able to try the oysters, either. The fork was too small or the oyster too slippery.

Marguerite wasn't having much success with her fork, either. "Aw, the hell with it," she finally muttered. She lifted a shell to her mouth and slurped its plump contents. After chewing rapidly, she chased the oyster with a gulp of champagne. A disapproving *Harrumph* came from across the table. Marguerite dropped her eyes and her cheeks colored.

I quickly scooped up an oyster the same way that she had and let it slide down my throat without chewing at all. Marguerite smiled. When I emptied my champagne glass in one draught, her smile turned to a grin.

The champagne was good stuff, I thought, sweeter than beer and with a more refreshing fizz.

Marguerite Turner and I were both more relaxed now. "How do you like playing for John McGraw?" she asked. I was glad she brought up baseball. The other talk at our table was about whether there would be war in Europe, a topic I didn't find particularly engaging.

"It's hard to say. I'm not sure that you're supposed to *like* playing for McGraw. I think I do, though. You have to play smart when you play for him. I like that."

"Is this your first year in the majors?"

"Oh, no. I played for the 1912 Red Sox most of the season." That team was one of the best ever; after breezing to the league title, the club beat McGraw's Giants for the world championship.

"Really?" Marguerite said, sounding impressed. "I was *at* the World Series that year. The first game, anyway, at the Polo Grounds. My brother took me for my eighteenth birthday. Did you play?"

"Did I what?" I was busy registering the new information: so, she would be twenty in October, almost two years younger than me.

"I said did you play in the Series?"

"Oh . . . uh, no. I got injured a couple of weeks before the end of the season, so the Sox released me."

"That's awful! You get hurt working for them, and that's how they show their appreciation?"

"Mmm. It was disappointing." I didn't see any need to mention that the injuries that ended my 1912 season didn't happen on the baseball field. "But I'll get into the World Series this year."

As we talked, we continued to inhale oysters, without the use of forks and without concern for what our table companions thought of us.

I thought it would be good manners to ask my date a question about herself. "You like baseball?" I asked.

"I *love* baseball."

"And you're a Dodger fan."

"Yes, but they're not my favorite. I still like the Boston Braves. I saw them play at the South End Grounds once when I was a girl."

"I played there! For the Braves, in 1911. That was my first time in the big leagues. Cy Young was on the team." That fact was the highlight of my two-week tenure with the Braves.

She pursed her lips. "1911. . . . The Braves finished fifty games out of first place that year, didn't they?"

"Worse. Fifty-four."

"You should watch out for the Braves this year."

I laughed. "Three years haven't turned them into pennant winners."

"They have the pitching," she countered. "That's ninety percent of the game."

Save me from women who think they know baseball. Pitching isn't more than seventy-five percent of the game. Eighty at most. "We'll see," I said skeptically.

"Would you play for the Feds?"

"No, I don't think they'll last. And it would kill my career. We can be blacklisted just for going to a Federal game." Besides, although the upstart Federal League had been raiding the established leagues for every player they could get, they'd never contacted me.

"Oh. That's too bad. I like going to their Brooklyn games. Washington Park is just a couple blocks from my flat near Red Hook." She said *my* flat. That means hers alone. As in no husband or mother—maybe not even a roommate.

She leaned toward me. "Would you excuse me," she whispered. "I have to go to the toilet." No decorous nonsense about nose powdering. I liked that. This was a girl it was easy to feel comfortable with.

I watched closely as she walked away. She didn't glide with small delicate steps but rather loped, as if still in her jungle attire. She'd seemed more comfortable in shirt and trousers than she did in a dress. In fact, she wore the dress with indifference if not awkwardness. She moved like a tomboy forced against her will to dress as a lady. I would bet that when she was a little girl she could climb a tree faster than any boy—and probably risked going onto higher branches.

"More champagne, sir?" A waiter held out a bottle with a white cloth wrapped around it. I nodded and he refilled my glass. The waiters were dressed in gay nineties style, in identical pink-striped shirts, black string ties, and green vests. As part of the costume, they all sported bushy black handlebar mustaches.

The hotel tried to maintain the ambience of two decades ago, from the ornate silverware on the tables to the gilt-framed paintings on the walls to the cut-glass chandeliers that showered flickering gaslight about the room. Unfortunately, the nostalgia even extended to the music. A five-piece band was struggling through a spiritless version of *"Bicycle Built for Two"* as if the bicycle had a flat tire. My preference ran more to ragtime, something I could tap my feet to.

As I was looking about the room, Florence Hampton caught my eye. She was at the table next to ours, across from me so I had a clear view of her face. She gave me a friendly smile. I returned it, then felt a small pang of guilt. I'd almost forgotten her in my preoccupation with Marguerite Turner. Then I remembered that she had passed me over for an umpire, and my guilt was assuaged.

There appeared to be too much competition for Florence Hampton's attention anyway. Seated on either side of her were two men I had seen earlier in the day at Ebbets Field: Sloppy Sutherland and his battery mate Virgil Ewing.

Sloppy Sutherland was elegantly attired, as always. He wore a blue cutaway jacket, a wing collar around his throat, and a large glittering stickpin in his necktie. His impeccably barbered black hair was slicked back with so much pomade that it sparkled in the gaslight. It was Sutherland's Beau Brummell aspirations that earned him his nickname, the same way three-hundred-pound behemoths are so often called "Tiny." He was better dressed than any of the movie stars, but he didn't wear his fine clothes easily. He seemed to be straining to appear dapper and graceful.

Virgil Ewing was also in a suit and tie, but he might as

well have stayed in his chest protector and shin guards. With his squat body, he could be one of only two things: a catcher or a fireplug. Ewing's bullet head rested directly on his shoulders with no neck in between. The coarse brown hair that crowned his scalp looked like he cut it himself without the aid of a mirror. His left cheek was puffed with a massive chaw of tobacco.

Sutherland whispered something in Miss Hampton's right ear; she leaned toward him and laughed. Then Ewing whispered in her left ear; she leaned toward him and laughed just as hard. Then it was Sutherland's turn again. I couldn't tell which one she was with, but I thought Sutherland was more her type than Virgil Ewing. Hell, *I'd* be more her type than Ewing.

Or maybe she was with both of them. The rumors about her again came to mind.

I also remembered that Coney Island used to be called "Sodom by the Sea," and preachers and newspaper editors liked to sermonize against the vices they said were rampant here. Being somewhat short of vices in my life, that reputation had a lot of appeal for me. Perhaps "nice" people didn't come to Coney Island, but it seemed the perfect place for movie actors and baseball players.

I was the only Giant here, though. Unless Tom Kelly counted. Kelly went back and forth between playing first base for the Giants and playing a leading man in motion pictures; he constantly threatened to jump from one business to the other unless he was paid more money. Kelly was dressed neatly but not in anything fancy. His main asset was a ruggedly handsome face, and he wore nothing to distract from it. He was seated at Miss Hampton's table next to his wife Esther, an actress and perennial ingenue who could have been the model for the Kewpie doll. Kelly never looked

at his adorable little wife, though. He seemed interested only
in Florence Hampton and the contest between Sutherland
and Ewing. Almost as interested as I was.

• • •

"She's very pretty, isn't she?" Marguerite Turner had returned
without my noticing.

"Who?"

"Florence Hampton, of course. You were staring at her."

"Well . . ." I wasn't sure if it was okay to tell your date that
another girl was pretty. But if I said no, I'd obviously be lying.
So I resorted to an old standby: evasion. "I was trying to
figure out who she's with," I said.

The band leader announced the first dance. To my surprise, Tom Kelly hopped up and took hold of Florence
Hampton's arm. He led her to the dance floor, though she
didn't look willing. His wife stared after them, her face red-
dening and her lips trembling.

I turned to ask Marguerite what was going on. She was
looking back at me expectantly. The other people at our
table scraped their chairs back and made their way to the
floor. Marguerite smiled, revealing a set of small pearly teeth.
Although she wasn't pretty in the same way as Florence
Hampton, there was something about her—especially when
she smiled—that I found powerfully attractive.

Then I realized what she wanted. And I tried to pretend
that I didn't. Please, anything but dancing.

"Uh . . . do you know who Miss Hampton is with?" I
asked, trying to divert her attention from the dance floor.

"Let's see," she replied slowly. "Right now she appears to
be with Mr. Kelly." It also appeared that Kelly and Miss
Hampton were arguing.

"I mean . . ."

"Yes, I know what you mean. To tell you the truth, I don't know. But I believe that is her business and hers alone. She's a friend of mine. I won't say anything about her that could be taken the wrong way."

"Okay." I dropped the subject.

Marguerite looked over at the band. Somebody must have told them to try some music from this century, for they were now playing a fast rag—not very rhythmically but at least with more energy than they had before.

I watched the dancers as they moved across the floor, and I tried hard to look too absorbed to realize that Marguerite wanted to join them. I noticed that many of the ladies were wearing slit skirts, some of them cut all the way up to the knees. The new style was supposed to make it easier to get in and out of automobiles, but it also allowed for more movement in dancing.

When the band launched into the next tune, Miss Hampton broke away from Kelly. Sloppy Sutherland quickly intercepted her. She took his arms willingly and danced with him closely.

As Tom Kelly returned to his table, his wife bolted past him and went to sit alone at an empty table in the corner of the room.

Marguerite began tapping her fingers on the table and swaying in her chair. "Gee," she said. "It's too bad Mr. Stengel had his card game tonight."

I laughed, remembering Casey as he left me at the studio. He'd contorted his face into a huge wink and said, "Good luck, kid." I was pretty sure he didn't really have a poker game, and I think I now owed him a favor.

"What's so funny?" Marguerite asked.

"Oh . . . uh, the pie. I was just wondering what kind of pie that was you hit me with. It didn't taste like anything."

She answered flatly, "That was movie pie. We make it ourselves. It's just a paste, no filling. And extra gooey so that it sticks. Real pie doesn't work so well." There was a hint of exasperation in her voice, and she was starting to look like she really did wish Stengel was here, maybe instead of me.

"I can't dance," I suddenly confessed. "But if you're willing to put your feet at risk, I would be honored if you would give me the next dance."

Her smile came back in full bloom. She grabbed my hand and said, "Why wait for the next one?"

With my free hand I downed the rest of my champagne. "I mean it about not knowing how to dance," I warned.

"Nonsense. Anybody can dance. You just move to the music." She made it sound simple, but at the moment I'd have rather been facing a Walter Johnson fastball.

• • •

Under Marguerite's instruction—I think she was leading—I started to get the hang of it. We worked into an easy step pattern that I could follow without causing her injury. As Marguerite and I maneuvered about, I kept an eye on the others around us, partly to avoid running into them and partly to distract my mind from what my feet were doing—I found the dancing went more smoothly when I didn't think too hard about each step.

The courting of Florence Hampton provided plenty of distraction, almost to the point of becoming a floor show. Virgil Ewing and Sloppy Sutherland continually cut in on each other to dance with her; each time the shoulder taps were harder and the relinquishment less willing. Tom Kelly appeared to have given up pursuing her; he sat at his table, his eyes fixed on Ewing and Sutherland, visibly seething.

"See? You dance wonderfully," said Marguerite.

"I do? I mean, thank you. So do you." Not that I was any judge.

When the band took a break, I led Marguerite back to our table. My legs wobbled a little. Not until I sat down did I realize how overheated and thirsty I was. Our champagne glasses had been refilled and we quickly emptied them. I then toyed with my empty glass, silently cursing its small size and wishing for a stein of beer.

Marguerite and I didn't say much; we sat quietly, just looking at each other. With the music stopped, it was easy to hear what was being said at Florence Hampton's table.

Virgil Ewing loudly suggested that Miss Hampton join him for a swim—no bathing dress needed, he added. He sounded desperate, as if he knew he was coming in second to Sloppy Sutherland and making one last bid to win her favors.

She glared her answer at him, her face flushing. Conversations hushed and people stared at them.

Florence Hampton then politely excused herself and went to sit with Esther Kelly. Mrs. Kelly looked happy to have some company, and Miss Hampton looked relieved to be away from her suitors.

Through the windows, I could hear waves lapping at the shore. Ewing's manners were awful, but his idea of a dip in the ocean had a lot of appeal. I could feel sweat running down my back, and my severe thirst was nagging me for relief.

A waiter carrying a champagne bottle on a tray passed our table. I leapt up and tried to hail him. I was sure he noticed me, but he turned away with a toss of his mustaches and headed toward Florence Hampton's new table instead. Great—just when I was starting to feel at home with this crowd, a waiter decides to remind me that Giants aren't welcome in Brooklyn.

I spotted another waiter and almost tackled him to secure a full bottle of bubbly for Marguerite and me. I filled her glass first, then my own. I kept refilling and emptying it, and my thirst was finally relieved. Just in time for me to be tugged back onto the dance floor.

• • •

We danced slower now, oblivious to the beat of the music. I didn't notice anything or anyone else in the room. All I was aware of was how very close Marguerite Turner and I were dancing. With my right hand on the small of her back, I could feel her body heat through her thin summer dress. And I could tell there wasn't much in the way of petticoats underneath. I also found that when I angled my head just right, her hair would brush softly against my cheek.

Actually, I don't think it was really dancing at all that we were doing—we simply propped ourselves against each other and swayed. But I did it successfully and without instruction.

"Tell me," Marguerite said. "Who's your favorite movie actress?"

My favorites were well-established and I answered like a schoolboy showing off that he knows the answer to the teacher's question, "Mary Pickford. And for comedy, Mabel Normand."

Marguerite giggled softly. "Not Florence Hampton?"

Was she worried that I was infatuated with Miss Hampton? "No," I said. "She's a nice lady, but she's not on my list of favorites."

Marguerite Turner was making a place for herself, though, and it had nothing to do with acting ability. Maybe it won't be her brother taking her out for her birthday this year. A brother . . . how protective? I wondered.

When the music stopped between dances, a waiter near the door called for attention, "Ladies and gentlemen!" After a pause, he announced, "Mr. Arthur V. Carlyle." No one else had been introduced that way.

Carlyle stepped through the door and stood still, surveying the room as if checking to see that it met his standards. He seemed to be doing an impression of theater impresario David Belasco and was dressed—overdressed—for the role in a crimson-lined opera cape and silk top hat. A black silver-headed walking stick was in his gloved hands. With all eyes on him, he methodically removed his cape, tugged off his gloves and put them in his topper, then handed it all to the waiter.

"Somebody order a ham?" Marguerite whispered, with a roll of her eyes.

I laughed, maybe a little too loudly.

Carlyle put a coin in the waiter's hand and walked onto the dance floor. The waiter looked down at his open palm with a scowl, then dropped Carlyle's clothes in a pile next to the door.

As the band struck up the next tune, I grabbed Marguerite. "Another dance?"

We'd barely started to move when I felt a hand clapped on my shoulder. "Mr. Rawlings!" Carlyle bellowed cheerfully, as if I was his dearest friend. "How is our newest thespian?"

I wasn't sure what that was, so I smiled and tried to shrug off his heavy hand.

"I see you've decided to forgive Miss Turner for her bad manners this afternoon," he said in his strange stilted voice.

"There wasn't anything to forgive," I answered.

"Very chivalrous of you, my boy. Well, you two have a good time. Hope to see you again, Mr. Rawlings." He made a slight bow and moved away.

Marguerite and I stared at each other, then burst into laughter. We resumed dancing still shaking from the laughs.

"What is that accent of his?" I asked. "I can't place it."

"It's *thea-tuh,*" she said. "Mr. Carlyle is a *legitimate* actor, you know. Not that he's been on the stage in years."

I was suddenly bumped from behind. I turned around, a low growl in my throat.

"I'm sorry," said Florence Hampton in a slurred voice. "Please excuse me."

"Of course," I said, but she was already staggering through the rest of the crowd, working her way across the floor. Her face was red, and she looked queasy.

Suddenly I didn't feel so good myself. Maybe I had to see Miss Hampton's face to realize it. My legs had been getting shaky for some time, but by dancing slower and holding Marguerite closer I had been able to compensate. Now the unsteadiness spread beyond my legs. I'd put nothing in my stomach all day but oysters and champagne, and they were starting to churn in my belly. The seaside smell of decay and fish seemed stronger, too, and I couldn't breathe fast enough to clear my head of the odor. I quietly sniffed at Marguerite's neck in the hope of detecting some perfume that might relieve me; she smelled clean but I could detect no additional scents.

"Do you mind if we sit down?" I asked, trying not to make it sound too urgent.

Marguerite nodded and we returned to our table. As I plopped down in my seat, my sweat-dampened clothes stuck to me, barely giving way enough to avoid tearing. I felt a little less woozy with the chair to support me.

Then all the champagne I had ingested bubbled up from my stomach and rushed to my head, trying to blow it off as if I was a bottle and my head was the cork.

I looked at Marguerite but didn't trust myself to open my mouth to say anything. The warning voice that lives in the back of my head was telling me to exit gracefully before I embarrassed myself.

It was Esther Kelly who gave me an out. She came back to where her husband sat. Pointedly ignoring him, she grabbed her handbag and fur-trimmed wrap and strode out of the dining room.

I quickly pulled out my watch and fumbled to flip open the cover. Giving it a cursory glance, knowing I wouldn't be able to make out the numbers anyway, I said, "Jeez, look at the time. I'd better be getting home, I guess. With the game and the movie and all, I'm pretty beat. And McGraw doesn't like us to be out late." I wished I could have said something about having a game tomorrow, but there was no Sunday baseball in New York. Closing the watch, I saw a photograph and realized I had opened the wrong side.

Marguerite eyed me quizzically.

I tried to think of the best way to let her know that I wanted to see her again and to subtly find out if she was similarly interested. A sudden spasm in my belly warned me that I had no time for subtlety. "Can I— *May* I call on you some time . . . soon?"

She answered simply, "Yes." And her smile told me she meant it.

Then I stood up and walked to the door, taking great pains to keep my body perpendicular to the floor.

I made it out of the dining room, then decided I didn't feel up to traveling much further. At the hotel's front desk, I paid two dollars for a room to spend the night.

Once in the small single room, it took only a minute to slip out of my clothes and into bed. As I settled my buzzing head onto the soft pillow, I knew that the light-headedness wasn't due to champagne alone.

My mind was filled with alluring visions of what was in my future: a trip to the World Series, appearing on a movie screen, and spending time with Marguerite Turner.

I remembered something my teammate Laughing Larry Doyle once said. I thought it couldn't have applied to anyone more than it did to me now: *It's great to be young and a New York Giant.*

# Chapter Four

There is something about the feel of a strange bed—a different sag of the mattress or firmness of the pillow—such that the instant you wake up in one, you know it's not your own. I was well-acquainted with this phenomenon from dozens of road trips and a hundred hotels.

So when I woke in the darkness in a bed that wasn't mine, I immediately assumed I was on the road with a roommate in a bunk next to me and a baseball game to play in the afternoon. I wasn't sure what city we were in or who we were playing, though I had the sensation that we might be under the sea, scheduled to play the Atlantis All-Stars. My head was closed up and humming, as if my ears were filled with water.

I silently cursed whatever had woken me. I could tell that the hour was that one-way bridge from late night to early morning—the time of day when it's too late to fall asleep again and too early to have had all the rest I needed.

Might as well get up and get oriented, I reluctantly told myself.

From experience so ingrained it was almost instinct, I prompted my body to take the critical first step: determine which side of the bed is against the wall before trying to roll out of it. Figuring out what day of the week it was and what city I was in could come later.

But even the minor task of getting out of bed proved to be too much for me. My brain couldn't relay the order to my body.

Oh, jeez. I suddenly remembered where I was and why. The champagne.

During the night, the champagne bubbles that had been gathering in my head must have exploded in little puffs of toxic gas. And the fumes they left seemed determined to remain bottled up in my skull until they killed me. I wiggled a pinky in each ear, trying in vain to open an escape vent.

Then, with a pang of urgency, my bladder let me know why I'd awoken. I forced my hands to feel around until I found the edge of the bed and swung my legs out. Flicking on a small electric lamp on the nightstand provided enough light for me to make use of the chamber pot.

When I finished, I killed the light and fell back into bed, wishing that my throbbing head could be relieved so easily. This wasn't my first hangover, but it was without doubt the worst. Never again would I touch champagne, I swore to myself.

After a little while, I could make out shapes in the room, illuminated by the first tentative glimmer of dawn.

Knowing that I wouldn't be able to fall back asleep, I prodded myself out of bed again, with the goal of finding the hotel restaurant and a strong cup of coffee.

My room faced the ocean, and as I dressed I could see the sun, red and diffuse, as it spread along the horizon. Shrieking sea gulls called attention to the break of day like roosters on a farm.

By the time I put my hat on, the entire sky was glowing

as if the ocean had caught fire. "Red sky in morning . . ." I muttered to myself, trying to remember the line. *Red sky in morning, somebody take warning.* Who was supposed to take warning? *Sailors* take warning. That was it. Well, good thing I wasn't a sailor. I figured the ominous sign didn't apply to baseball players.

•   •   •

In the hotel coffee shop, I guzzled two cups of its specialty, black and hot. A dozen other early risers seated around me dug into more hearty breakfasts that filled the room with the odor of greasy bacon and sweet syrup—smells that did nothing to alleviate my still queasy stomach.

I decided to go home to continue my recovery. After turning in my room key at the desk, I stepped outside and was greeted by a refreshing gust of salt air that washed into my nostrils and tingled the inside of my nose. I changed my mind about going right home and instead walked around to the back of the hotel, toward the ocean, to breathe in more of the invigorating air.

The hotel had one rickety pier projecting from the beach out into the Atlantic Ocean. No boats were moored to the pier, and except for me the beach was deserted. As I plodded through the sand, making my way to the dock, sea gulls made diving runs at me, still shrieking as if there was someone they had yet to wake. I wished for a fungo bat and a bag of baseballs to shut a few of them up.

I walked across the poorly fit weather-beaten boards of the pier as far out as I could go. Standing at its edge, I tried to inhale everything that I could from the ocean, and I imagined the waves that crashed on the pilings were being sucked in by my deep breaths. After a few lungfuls of the sea air, I felt almost lifelike.

The Sea Dip Hotel was on the border between the respectable and the disreputable sections of Coney Island. From my vantage point on the pier, I could see the fashionable resort hotels of Manhattan Beach and Brighton Beach to the east and to the west, the seamy side of the island, the amusement parks: Steeplechase, Luna, and the burned ruins of Dreamland.

Turning about, I started to walk back. The sun was now its proper shade of golden yellow, the cloudless sky was correctly blue, and I could tell it was going to be a hot and humid one again today.

I was just about off the pier, no longer over the water, when a sea gull made a low run at my head. I ducked down in reflex, and through a gap between the planks, I saw somebody laying on the sand underneath. Sleeping, I thought.

Then I got down on my knees and looked closer. No, not sleeping.

It was a woman. She was on her back, with matted hair covering her face and no cover at all on her naked body. Her arms and legs were bent into positions that I was sure she hadn't assumed voluntarily. The tide had probably washed her ashore, dumping her on the beach like a piece of twisted driftwood.

I hopped off the side of the dock and slowly approached her. When I was close enough to see her skin, I knew for certain she was dead. Her skin had a bluish tinge that was no color for a human being to be. Sand was sprinkled over her; it sparkled in yellow stripes across her body, lit by the sun through the cracks in the pier above. The purple and yellow baseball diamond that I'd seen in the Vitagraph studio flashed before my mind's eye.

The woman had no localized injuries that I could see—no knife cuts or gunshot wounds, no ugly bruises. She was simply dead all over.

Green seaweed was tangled in the blondish hair that covered her face. I bent down to pull away some of the seaweed and her hair moved away with it. The face was bloated, the lips were purple, and the open eyes no longer had a personality behind them. But they had an identity—they were the white lifeless eyes of Florence Hampton.

I felt a sudden vacuum in my gut, as if a vital organ had just been plucked out of me.

The proper thing to do was to close her eyelids, but when I reached down, I found I couldn't bring myself to touch her skin. So I took my boater off and laid it over her face. Then I slipped off my coat and covered her body—not to preserve her modesty but because she looked so cold.

I then shooed away the sea gulls as best I could and trudged back to the hotel, knowing nothing could help her now. I felt no panic as I walked. Just numbness.

I had seen Florence Hampton too recently, her memory was too fresh in my mind for her to be dead. I could still hear her voice echoing from yesterday when she laughed loudly at Casey Stengel in Ebbets Field and when she softly asked if I was all right after I tripped in the movie studio.

• • •

At the hotel's front desk was the same idle clerk I'd given my key to. "There's a dead woman out back by the pier," I told him.

"Oh. Well, I'll make sure somebody looks into it," he said. He sounded as composed as if I'd told him a towel was missing from my room. Did this happen so often that it was routine for him?

"She's—" I hesitated, unsure how much I should say. The last time I found a body, it caused me all sorts of problems. "She looks like Florence Hampton, the movie actress," I said.

The clerk's eyes widened. Then he grabbed a telephone and squawked into the mouthpiece, "Get me the police."

In less than five minutes, four policemen arrived. Three of them went to check on the body, while the fourth questioned me in the hotel lobby. His questions were brief and perfunctory. I told him my name, when I found her, that I had been alone on the beach, that I had seen nothing strange other than the body itself, and that I had covered her with my hat and coat but didn't want them back. I volunteered no additional information. I said nothing about being sure of her identity, nor that I had been at a party with her the night before.

After satisfying the easily satisfied officer, I went to the trolley station to go back to Manhattan.

• • •

By the time I got home, my headache was back with a ferocious intensity and my apartment was sweltering with the heat of another scorcher.

I first went into the kitchen. After I threw some wood into the belly of the stove and lit a fire, I overloaded the coffee pot to make a brew powerful enough to do battle with the champagne bubbles still percolating in my brain.

While the pot heated up, I stripped off all my clothes and flung them on the couch. Then I plugged in an industrial-sized electric fan to stir the air.

When the coffee was done, I brought a mug of it in to the sitting room and settled into My Chair—a deep oversized wing chair with green leather upholstery and brass tacks studded around the seams.

I took a sip of the gritty black liquid and waited for my brain to come back to life. While I waited, I chewed on the grounds that stuck in my teeth and tried not to think of Florence Hampton, not even of Marguerite Turner. I didn't want to dwell on anything that had happened in the last twenty-four hours because I didn't want to imagine their consequences. Right now I wanted to focus on the familiar surroundings of home and be comforted by them.

Having a place of my own was relatively new to me, and I relished the independence that came with it. For years, I was a gypsy infielder, playing for factory teams and barnstorming squads, never spending more than a few months in any one place. My only homes were cheap boarding houses and hotels with low enough standards to take ball players.

Now the Giants were paying me $2,700 a year, more money than I ever thought I'd earn at baseball. Enough for me to lease a one-bedroom apartment on 158th Street near Broadway, a few blocks from the Polo Grounds. It wasn't cheap—$42 a month—but it had all the modern amenities: an electric outlet in every room, all-night elevator service, and guaranteed fireproof. I even had a view of the Hudson River from my fifth-floor window.

Most important, though, it was self-contained, with a kitchen, a bathroom, and a telephone in the parlor. No more nosy landladies to sneak past, no more sharing bathrooms with other boarders. I was now king of my own castle. If I wanted to, I could spend the entire day sitting naked in the parlor. All in all, for a little ol' country boy from New Jersey, I was doing pretty well for myself.

The only problem with the apartment was that I wasn't quite sure what I should put *in* all these rooms. At least hotels and boarding houses were furnished. My white walls were as bare as the hardwood floors. And with the exception of my chair and bed, the only furniture was what had been left by previous tenants: a ratty brown horsehair sofa, a small bookcase that looked as if it had been constructed from old packing crates, a pine dresser with drawers that stuck, and a few small mismatched tables. "Early American Abandoned" would best describe the decor. But it was home and it was mine.

The lack of sleep from the night before sent a welcome wave of drowsiness over me. I put the half-full coffee cup on the floor and closed my eyes.

• • •

The gas bubbles were trying to beat their way out of my skull. And they had organized now, hammering away in unison like the waves that crashed against the pier behind the Sea Dip Hotel. Three bangs at my head then a pause. Three more bangs, harder. Wait a minute . . . waves don't break in sets of three.

My eyes popped open. With the next pounding attack, I realized the knocking wasn't internal. It was my door. Who the hell would be here on a Sunday morning—was it still morning?

I ran into the bedroom and slid into a robe. "Coming!" I yelled, trying to forestall any more raps. I made it to the door just as the knocking resumed and yanked it open.

There stood the grim reaper, come to claim me. Just like in the pictures: a skeletal figure garbed in somber black, with a death pallor on his gaunt face.

But instead of a scythe, he carried a rolled-up newspaper. And on his long thin nose he wore steel-rimmed spectacles that magnified his sunken gray eyes. He was an inch or two shorter than me and many pounds lighter. Recognition twinkled in the back of my brain. This was no apparition. I knew this person from somewhere.

Exhibiting a sudden sign of life, he stuck out a bony hand. "Hello, Mickey."

The sniffy voice pinned down his identity. "Karl Landfors. I'll be damned." I grasped his hand and found it wasn't a pleasant thing to touch. "Uh . . . come in."

He removed his derby and stepped in. "Thank you."

Then there was an awkward silence. We'd lost touch with each other, and I wasn't sure who was responsible for the break. I tried to remember when I'd last seen him. I knew it had to be less than two years ago, but so much had happened—and Landfors's sparse brown hair had receded so much more—that it seemed longer.

I offered a seat.

"No. I'm fine, thank you." A reasonable answer since he could see that the couch was covered with clothes. And My Chair had a forbidding look that warned, "No one sits here but my master."

"Interesting apartment," he observed. "Different." He said "different" in a way that came out as "dreadful." My apartment suddenly felt smaller with two grown men in it and not quite so nice.

"Let me, uh . . ." I started scooping up clothes. "In case you change your mind." I hustled the bundle into the bedroom and threw it on the bed. Stepping back into the sitting room, I closed the bedroom door behind me. "Well, how about some coffee?" I offered.

"Coffee. Yes, I could use coffee, thank you."

I went into the kitchen. "With cream, if you have it," he called after me.

I knew I didn't have any. I opened the ice box anyway to appear as if I was making an effort. It contained just three bottles of ginger ale. "Sorry, all out," I reported.

"Oh. Well, black then, I suppose."

There was enough in the pot for one cup, if I included the dregs. I did, emptying the pot into my other coffee mug. No steam came from it. I dipped a finger in—tepid, at best. I must have dozed off longer than I thought. Well, it would have to be good enough for Landfors. It was too hot to start another fire.

As I brought him the mug, I asked, "You still working for the *Press?*"

"Oh yes."

"I thought you might have left after your book came out." Landfors, a muckraking reporter for the *New York Press,* had published *Savagery in the Sweatshop,* a volume that was supposed to expose sweatshops the way *The Jungle* had revealed the horrors of the meat packing industry. "I bought a copy."

"So you're the one. What did you think of it?"

"It was . . . uh . . . different." I'd only gotten through the first three chapters. Karl Landfors was no Upton Sinclair.

Landfors availed himself of the cleared couch. I set the coffee in front of him, then settled into my chair. He took a sip and his face curdled. When it recovered, he asked, "Did you see today's paper?" I guess we'd finished catching up on the last two years and were now onto today's news.

"No . . ." Uh-oh. Was Florence Hampton already a newspaper story? If she was, I hoped I wasn't in it.

"Here." Unrolling the paper, he handed it over to me. "Hot off the press."

It was an EXTRA edition of the *New York Press*. A banner headline screamed

*Germany Invades France, Declares War on Russia.*

This explained Landfors's dazed look—it was the sort of thing that interested him. I wasn't sure what it had to do with me, though. I knew war was awful, but it was too remote for me to feel affected by it. "Well . . . it looks like there's a war starting," I said, summing up my grasp of the situation.

"Page three," he grunted. "Top left." His conversational skills hadn't improved any in the past two years.

I flipped to page three. And there it was.

*Florence Hampton Dead!*

a two-column headline announced. Below that, in smaller type:

*Motion Picture Actress Found Drowned
on Coney Island Beach.*

I murmured, "I *saw* her. Just yesterday." I chose not to add that I'd also seen her this morning.

"I know. That's why I'm here."

"What do you mean you know?"

"It's in the article."

I skimmed it and saw in the third paragraph:

> On Saturday afternoon Miss Hampton com-
> pleted her last motion picture, *Florence at the
> Ballpark*. According to the Vitagraph Com-

> pany, the picture features popular Vitagraph
> leading man Tom Kelly as well as baseball
> players Casey Stengel of Brooklyn and Mi-
> chael Rawlings of the Giants . . .

"It's *Mickey,*" I muttered.

> Elmer Garvin, Miss Hampton's director at
> Vitagraph, says, "Her final picture is also her
> finest. We plan to release it as soon as possi-
> ble so her fans can see her and say farewell."

"Let me save you some time," Landfors said impatiently.

"Okay." I sat back, lowering the paper.

"She was found dead at about six this morning. Presumed drowned. Presumed to be an accident."

Whatever Landfors was driving at escaped me. Why was
*he* so interested in the death of Florence Hampton? "No
offense," I said. "But why did you come here to tell me this?"

"Because I'm not convinced it was accidental."

"Why not?"

"Just a feeling. There's something the paper didn't say:
she was nude."

I already knew that. "Was she . . . you know . . . attacked?"

"I don't know yet. There were no obvious signs, but the
medical examiner hasn't done an autopsy yet."

He hadn't answered my first question. "But why tell *me?*"

"I'd like you to look into it."

*"Me?"*

"Yes. You'd be perfect. For one thing, she was involved
with baseball . . . and baseball players. For another, you saw
the people she was with just before she died. And you've had

experience in investigating matters of this sort." He paused before adding, "And you found her body."

"You know? Was it in the paper?"

Landfors shook his head. "I talked to the police and the hotel clerk. They gave me your name. Ten bucks to the cop and five to the clerk got their promise not to give it to any other paper. Then I made sure we didn't use it either. I thought you might prefer not to have it known."

I said, "Thanks," but I wasn't sure he'd done it strictly as a favor. More likely as leverage to get me to help him.

"No problem," he said. "Anyway, about helping with the investigation . . ."

"Yes, of course I'll help." I would have agreed even if he hadn't had anything to hold over me. I already owed him. The "matters of this sort" Landfors referred to was a murder case, one that involved Fenway Park, one that he'd helped me solve when I was about to be framed for it. The least I could do for him was ask some questions about a drowning. "From what I saw, there's nothing to investigate, though. There wasn't any blood and no bruises or anything. I think she just drowned."

"We'll see," Landfors said doubtfully.

I still wasn't sure *why* he wanted my help. I thought he only covered politics. "Why are you interested in this anyway?" I asked. "For a story? You want to find out something the other papers don't?"

He shook his head. "No. It's to prevent a story."

I said nothing, hoping the silence would prompt him to continue.

He leaned forward and rested his elbows on his knees. Then he placed his hands together as if in prayer and hooked his chin over the peak of his fingertips. "Have you heard of James Bartlett?" he finally asked.

"Mmm . . . no."

Landfors nodded, not surprised. "He's a politician. One

of the good ones—and there aren't many. He's with the District Attorney's office in Manhattan. Assistant D.A. And he's running for City Council. I want to see him win."

"He's a Socialist?" I remembered that Landfors had voted for Eugene Debs.

"No, but he's a Progressive. And he's opposing Tammany Hall."

I was still missing the point. "How does this connect with Florence Hampton?"

"Miss Hampton's romantic entanglements weren't limited to baseball players. She was . . . she was involved with Bartlett."

"And if it got out, that would hurt him in the election."

"It would *kill* his chances. Bartlett's married, with three kids. The Tammany hacks would smear him."

I didn't feel much sympathy for Bartlett. "Sorry, but I don't see that he's such a great guy if he's cheating on his wife and kids."

"Bartlett's a good man. His judgment just failed him. I understand Miss Hampton has . . . *had* some very enticing qualities." He understood right. "Bartlett is the best chance there is to clean up city government, and I don't want to see him shot down because of a personal indiscretion."

I decided I'd still help, but only as a favor to Landfors, not to help James Bartlett. "What do you want me to do?" I asked.

"Nothing for a couple of days. I want to see what the medical examiner finds first. I'll get in touch when I have some more information." He grabbed his hat and stood up. There was no pretense that this had been a social call, so with his business completed he was ready to leave.

I walked him to the door. Just before I closed it behind him, he said, "Thanks, Mickey." His voiced cracked when he said it.

*Chapter Five*

The top of the Vitagraph smoke stack was hidden in the heavy ash-gray Monday morning haze that blanketed Flatbush.

Marguerite Turner told me that the studio began work at dawn to take advantage of the light, so I got up before daybreak to be there by seven o'clock.

Karl Landfors had told me not to look into Florence Hampton's death until I heard from him, so I decided to start immediately. If things worked out as I expected, I figured I'd have the investigation wrapped up by the time he contacted me again.

I walked up the driveway to the studio entrance, lugging a satchel with my uniform in it for the afternoon game at Ebbets Field.

The Vitagraph guard, a large fit man of about forty, stepped in front of me. He spread his feet and crossed his hands behind his back in a rigid military "at ease" position.

"I'd like to see Marguerite Turner please."

He shook his head. "I'm sorry," he said in a voice that

was more genial than his appearance. "The studio's closed today. You'll have to come back tomorrow."

"Closed?"

"In memory of Miss Florence Hampton. It's a day of mourning."

"Oh. Well, would you have Marguerite Turner's address?"

"I can't give that out."

Through the gate, I could see lights glowing in two windows of the building across the courtyard. "Isn't *anybody* else here?"

"Well . . . there's some work being done in the laboratory . . . editing Miss Hampton's last picture, I believe." He sounded as if he felt even this much activity was disrespectful to her memory.

"Oh! Is Mr. Garvin here then? He knows me. I was in that picture."

"You were, huh?"

"Yes. My name's Mickey Rawlings, I play for the Giants." That didn't seem to be enough to convince him that I was a ball player. I opened my satchel and pulled out my uniform jersey. "See?"

The guard hesitated, then said, "Come with me." He opened the door to his tiny booth and waved me inside. He followed, filling the booth beyond its capacity. I was pressed against a small desk that dug into my hip.

My host took the receiver off a wall phone. Next to the phone was a large photo of Teddy Roosevelt in his Rough Riders uniform. On an adjacent wall was a smaller picture of the guard as a young man in the uniform of the NYPD.

"Mr. Garvin," the guard said into the phone. "This is Joe Gannon at the front gate—yes sir, I'm sorry to bother you. But there's a young fellow here—" He cupped his hand over the mouthpiece and asked, "What's your name again?"

"Mickey Rawlings."

He repeated my name into the phone. "Says he was in the baseball picture," he added. "He'd like Miss Turner's address." After listening a while, Gannon said, "Yes, sir. Good idea, sir. Sorry to have bothered you." He hung up, then reached past me to a desk drawer.

"What did he say?" I prodded.

Gannon pulled a small ledger from the drawer and began leafing through the pages. "He says the picture will be finished tomorrow and the premiere will be Wednesday night. At the Vitagraph Theatre, probably. And he'd like you to be there." Gannon started copying from the ledger onto a slip of yellow paper. "Call back tomorrow and he'll give you the details."

He handed me the paper. It had Marguerite Turner's name, phone number, and address on it. "Meanwhile, you might want to find yourself a date for Wednesday," he suggested with an encouraging grin.

• • •

I hopped off the trolley at Third Avenue and First Street, just outside the left field fence of Washington Park.

When I was a boy, I often came to see the Dodgers play in the ramshackle wooden stadium. I was almost a regular in 1900 when Wee Willie Keeler and Iron Man Joe McGinnity led the Dodgers—then called the Superbas—to the National League pennant; since there were no other major leagues at the time, it made Brooklyn the century's first world champions.

Across the street from the ballpark, the Brooklyn Rapid Transit power plant was spewing dung-brown smoke into the low-hanging sky. Behind the power plant was the Gowanus

Canal, an open sewer that saturated the air with its vile stench. As dreary as Pigtown was, it was more attractive than the east end of Red Hook.

I found Marguerite Turner's address a block and a half away on Whitwell Place, a street with more potholes than cobblestones. Her apartment building was a sagging four-story structure of dull brown brick. Someone had once put a coat of bright red paint over the bricks, but only a few scattered flecks still clung to them. The air had probably dissolved the paint job.

I climbed the front steps, taking care not to touch the rusty wrought iron railings. A weathered piece of flimsy wood was nailed to the door where a pane of glass had once been. I thought of the many "Homes of the Stars" photo spreads I'd seen in the movie magazines—none of them ever looked like this.

In the hallway was a row of mailboxes, one of which had a handwritten card on it that read "M. Turner, Apt. 23."

Now that I was inside her building, I was having second thoughts about being here. She's not expecting me. . . . I should have called first . . . she might be too upset over Miss Hampton's death to want company . . .

My eagerness to see her finally won out. I knocked gently on the door of apartment 23. In less than a minute it was pulled open.

Marguerite appeared in worse shape than her building. What looked like a hair explosion had left long frizzy locks hanging across her face and about her shoulders. Her nose, not exactly dainty to start with, was red and swollen and chafed around the nostrils. And her heavy-lidded eyes were puffy and wet.

I could tell this was not a good time for me to visit.

"Oh, hi," she said, with as much enthusiasm as if I'd come to collect the rent. "Come in."

"Thanks," I said. "I'm sorry about Miss Hampton. I know you were friends."

"Huh. Some friend I was." She looked like she was about to burst into tears, and I was wondering what to do if she did. She waved me toward an overstuffed chair. I left my bag and boater next to the door, then took the seat. Marguerite sat down cross-legged on a straw-colored sofa. She was wearing baggy brown corduroy pants that looked too heavy for this heat and a red-checked gingham shirt with its long sleeves rolled back at the cuffs.

The apartment had a similar layout to mine, with one big difference: hers looked inhabited. There was comfortable furniture in the parlor, fringed throw rugs were on the floor, and white lace curtains—one of the few feminine touches—diffused the sunlight from the windows. The place wasn't especially neat, but it was clean and in better repair than the exterior of the building; what disorder there was—some clothes on the furniture and records on the floor—just made it seem all the more homey.

Marguerite pulled a billowy white handkerchief from a shirt pocket and blew her nose with a resonant honk.

"Are you okay?" I asked.

"Nooo . . ." was her barely audible answer. She folded her hands in her lap and looked down as her fingers twisted and squeezed the handkerchief. Her slim tanned wrists looked smooth and feminine in contrast to the masculine clothes. "She was my friend and I couldn't help her," she said plaintively.

"There was nothing you could have done."

"I could have talked to her. I tried for a while, but then . . . I just gave up."

I wasn't sure how talking to someone could save her from drowning. "What do you think happened?" I asked.

"I'm not sure . . . she just changed after her husband died. She wouldn't talk to me anymore."

I'd meant what happened the night she drowned, but if it made her feel better to talk about her friendship with Miss Hampton, that was okay with me. "The two of you were close?"

"I thought we were. We used to talk about everything. Just after I started with the studio, Vitagraph went on location to Port Jervis. Beautiful mountains and forests there. We made westerns and Indian pictures and anything else we could think of to use that scenery. The whole company stayed at the Caudebec Inn, and Libby and I shared a room. She took me under her wing—"

"Who's Libby?"

"That's what I called Florence. It was a wonderful time. We'd stay up until two or three in the morning chatting like schoolgirls."

"When did you start in the movies?" I thought it might be a good idea to steer the conversation away from Florence Hampton for a while, at least until she looked less likely to break into tears.

"Three years ago. Three years. . . . I never thought the picture craze would last this long. Someday I'm going to show up for work, and the studio will be closed. Something new will catch the public's fancy and my career will be over. Like Libby's . . . hers is all over. Everything is over for her."

Changing the topic sure didn't work. Maybe it would be better to let her go on about Florence Hampton and get it out of her system. "You said Miss Hampton changed after her husband died?"

"Mmm . . . yes. Could I call you Mickey?"

The question caught me by surprise. "Yes, of course."

"Good. And I'm Margie. Elmer Garvin makes us call everyone Mr. and Miss at the studio—he keeps trying to make us behave respectably, improve our reputation. Actors are thought to have low morals, you know. Oh, but you must run into the same thing, being a baseball player. Anyway, it sounds so unfriendly to me. So please don't call Libby Miss Hampton."

"Okay." I didn't think it proper to refer to her by Margie's private nickname for her though. "How's Florence?" I suggested.

Margie's face froze and she stared into the air. "She's dead," she said. Then she burst into humorless giggles. And then the giggles turned to harsh heaving sobs. I just looked at her, sympathetic but powerless to stem her sorrow.

Sudden shouts from the apartment next door came through the thin walls. Then a door slammed and a picture on Margie's wall slid askew. Dozens of framed portrait photographs, showing the kind of grim-faced people who wouldn't be displayed unless they were relatives, covered the wall. They were all crooked.

"They're always fighting," Margie said, staring toward the source of the noise. Then she turned to me and started to talk dispassionately, as if reciting a tale of people who were strangers to her. "Libby met William Daley two years ago, and she fell in love. Hard. And he loved her. Last year they married, a June wedding. I was a bridesmaid.

"Libby hadn't turned thirty yet and she couldn't have been happier. Everything in her life was wonderful—the movies, her new husband. She still talked to me then, mostly about having children. She had a future. Then her husband goes off on that fool trip, thinks he's going to teach the Chinese to play baseball . . ."

I knew the trip she was talking about. Last winter, Daley had organized a baseball tour of Asia and Europe that featured some of baseball's biggest names.

I also knew how the tour had ended. "And Daley died on the trip," I said.

She nodded. "Bad oysters. He ate some bad oysters . . . and that's it. He's dead, and Libby's life is ruined." I remembered the zeal with which Margie consumed oysters at the Sea Dip Hotel. Maybe she imagined she was avenging William Daley's death. "She was married to him for eight months, didn't see him for the last four, and then . . . she's a widow."

"Didn't see him? She wasn't with him on the trip?" Why wouldn't a new bride join her husband for a world cruise?

"No . . . maybe that's what bothered her so much. Maybe she thought if she'd been with him she could have helped him. But she couldn't go on a ship. She was terrified of water."

"Afraid of water?"

"Uh-huh. Ever since she was a little girl. She told me."

"But she went swimming Saturday night. That's how she drowned."

"She couldn't swim. She must have fallen in."

"But she had no clothes on. You don't take your clothes off to fall in. You take your clothes off to go swimming."

"I told you! She couldn't swim!" Margie sounded angry that I couldn't comprehend this simple fact. It wasn't all I couldn't comprehend.

"How do you know she had no clothes on?" she suddenly asked in a calmer voice.

Oops, I guess I let that slip. Did I want to tell Marguerite that I was the one who found Miss Hampton's body? No, for some reason I didn't. "I have a friend," I said. "He's a reporter. And he told me."

"Why?" Her eyes probed me sharply.

"He thought I might know something about what happened. Or . . . that I might be able to find out for him."

"Is he writing something about her? I don't want that. There've been too many horrid things written about her already."

"No. He promised me it's not for print."

"Her death wasn't an accident, was it." Her question sounded like a statement of fact.

"I don't know. I thought it was. I figured she met Virgil Ewing after the party and they went for a midnight swim. You remember when he said . . ."

Margie nodded.

"She was naked and she was found drowned," I said. "If she wasn't swimming, why would—" I halted as I realized there was another reason to take your clothes off. But from what I'd heard of that activity, it didn't generally result in drowning.

I changed tack. "After I left the party, what happened? Did it seem she was more with one fellow than another? Did it look like she'd be leaving with one of them?"

"Nooo. . . . Things were the same. All the men fighting over her. Then— Oh! She left alone. I saw her, I remember she wasn't looking well. It was just a little while before I left."

"Wait a minute. I just thought of something: why would Virgil Ewing even ask her to go swimming if she's afraid of water?"

Margie chuckled. "He wouldn't know about it. Libby wasn't one to admit she was afraid of *anything*. I'm probably the only person who knew. She let it slip during one of our late-night chats."

"Hmm. . . . Well, maybe I should talk to some people and see what I can find out about all this." I was thinking in particular of speaking with Virgil Ewing, Sloppy Sutherland, and Tom Kelly.

"Why you?"

"I want to find out what happened."

"So do I. And she was *my* friend."

Was this a competition? "I don't know . . . I just thought . . ."

"Why don't we *both* try to find out what happened?"

"Together?"

"Together," she said.

Together sounded good.

•   •   •

Not until after the game, while riding home on the Third Avenue El, did I realize that I'd forgotten to ask Margie about going with me to the movie premiere. Even if I had remembered, I wouldn't have brought it up though. It wouldn't have been appropriate under the circumstances.

I had the feeling that before anything could develop between Margie and me, Florence Hampton's death would have to be put behind us. And the best way to do that was to find out how and why she died.

I tried to imagine what could have happened to her Saturday night.

I started with the simplest explanation: after the party she meets with Virgil Ewing—or with somebody who heard Ewing's suggestion and thought it a good idea. Anyway, she meets one of her suitors and they go skinny dipping. She has a cramp, or is too drunk to swim, and drowns.

Two problems with that scenario. One, why didn't her

swimming date report her death? It could be because the publicity would hurt his career—and if it was Tom Kelly who was with her, it could also cost him his marriage. The second problem was tougher to explain: if she was so afraid of the water, she wouldn't have gone swimming in the first place. Maybe Margie was wrong about that, but why would Florence Hampton tell her she couldn't swim if it wasn't true?

Okay, so how could somebody who's afraid of the water end up naked in the Atlantic Ocean? Again, she meets someone on the beach. Not for swimming, but for a romantic rendezvous. It gets to the point where their clothes are off. Then what? She gets sick—the heat and the champagne overwhelm her—and maybe she passes out. Her partner brings her into the water to revive her. But then how would she drown? If she passed out, he wouldn't just dump her in the water, he'd hold her up.

Maybe she didn't get sick. Maybe there was an argument and she was beaten or choked—but not too badly, or the police wouldn't have called her death an accident. And I hadn't seen any marks on her body. Anyway, then she gets thrown into the water. Did the man who threw her in know she couldn't swim? Was it murder? Or was it unintentional, just a way to punctuate an argument that got out of hand?

Whatever did happen, I was convinced that someone was with her when she died. And I was starting to believe that her death was no accident.

• • •

Things no longer looked as bright as they had when I was dancing with Margie Turner on Saturday night.

Even the baseball diamond, the one place where hope always survives no matter how lopsided the score, seemed dimmer. Not only did the Dodgers beat us again Monday afternoon, but the mood of the ballpark was funereal. Florence Hampton's death left the Brooklyn fans too glum to cheer their team's victory.

Before the game, Charlie Ebbets addressed the crowd through a megaphone set up behind the pitcher's mound. He said polite, insipid things about her. I thought he should have treated her better when she was alive—it was just two days ago that he threw her friends out of the ballpark. Come to think of it, I never did find out what that was all about. Why wouldn't he want his ballpark used in a movie?

# Chapter Six

The flags around the outfield fence were still at half-mast, the same as they had been yesterday afternoon. But it was the Pittsburgh banner that was nearest the right field foul pole today. By beating us in the first two games of the series, the Dodgers had pulled themselves out of the National League cellar and into seventh place.

There was some relief from the heat today, provided by scattered clouds and gusting breezes. Winds can swirl strangely in a ballpark, and they blew today with home team bias. The Dodgers' flag flew straight out, as if the breeze was giving them a good omen. The Giants' hung limp next to the left field foul pole.

I stood on the top step of the Giants' dugout, absentmindedly tightening the leather lacing on my glove. It was two-thirty on Tuesday afternoon, half an hour before game time for the series finale, and the park was already standing room only. Crackling chatter and guttural shouts from the crowd filled the park with a frenzied din. The Dodger fans were in a blood lust, eager to see Brooklyn sweep a series from the Giants.

Last evening's crowd had been restrained, almost somber, in mourning for Florence Hampton. Now the lowered flags seemed to be the only things grieving.

Across the diamond, the Dodgers' hunchbacked batboy emerged from the dugout. A hunchback was considered the most powerful good luck charm a baseball club could have, and many teams had them as mascots. Virgil Ewing then stepped out in his catcher's gear and gave the boy's hump a rub for luck before going to warm up Sloppy Sutherland. The boy went about his business, lining up the team bats in front of the Brooklyn dugout. With their barrels pointing toward the infield and the Giants' bats arrayed the same way on our side of the field, they looked like the cannons of two battleships about to fire broadsides at each other.

I walked out to second base, not so much to inspect the ground as to suggest to John McGraw that I was ready to play that position today. In the locker room, I'd seen that Larry Doyle, our regular second baseman, had a swollen right ankle splotched with angry red scabs where Brooklyn's Zack Wheat spiked him yesterday. Since the amount of playing time I got depended largely on injuries to the starters, I paid as much attention to my teammates' pulled hamstrings and split fingers as I did to batting averages and fielding percentages.

McGraw came up to me as I was kicking the second base bag. "Doyle's okay to play," he said in answer to my thoughts. Then he looked to right field where Stengel was again bouncing balls off the flypaper sign. "What's that crazy sonofabitch doing?" McGraw muttered. "He think the ball's going to stick to it?"

Since McGraw had just vetoed my starting hopes, I took some pleasure in correcting him—not something that was done often. "Uh-uh," I said. "See, he's throwing at the crease. So he can see how to play it off the wall."

McGraw watched a minute more, then conceded I was right, saying, "I'll be damned." He gave me a long look, nodded, and marched off to the Giants' bullpen where Jeff Tesreau was warming up.

I walked back to the dugout, my head down.

"Rawlings!"

I turned to the field to see who was calling me.

"Rawlings! Mickey Rawlings!"

The shout wasn't from the field; it was from the stands in front of me. Somebody was calling me by name! I lifted my head, almost eager for the heckling to start. I didn't feel at all persecuted. Actually, I felt rather honored.

But no abuse came. Just my name repeated again, with no hostility in the voice. I looked into the stands, knowing full well that a visiting player shouldn't acknowledge the crowd and wondering if I was being suckered in by an especially devious heckler.

Then I saw a black derby near the rail and under it a face that looked like a skull with spectacles. I didn't feel flattered anymore. This was no obnoxious Dodger fan about to shower me with vile abuse. It was only Karl Landfors.

He waved to me and I walked up to the rail in front of him.

"Hey, Karl," I said. "What are you doing here?" Not the friendliest of greetings, but I'd sooner expect to see Henry Ford driving a Chevrolet than Karl Landfors at a baseball game.

Landfors looked behind him with exaggerated caution. Then he leaned over the railing and cupped his hands around his mouth, not as a megaphone but to hide what he was saying. "I have the autopsy report," he whispered.

"The what?"

"The autopsy report on Florence Hampton." He pulled a folded paper from an inside pocket of his black undertaker's coat.

Karl Landfors sure was an odd one. He comes to a ball-game not with a glove to catch a foul ball or a picture to be signed, not even with bottles or vegetables to throw at the visiting players. No, he comes to a baseball game with an autopsy report.

"She drowned," he announced.

"Everybody knows she drowned."

"They *assume* she drowned. There's a difference. The autopsy *proves* it. Her lungs were full of water."

"Jeez, Karl, I can't talk about that now. I got a ballgame to play."

"Oh. You're playing in this one?"

I wanted to grab his necktie and give it a hard twist. I also wished I could have answered yes.

"Rawlings! Get your ass over here." That yell came from behind me and it was the voice of John McGraw.

I pulled the paper from Landfors, then handed it back, saying loudly, "How can I give you an autograph if you don't have a pen?" I added quietly, "Meet me after the game."

"I'm not staying for the *game.*" He sounded appalled by the notion that he'd watch a baseball game.

"Suffer through it. I'll meet you in the rotunda."

I trotted up to John McGraw. He showed me the lineup card. I was on it, playing second and batting eighth. I wished I could have shown it to Karl Landfors.

• • •

The Dodgers started Sloppy Sutherland again on only two days' rest. With no hope of getting to the World Series, they were going all out to sweep this series. Sutherland continued where he left off on Saturday, as if the two days off were just a break between innings. He dominated the game, slipping his talcum pitches past the fruitless swings of the Giants' hitters. Big Jeff Tesreau, on a pace to win thirty games for us this year, had less luck with his less elegant spitballs. After five innings, we were down 6–0.

In the top of the seventh, the tension between the teams suddenly boiled over. Sutherland must have thrown too close to Chief Meyers, because Meyers was charging the mound, bat in hand. We were going to have a donnybrook!

I leapt off the bench ready to fight the first Dodger I could lay my hands on. Then I saw it wasn't Meyers who was going after Sutherland, it was Virgil Ewing. Meyers was just trying to hold him back as Ewing screamed about being crossed up on signs. From the third base coach's box, McGraw yelled at the Chief, "Let the bastards kill each other!" Wilbert Robinson bolted out of the Dodgers' dugout and jiggled his way to the mound. The Dodger manager interposed his girth between Ewing and Sutherland and kept them from coming to blows. Umpire Bill Klem finally dragged Ewing back behind the plate.

The Giant players sat back down, even more frustrated than before. We were already behind the Dodgers on the scoreboard; the least they could do was give us a chance to even things up with a brawl. But no, they wanted to fight among themselves. This Dodger team was not a civilized bunch. Maybe not a smart bunch either—how many signs do you need for a guy who only throws one kind of pitch?

With two outs in the top of the ninth and the Dodgers still up 6–0, our first baseman Fred Merkle knocked a long triple

to the center field wall. I was up next to either end the game
or keep the rally alive.

As I moved into the batter's box, Virgil Ewing squirted a
thin stream of tobacco juice at a pigeon bobbing along the
ground near the backstop. He nailed the bird in the tail
feathers, sending him into flight. I was impressed—Ewing
hadn't bothered to lift his mask; he'd spit clean through the
bars. There aren't many who can do that. I thought Virgil
Ewing might have some unexpected talents in him.

I looked back toward third base. Merkle was dancing off
the bag eager to score. John McGraw, the only man in baseball who wore an infielder's mitt in the coach's box,
pounded his fist into the glove twice. I wasn't sure that I saw
right, so I backed out of the box. McGraw repeated his move,
hitting the glove twice with his right fist. It was the sign for a
squeeze play.

It didn't make sense—we needed six runs, not one. I
should be swinging away. Then I realized: McGraw figures
the game is lost, so he wants to cost Sutherland his shutout
and salvage some kind of victory. Well, it doesn't matter what
makes sense; all that counts is that McGraw wants me to lay
down a bunt, so that's what I have to do.

And I did. On Sutherland's first pitch, Merkle broke for the
plate and I laid a perfect bunt up the first base line. I beat out
the throw for a single and an RBI. And from the stands came
a deafening roar of boos that could be heard in Hoboken.
The Dodger fans had wanted Sutherland to get the shutout,
and I became the most hated man in Flatbush.

I took only a token lead off first base. No way was I going
to try to steal a base now. I wouldn't get out of the ballpark
alive if I did.

When Jeff Tesreau got up to the plate, Sutherland went
into his stretch. Then he whirled and caught me by surprise

with a pickoff throw—not to the base but at my head. I ducked and it grazed my shoulder as it flew into foul territory.

I was too stunned to take off for second base right away. I recovered and started running but too late. Casey Stengel fielded the overthrow and threw me out at second base to end the game.

Sloppy Sutherland didn't trot off the field with the out. He stayed on the mound and followed me with his eyes as I ran to the Giants' dugout. The look in his eyes told me that he hadn't settled with me yet.

•  •  •

The marble rotunda of Ebbets Field was known for two things: its ornate design and the bottleneck it created for fans entering or leaving the ballpark. To avoid encountering any of them, I kept Landfors waiting there for almost an hour before meeting him.

He was standing in the center of the round floor, staring up at a huge chandelier that hung from the domed ceiling. The room was about 80 feet across, with a dozen ticket windows and turnstiles around it in a semicircle. The floor was tiled in white, with some red tiles laid in to look like the stitches of a baseball. The light fixture Landfors was admiring was ringed by oversized baseball bats, each supporting a baseball-shaped globe.

"Sorry I took so long," I said.

"Quite all right," he answered, and it sounded like he meant it. Maybe a day at the ballpark had done his disposition some good.

"How'd you like the game?"

"It wasn't bad, really. As a matter of fact, once I started

pulling for the Dodgers, it was almost enjoyable. They really beat you bad."

I shot him a look. He comes to see me at ballgame and then roots against me? Well, I had to give him some credit— at least he didn't root for the umpires.

Landfors wanted to find a saloon near Ebbets Field where we could sit down and talk. I didn't want to risk going into a Brooklyn bar. I might be recognized as the guy who cost Sloppy Sutherland his shutout, and Landfors wouldn't be much help in a barroom brawl. I did agree on a bar, though. I could use a postgame beer, and Landfors was easier to be around after a few brews.

I wasn't going to feel comfortable until we crossed the East River back into civilization, so we left the park and hopped a trolley to Manhattan.

As we stood on the packed trolley, grasping onto leather straps, Landfors filled me in on the autopsy results. We talked into each other's ears, not to be secretive but because we were pressed so close together.

"It's official," Landfors said. "Florence Hampton drowned. Period. No evidence of foul play."

From past experience, I knew that "official" doesn't nec- essarily mean correct. "Do you think the report is right?"

Landfors thought a minute. "There doesn't seem to be anything to indicate that her death is anything but an acci- dental drowning. Some abrasions on the skin, but that's from the sand scraping her when she was washed up on the shore. No contusions—uh . . . no bruises, that is. And no sign of sexual assault."

Somewhere there was a flaw with the accident conclu- sion, but I wasn't sure what it was. "Why was she naked?" I asked, poking around to find the error. I answered myself,

"Either to go swimming or to have sex. But she couldn't swim."

Landfors twisted his head so quickly that his spectacles hit me in the nose.

"A friend of hers told me she couldn't swim," I explained. "She was deathly afraid of water." As it left my lips I realized "deathly" wasn't the best word to use.

"And the autopsy showed she hadn't had sex," Landfors added.

"Was she interrupted?" I guessed. "Maybe she met somebody on the beach, and . . . and they stripped, but before they could do anything she drowned."

"How did she end up in the water?"

"Mmm. . . . Maybe there was an argument—a fight. The man she's with gets angry for some reason, and he drowns her. Or how about this: there's a third party. Somebody catches her with a man, gets jealous, and pulls her into the water and drowns her."

"A third party?"

"Yeah, you should have seen all the guys going after her at the party." I quickly filled Landfors in on the party at the Sea Dip Hotel and how Ewing, Sutherland, and Kelly were all competing for her attention. I didn't leave out anything—except for Marguerite Turner being my date. I preferred that Landfors didn't know about her. "Maybe Sutherland caught her with Virgil Ewing," I suggested. "Or Ewing caught her with Sutherland. Or Tom Kelly—he's the jealous type. Oh, jeez. Esther Kelly, Tom Kelly's wife, she left the party early. What if she waited for Miss Hampton to come out, then followed her and killed her because she was jealous?"

"She drowned Florence Hampton and then took her clothes off?" Landfors sounded dubious.

Picturing Esther Kelly, I decided his skepticism was well-founded. "No, I guess not. She's not big enough to have overpowered her."

"How about this," Landfors countered. "Esther Kelly finds her having sex with her husband, so her clothes are off, and she's in no position to defend herself."

That was dumber than my idea. "She drags Florence Hampton into the ocean with Tom Kelly on top of her, and he just lets himself be dragged along for the ride?" I scoffed. "Besides, wouldn't she kill her husband then? He was the one who was cheating on her, not Miss Hampton." I thought of James Bartlett with distaste and promised myself that I wasn't doing this to save his political career.

"I don't know," Landfors said. "What if Esther Kelly and Florence Hampton got into a fight and Tom Kelly tried to stop it? Somehow she gets killed."

"But how did she get drowned?"

"I don't know," he conceded again. "She would have struggled. And there was no sign of a struggle—no bruises on her and nothing under her nails from someone else." Landfors was right. She'd have fought like hell.

Nothing we could come up with led us to the final result: Florence Hampton, drowned, naked, and without bruises. It was a you-can't-get-there-from-here situation. One thing I was sure of, though: she hadn't been alone. The only way for her to have gotten in the water was for somebody to have been with her. I just had to find out who.

Landfors and I both thought about things silently for a while. We'd crossed the Brooklyn Bridge when he said, "Well, the thing to do is for you to talk to those men who were with her at the party. I think we can omit Esther Kelly."

"Talking to Sutherland and Ewing won't be easy, Karl." Especially not Sutherland, I thought—and especially not after today's game.

"Why not?"

"They're *Dodgers.* I'm a Giant."

"So? You're all baseball players."

"Giants and Dodgers hate each other. Always have, always will." Landfors was a smart guy, even went to college, but there were some fundamental facts of life he didn't understand.

"Forgive my ignorance," he said facetiously. "But the logic of that escapes me."

I explained to him that the rivalry between Brooklyn and New York baseball teams was already a fierce one when my grandfather saw the Brooklyn Atlantics play the New York Mutuals in the 1850s. Landfors still looked lost. Then I mentioned that the Manhattan clubs were made up of gentlemen and the Brooklyn clubs of mechanics and firemen.

"Ah," Landfors said. "Proletariat versus bourgeoisie." He had a satisfied look on his face as if he finally understood.

I'm damned if I did though. All I could think was that next time I'd wait until I had a beer in front of me before enduring another conversation with Karl Landfors.

# *Chapter Seven*

I could feel my collar shrinking, tightening around my throat until it had a stranglehold that barely let me breathe. A clammy shroud of sweat covered my body.

Nobody told me I was going to have to face reporters.

Only four days earlier, Florence Hampton completed her last picture. Now, on Wednesday night, it was being unveiled to the public with enough fanfare and spectacle to make P. T. Barnum proud.

Instead of using its own theater on 44th Street, Vitagraph leased the opulent Strand Theatre on Broadway for the premiere. The marquee proclaimed:

*FLORENCE HAMPTON*
*in*
*FLORENCE AT THE BALLPARK*
*Her Final Picture! Her Greatest Role!*

The sidewalk area under the marquee was cordoned off with purple velvet ropes. I was confined inside them, along with the other guests and stars of the Vitagraph Company. Spotlights set up across the street cut through the dusk, sweeping across the front of the theater with translucent cones of white light, too often pinning me in their beams. I felt like a display in a museum. My only comfort was that Marguerite Turner stood next to me, her hand on the crook of my arm.

I'd finally called her this afternoon and asked her to accompany me. She sounded delighted that I asked and cheerfully agreed. Later I found out that the studio had already told her she was to be my escort.

The army of movie fans that pressed against the ropes outside the Strand was nothing like a ballpark crowd. They were too quiet—no cheering, no arguing, and of course no heckling. Just silent mournful staring. It was like they had come to Florence Hampton's wake.

I don't think the mood of the crowd mattered to Elmer Garvin, though, as long as they shelled out their two bits a ticket.

On a carpeted platform next to the theater entrance stood Arthur V. Carlyle. It was his job to announce the featured guests, who then had to climb the platform and answer reporters' questions. Elmer Garvin had already faced them, choosing to give a long speech rather than answer questions directly. So had Tom and Esther Kelly; Tom did all the talking, even answering questions addressed to his wife.

With his booming *thea-tuh* voice Arthur Carlyle introduced Casey Stengel and Constance Talmadge. She was a bit player best known for being Norma's sister; Vitagraph assigned her as Casey's date to get her some publicity. I felt some pride that my date was a bigger movie star than his. I also felt my throat constrict a little tighter—Margie and I would be next on the platform.

"What's it like making a movie, Casey?" a reporter shouted in a practiced voice that sounded insistent and bored at the same time.

"Well, I'd have to say it's a great deal of fun. Not as much fun as playing on a baseball field, which is of course another kind of performance, but it's different in its own sort of way. Both of which have their advantages over dentistry, however. Now when I was in dental college in Kansas City, which by the way there aren't many left-handed hitting dentists . . ." Jeez, if Casey kept it up, I might not have to take the stage after all. I'd owe him another favor if he did.

But no such luck. Elmer Garvin beckoned frantically to Constance Talmadge. She tugged Stengel off the stage as he was explaining why tobacco chewers throw the best spitballs.

Arthur Carlyle stared after Stengel, his mouth agape. When he recovered, he announced, "Ladies and gentlemen! I am pleased to present another young man—another baseball player—whose first acting performance is being screened this evening. And with him is a young lady whom you already know as one of Vitagraph's most popular actresses. Ladies and gentlemen, Mr. Mickey Rawlings and Miss Marguerite Turner." I thought it rude of Carlyle not to announce the lady first.

I made it up the platform without tripping. Immediately, I was blinded as photographers put their flash lamps to use, producing little explosions of light and smoke. It reminded me of the spotlight in the Vitagraph studio, and I was grateful that the spotlights here were safely across the street where I had no chance of knocking into them.

"Did you enjoy working with Florence Hampton, Rollins?" a reporter yelled.

I nodded yes and hoped the reporter would check the spelling of my name before he wrote his article.

"A nod makes for a lousy quote," he followed up.

"Yes," I elaborated. "I enjoyed working with Miss Hampton."

"Gee, thanks, Rollins. That's a whole lot better."

I hoped the next question would be for Margie.

"Hey, Rawlings!" another reporter called in a shrill voice. "I can see how Stengel got in the picture—he's a big name. But how did *you* get a part? You're not even a starter. Was it Miss Hampton's idea?"

I said nothing. I wasn't going to tell him that John McGraw didn't want one of his starters used for the picture.

"Just how well did you know Miss Hampton?" the high brittle voice continued. "I hear she *liked* ball players."

I bristled at the insinuation. Who the hell *was* this guy? My right fist balled, and I felt Margie slide her hand down my arm. She gently pried my fist open and gave my hand a comforting squeeze.

"You were at a party with her Saturday night, last time she was seen alive. And you left early. Didn't meet Miss Hampton for a midnight swim, did you?"

Why was he saying these things to me? In front of all these people . . . and Margie . . . ?

More blinding explosions went off as photographers shot more pictures.

Margie led me off the platform. I tried to pick out the reporter's face, promising myself that I was going to do some damage to it—if not tonight, then someday. But the spotlights and flash lamps kept him shielded by a white glare.

• • •

I was still trembling with anger after we were seated in the theater. Margie kept her hand on my forearm, giving it an occasional pat. "Some of the newspaper reporters are just awful," she said. "The fan magazines are much kinder. Don't let it bother you." I tried to smile, but I was bothered intensely.

We were in the front row of the auditorium, seated just behind the full orchestra that had been hired for the event. We sat in roomy armchairs with white velvet upholstery and gilded wood trim.

The Strand Theatre opened in April as the first theater built exclusively for showing motion pictures. It had a seating capacity of 3,000 and every seat was filled this evening. I'd played in major league ballparks with smaller crowds.

Before the show, Elmer Garvin took the stage. "Ladies and gentlemen," he said. "As you know, we've suffered a tragic loss in the Vitagraph family. Since there were no public services for Miss Florence Hampton, it is fitting that I take a moment to say a few words about her." Garvin then went on to say quite a few words about the virtues of the Vitagraph Company.

After Garvin's speech, the orchestra burst into a deafening overture. They played at a volume that ensured that patrons in the last row could hear them clearly and almost blew those of us in the front row out of our seats. A rippling burgundy curtain was raised, revealing a dazzling white screen of immense proportion. The house lights dimmed, and the movie program was under way.

Before the main feature, some short one-reelers were shown, including the latest episode of Marguerite Turner's *Dangers of the Dark Continent* serial. As it unfolded, I discovered one of the joys of dating a movie actress: I could stare at her on the screen in a way that would be fresh to do in person.

I did stare when I first saw her tonight. She looked stunning, in a shimmering peach gown that fit her snugly. Her hair was done up in a neat bun, and rouge highlighted her cheeks.

*Florence at the Ballpark* suddenly appeared on the screen in fancy script lettering. Then a title card that read *starring Florence Hampton* with a smiling portrait of her in an oval next to her name. A wave of applause swept through the audience.

The rest of the credits rolled by, for Tom Kelly and Casey Stengel. When *And introducing Mickey Rawlings of the New York Giants* came on, Margie gave my hand a quick double squeeze. I didn't even mind that Casey was "featured," while I was merely "introduced."

Then the movie started. And in five minutes I could tell it was going to be awful. The photography was good, in crisp black and white. But the dialogue that appeared on the title cards was sappy, the words supposedly spoken by Florence Hampton making her sound dumb and weak. There were far too many irrelevant shots of her, too, most of them from movies I'd seen before. Elmer Garvin must have taken clips from other pictures to pad the film.

I didn't like the way people were exploiting her death. Elmer Garvin was using her image and the public's sympathy to cash in at the box office. That reporter outside was trying to sell papers by smearing her name with scandal. I could imagine what he'd do if he found out about her affair with James Bartlett.

The scene of Casey Stengel and me finally came on, and as I watched us go through our bat-tossing routine, I momentarily forgot about Florence Hampton. I looked pretty damn good up there—maybe it was the artificial backdrop of the diamond that made me look better by comparison, but I thought I cut a fine figure on the screen.

When Florence Hampton walked past us with Tom Kelly in his umpire outfit, there was a close-up shot of my reaction. And I couldn't believe what I saw myself say. The title card read "Shucks," but three thousand lip readers in the audience knew what I really said and laughter boomed throughout the theater. I looked to Margie at my right; she was doubled over, convulsed with belly laughs. On the other side of her, I could see Casey Stengel grinning so broadly that the tops of his jumbo ears nearly met above his head.

I had an impulse to slip down in my chair and hide. The sight of Stengel gave me an idea, though, one that I clung to as I tried to forget my embarrassment.

• • •

The picture was over, mercifully over, and most of the audience had left the theater. The movie people remained in the lobby, waiting to make exits as carefully choreographed as their entrances had been.

The ladies, Margie and Constance Talmadge included, were gathered in a corner of the lobby, fixing each other's hair and touching up their makeup.

I walked over to Casey Stengel, who was standing next to the popcorn machine hungrily eyeing the few kernels that remained. "Hey, Casey," I said. "You looked good on the screen."

"Well, thanks. So did you. Maybe when we're not playing baseball any more we can go to work for the pictures. Which wouldn't be a bad sort of business to be in. It's a whole lot better than wrestling alligators. There was this fellow I knew in Missouri who used to play left field for the Rolla Tigers, or was it Sedelia? Anyway, after he stopped playing ball—"

"Uh, Casey. I wanted to ask you something before the girls get back . . ."

"Oh, sure. What's on your mind?"

"At the party—on Coney Island—well, Sloppy Sutherland and Virgil Ewing were both dancing a lot with Florence Hampton. Almost fighting over her. But I don't know who she ended up with. So I want to talk to Ewing and Sutherland and see if they know what happened to her afterward."

Casey frowned. "Yeah?" he said guardedly.

"Well, it's not really *my* idea," I fibbed, trying to allay his suspicion. "To tell you the truth, Margie—Marguerite Turner—wants me to talk to them. She was a friend of Miss Hampton's and wants me to see if they know anything. I don't see what good that'll do, but Margie . . ." I shrugged. "You know how it is."

Casey smiled with understanding. I was simply following the bidding of a woman. No further explanation was necessary.

"But I don't know if they'd talk to me, being a Giant and all," I went on. "Especially after the game yesterday. I thought you might introduce me to them. If you don't mind . . ."

"No trouble at all. I'd be glad to. Ewing and I get along pretty well, sometimes play cards together when we're on the road. Sloppy Sutherland, though, he's a tough one to find when he's not on the ballfield. He likes to go with the uptown crowd . . ." Casey's eyes went back to the popcorn machine. "Damn, I'm hungry. Say, are you coming to the party?"

We were all supposed to go to the rooftop show at Madison Square Garden after the picture. But I remembered the Garden as the place where its architect, Stanford White, was murdered. Between that and the way the last Vitagraph party turned out, I had no enthusiasm for going there.

"No, I don't think so. We got a game against the Cardinals tomorrow, and I'm not really up for—"

Margie walked toward us, and with one look at her, I changed my mind. In fact, I thought maybe I'd even try that dancing business again.

# Chapter Eight

*Is she next?*

I read the photo caption again and again, not believing that the question could have been put into print.

But that's what it said. On the front page of the *New York Public Examiner* was a photograph of Margie and me in front of the Strand Theatre. The grainy photo showed me with an angry expression. The photographer must have timed his shot to catch my reaction to the infuriating questions about Florence Hampton.

Bad as the photograph was, the wording underneath it was worse: *Baseball player Mickey Rawlings with new actress friend Marguerite Turner. Is she next?*

The accompanying article was written in sentences that read like a series of lurid headlines. According to the story, I was "a baseball player of little renown who currently warms the bench of the New York Giants." Florence Hampton was "a notorious ex-showgirl whose wanton ways caught up with her Saturday night." And since I "didn't deny a close relationship with Hampton," the paper concluded, "it is believed Rawlings met her for a midnight swim." As for Margie:

"Miss Turner seemed unaware of the perils of associating with Rawlings."

The *Public Examiner* was trash, the kind of paper you claimed to have found on the trolley if you were caught with a copy. Just last month it reported in bold headlines that President McKinley hadn't really been assassinated, that he had been living in South America for the last thirteen years.

Although the paper was known for being unconcerned about facts, people did read it and some of them even believed its stories.

The byline to this story read: *by William Murray.* I had his name now. And I could still hear his shrill voice from last night. I stopped worrying about the article long enough to indulge in some delightful daydreams of meeting him fist to face.

A copy of every paper that my local newsstand carried was piled on my couch. I'd gone through every one, every page. Except for the *Public Examiner,* the front pages for Thursday morning, August 6, were dominated by more important news: the expanding war between Germany, Russia, France, Belgium, England, and a bunch of smaller countries in a place called the Balkans. Most of the papers had the reaction of President Wilson and his promise to stay neutral.

Most of them also reported on the opening of *Florence at the Ballpark* but on an inside page and without the vicious slant of the *Examiner.*

It only takes one paper to start a smear though.

I worried what Margie would think when she saw it. Not only about the *Is she next?* question—she'd know there was nothing to that—but also about the "warms the bench of the New York Giants" line. That was really low.

And just when things were going so well between us. Not only did I go to Madison Square Garden with her, but we danced more than any other couple and were among the last to leave.

Wait a minute. *Would* it be obvious that there was nothing to the *Examiner*'s insinuation? What if the police saw it and decided to question me again? Would I need an alibi?

I tried to figure out what time I'd left the party Saturday night and found I had absolutely no idea. I remembered opening my watch, but I never saw the watch face, just the photograph on the back cover.

And no one was with me to verify that I stayed in my hotel room that night.

This is ridiculous. I don't need an alibi. Not because some sleazy penny paper wants to invent a scandal. Oh jeez. What if that reporter finds out that I discovered Florence Hampton's body?

I tossed the *Public Examiner* on the pile with the other papers, then leaned back in my chair to try to relax. We were opening a homestand at the Polo Grounds this afternoon, and I had only a few hours to get my thoughts focused on baseball.

But my thoughts had a mind of their own.

I started wondering what the papers would print if they knew about Miss Hampton's affair with James Bartlett. Hell, if they could smear a "baseball player of little renown," imagine what they could do to a politician. The idea of a politician in a sex scandal would send the papers into a feeding frenzy.

The notion of tipping the papers off about Bartlett passed briefly through my mind. They'd forget about persecuting me if they could sink their fangs into a political candidate.

I let the idea pass on through and fade away. I had no sympathy for Bartlett, but I could never double-cross Karl Landfors that way.

Then some more ideas about James Bartlett came to mind. And these seemed worth pursuing.

•   •   •

"Karl Landfors, please."

"One moment."

I waited for the *New York Press* switchboard operator to connect me.

Landfors answered with a grumpy "Yeah?"

"Karl, it's Mickey. I have an idea."

"Yeah?"

For a guy who was full of ten dollar words, he wasn't giving me a nickel's worth. "Listen, Karl. I have an idea about somebody else who might have wanted Florence Hampton killed."

"Who?"

"Tammany Hall. Or whoever runs it, anyway."

"Where'd you come up with *that* idea?"

"From you. You said James Bartlett was running for office, opposing Tammany Hall. And you said if they found out about him and Miss Hampton, they'd use it to smear him. Right?"

"Right . . ."

"Well, what if they *did* know about her, and they killed her. So now there's a lot of attention on her death. And maybe with all that attention, it comes out that Bartlett was involved with her. Then he's ruined, right? What do you think?"

"I think that's utterly absurd. You don't understand how these people work. They don't kill people."

"They don't?"

"No. Well, not usually. They don't have to. You remember Sulzer?"

"Of course." Landfors must have thought I knew nothing that wasn't reported on the sports pages. It was just a year ago that William Sulzer was impeached as governor of New York.

*"That's* how Tammany Hall operates. They got Sulzer elected, Sulzer didn't do exactly what they wanted, so they trumped up some charges against him and got the state legislature to impeach him. Bingo. Sulzer is history. See? They don't need to kill people to get what they want. Besides, it's risky. It could backfire on them if they got caught."

"Oh. Well, I had another idea then."

"I hope it's better than the last one."

Actually, I knew it was even more far-fetched, but I figured I'd tell him anyway. It wasn't going to lower his opinion of me any. "What if it was Bartlett's *supporters* who killed her? What if—"

"You've *got* to be kidding."

"No, listen. What if they wanted her to end the affair with Bartlett so that he wouldn't get caught. And she wouldn't, so they killed her to put an end to it."

"Oh for chrissake! Make up your mind. First she's killed to expose the affair, then she's killed to keep it quiet. Look: forget the political angle. You don't know anything about it. *I'll* look into Bartlett. You work on the baseball players and movie actors." Then he must have remembered that I was doing him a favor this time, because he added in a gentler voice, "All right, Mickey?"

"Yeah, okay." I was ready to hang up, then added, "Oh, one more thing, Karl. You know a reporter named William Murray?"

"William Murray. . . . I've heard the name. But I don't know him personally. He used to be a theater critic, I think."

"Do you know what he looks like?"

"No, never met him. Why?"

"Oh, no reason."

"She's a pretty girl, Mickey."

"Who?"

"Marguerite Turner, of course. You, on the other hand, look like a gargoyle in that picture."

"Oh. You saw . . ."

"Of course I saw it. We're a newspaper; we get all the other papers, even the *Public Examiner*. Are you sweet on her?"

"She's okay." Margie Turner wasn't a topic I wanted to discuss with Landfors. "Back to Bartlett though—"

That was something *he* didn't want to discuss. *"Forget Bartlett,"* he said with an exasperated sigh.

"Yeah, okay. I better go."

Funny thing was, as I hung up, I did have another thought about James Bartlett. If he was having an affair with Florence Hampton, when and where did the two of them meet? Maybe at night, on a Coney Island beach.

•   •   •

At three o'clock in the afternoon, Christy Mathewson led us out of the center field clubhouse and onto the outfield grass of the Polo Grounds. The turf felt reassuring under my spikes, and in general I felt on firmer ground here. This was what I knew—the baseball field. Not movie studios or newspapers or political machines. I was at home here.

My teammates looked similarly happy to be back in the park, with the fiasco in Flatbush behind us.

Technically, this was also the home field of the Yankees; the American Leaguers had left Washington Heights at the end of the 1912 season, abandoning their old Hilltop Park on Broadway and 166th. Until they could build a new stadium, we were letting them share ours. The Yanks were just tenants though. The Polo Grounds was truly home to only the Giants.

It was a long trek from the clubhouse to the dugout. I'd seen ballparks that were square and ballparks that were round and some that were shaped like jigsaw puzzle pieces to fit into odd-shaped building lots, but the Polo Grounds was the only one I knew that was built like a bathtub. It was less than 300 feet down either foul line, and about a mile and a half to center field. I could barely make out the pitcher's mound in the distance, and home plate wasn't visible at all. What dominated the view in front of me was Coogan's Bluff rising above the double-decked grandstand. Not only was the shape of the ballpark unique, so was its location: wedged between a cliff on one side and the Harlem River on the other.

It was baseball weather today—clear blue sky, temperature in the 70s, and a slight breeze blowing out to left field. As we moved closer to the infield, cheers and applause rippled through the early crowd that came to see batting practice. Bouyed by the home team fans and invigorated by the weather, my Giant teammates carried themselves like champions and I knew our slide in the standings was coming to an end.

Unfortunately, the visiting third-place Cardinals didn't know it. Behind the two-hit pitching of Slim Sallee and a sacrifice fly by their manager and second baseman Miller Huggins, the Cardinals shut us out 1–0.

It wasn't a bad loss though. The game was errorless and well-played by both teams; the Cards just came out ahead this time.

The mood in the clubhouse after the game was quiet but

not glum. It was a loss, so we couldn't be happy, but I could see a new confidence in my teammates. If we played the rest of the season the way we did today, we'd have the pennant locked up by Labor Day.

After showering and changing, I felt confident enough to talk to John McGraw about something that had nothing to do with the game. I'd had another one of my great ideas: who would be better to ask about Tom Kelly than John McGraw? I figured since McGraw had a grudge against Kelly for jumping the team, he wouldn't hesitate to tell me if he knew any dirt about him.

McGraw was in his office, still in uniform, his feet on a desk and a newspaper in front of his face. It wasn't a large room, just something to give him a little privacy from the players.

"Mr. McGraw?" Behind his back, he was often referred to as "The Little Round Man"; to his face, he was always "Mr. McGraw."

He lowered the paper enough to look at me over the top of it. "Yeah, kid?" His eyes had an anger in them, and I remembered that it was winning, and only winning, that mattered to McGraw. "Well-played" didn't count unless it put the game in the win column.

"I was wondering about Tom Kelly. When he played for you—"

"Kelly!" he roared. "You thinking of doing like he did? Think you're gonna be a goddamn movie star now?"

"No! No, I just—"

"You forget about them goddamn moving pictures!" He threw down the paper and I saw it was the *Public Examiner*. Jeez, my timing needed work.

Now I just wanted to get out of his office as quickly as possible.

"You keep the hell away from them goddamn movie people," he ordered. "They're only gonna get you in trouble. You want to find yourself back in Beaumont?"

"No!" One season in East Texas was enough for a lifetime. And enough for an afterlifetime—it was a better illustration of hell than any fire and brimstone sermon by Billy Sunday.

"Then you worry about baseball and winning the pennant." He slapped his hand down on the newspaper. "I read any more crap like this, and you're not playing for John McGraw anymore. Got it?"

"Yes." And I did. I backed out of his office and hustled out of the park. He had me feeling guilty and worried.

It took a while for me to realize it was McGraw who'd chosen me for the movie in the first place. If I got into trouble because of it, wouldn't it be his fault?

*Chapter Nine*

**F**riday morning never dawned. The sun wasn't powerful enough to penetrate the dark massive clouds that stormed above the city.

I woke to a steady drum roll of rain pelting the awning over my bedroom window. Rumbles of thunder echoed in the background.

The rain cooled the air so much that my bedroom was almost chilly. I pulled the blanket up to my chin and plumped the pillow under my head. Listening to the gurgle of rain water running through a down spout, resting my eyes in the soothing dim gray light, and breathing air so brisk that it felt alive, I wallowed in the utter coziness of it all.

New York hadn't been this cool since spring, and it reminded me that fall would soon be here. And with fall, the World Series. I just hoped the Series would hurry up and get here while the Giants were still in first place.

I tried to imagine myself playing in the World Series. Would it be in Philadelphia's Shibe Park, against Connie Mack and his Athletics? Or would we be facing my former Red Sox teammates in Fenway?

Neither ballpark came into view. The only scene I could picture was me sitting next to John McGraw on a dugout bench as he fills out a lineup card. When he finishes, I can see that I'm not on it. Then he crumples it up, throws it on the ground, and writes a new one with a different batting order. My hopes rise only to be dashed again. He writes one lineup card after another, filling the dugout floor with his rejects, and not writing my name on one of them.

My sense of physical comfort was eventually overrun by a nagging voice in my mind. It was telling me that McGraw was right—I was in trouble.

I tried to figure out how I had gotten into such a confounding mess so quickly. What had I done wrong?

I jumped back to the beginning and quickly reviewed all that had happened.

Six days ago, I'm sitting in the visitors' dugout of Ebbets Field, wanting nothing more than to get in the game. Then McGraw jerks his thumb at me, and I'm in a movie with Florence Hampton. Miss Hampton drowns, and Karl Landfors shows up to call in a favor: he wants me to investigate her death to protect some politician. Then a hack reporter wants to invent a scandal, so he does a front-page story suggesting I was involved in Miss Hampton's death. McGraw sees the story and gives me hell . . .

Jeez. As far as I could tell, not only hadn't I done anything wrong, I hadn't really *done* anything at all. Other people had just aimed me where they wanted and pushed me along.

Well, I wasn't going to be pushed any more. If I was going to get *out* of trouble, I was going to have to do it myself and set my own direction.

• • •

Although in setting my own course, I wasn't going to aim for any head-on collisions with the more obvious hazards. Having learned from past mistakes, I knew it was wiser to steer around them when I could.

Chief among the obstacles was John McGraw. He wasn't somebody to cross, especially if he had your career in his hands. Never mind .250, I'd have to be batting over .400 before I could risk going against his orders.

Karl Landfors, on the other hand, had no such power over me. He was in no position to give me orders.

So I decided I would go and see James Bartlett for myself.

By late morning, it was pouring so hard that the afternoon game at the Polo Grounds was sure to be canceled. Confident that I had the day off, I headed down to lower Manhattan with only my straw hat to fend off the raindrops. The only time I ever remembered to buy an umbrella was when it was already raining, and by then I was always too wet for it to help.

After a forty-minute ride on the 6th Avenue El, I arrived at Park Row to find an overabundance of government buildings. I didn't know which one would house a district attorney's office. What did government do to need all these buildings and offices, anyway?

I walked around the block. There was elegant old City Hall with its domed clock tower piercing the cloud-covered sky. Behind it was the Tweed Courthouse, named after Tammany Hall's infamous "Boss" Tweed. On Centre Street was the new Municipal Building, rising forty stories from the imposing colonnade at its base to the statue that crowned its tower.

I figured if Bartlett's an assistant district attorney, that makes him a lawyer, so the courthouse would be the sensible place for him to be.

I tried the courthouse. That wasn't it.

Then City Hall. No, that's for the mayor and the city council.

Finally, the Municipal Building, which I thought was just too damn big to find anything in it. I walked through the pillars of the front court and under the central archway, which allowed Chambers Street to run through it, dividing the building's ground floor.

In the north entrance hall, I looked over the listings in the lobby directory. There were tax offices, and the Department of Sanitation, and license bureaus for just about everything—liquor, dogs, cabs, marriages, milk. And on the sixteenth floor: the District Attorney's office.

That's where my mission came to an end. There was no one named James Bartlett who worked in the Manhattan District Attorney's office. Not an assistant district attorney, not a secretary, not a janitor.

Karl Landfors had lied to me.

•  •  •

Casey Stengel, on the other hand, came through for me. He called in the afternoon and offered to bring me to a Brooklyn pool hall to meet Virgil Ewing.

At seven o'clock I was riding the Fulton Street elevated, on my way to take him up on his offer.

The rain had exhausted itself by now, and the clouds had parted enough to let an orange sunset squeeze through and cast its hue on the city.

I got off at Willoughby and walked half a block toward Pearl Street. The air felt clean after the rain, the summer dust all washed out of it. Puddles large enough to be small ponds filled the streets, and squealing barefoot children filled the puddles. Some played with toy boats; most just played with other children, splashing and dunking each other while passing automobiles sprayed muddy cascades over them.

Casey Stengel was at our appointed meeting place in front of the Loew's Royal Theatre. He was demonstrating his batting stance to a group of street urchins, while regaling them with a story about—actually I couldn't tell what his story was about, except that it had something to do with baseball. I wasn't sure if the kids could tell either, but it didn't seem to matter to them. They were enthralled by Stengel, and I remembered what was best about being a big-league baseball player: the adulation of youngsters. To a kid—especially a boy—one baseball player is worth ten movie stars.

"Hey, Mickey!" Stengel called when he spotted me. He dismissed his audience with the parting advice, "Remember to lay off the high ones, boys."

We walked down the street together for another block. "Here we are," he said when we reached Marsten's Billiard Parlor. A swinging sign over the front door advertised: *Pool, Billiards, Snooker.*

"I told Ewing I'd be bringing you around tonight," Casey said as we walked in. "By the way, don't call him Virgil; Virg is okay, or Ewing, but not Virgil. He doesn't like it. Although I don't see anything wrong with the name myself. It's better than Lave Cross—his name is really Lafayette. Now isn't that a helluva moniker for a ball player? But that's not the strangest name I ever heard. There was this fellah . . ."

With one look I could tell that Marsten's Billiard Parlor was for serious players. This wasn't a saloon with a pool table or two, where playing pool was something you did while drinking beer. Marsten's was all pool tables and no bar.

More than twenty tables were neatly arranged in two rows. Well-dressed but tough-looking players had every one of them in use. Tall chairs lined the walls, their seats filled by silent men who paid rapt attention to the games in progress. Polished brass cuspidors were placed at frequent intervals on the carpeted floor, and ceiling fans turned slowly overhead to circulate cigar smoke. Frosted white lights hung low over each table; their brightness brought out the rich color of the felt, a green almost as pretty as well-kept infield grass.

Casey led the way to the back, where there was a smaller room on a level a foot higher than the main floor. Only one table was in the room; it had elaborately carved woodwork with inlaid ivory markers and leather net pockets.

Virgil Ewing was lining up a shot with a pool cue that looked like a straw in his meaty hands. He was wearing a yellowed undershirt that clung tightly to his barrel chest and droopy gray trousers that hung from one suspender. His face, red with concentration, was distorted by a lump the size of a cue ball in his stubbly left cheek.

Half a dozen other men and a boy I recognized as the Dodger bat boy were in the room watching Ewing. One man had a cue stick in his hand and a resigned look on his face; he was sitting in a chair and looked like he'd been there for a while.

I'd played pool myself a few times. At first I thought nothing could be easier than to hit a ball that's sitting still. Then after some friendly games that invariably ended up costing me money, I realized it was harder than it looked.

Virgil Ewing quickly pocketed four balls. After each shot, the cue ball was left in perfect position for the next one.

The boy kept score by sliding a marker on a string, and he gave a small cheer at each shot Ewing made. He was about twelve years old, with a friendly innocent face and a small slim body that was hunched at his right shoulder. He was wearing his Dodgers cap with obvious pride and seemed equally proud to be in a pool hall with grown men. A batboy for the Brooklyn Dodgers by day and a pool hall denizen by night—he must be the envy of every boy in his neighborhood.

Ewing paused from his shooting to chalk the tip of his cue.

"Virg," Stengel said. "This is Mickey Rawlings. You two met before, I think."

I nodded hello and offered my hand to Ewing. He shook it with a hard grip. "How you doing?" he drawled.

Ewing's opponent, a lean pale man who looked as if he spent a lot of time in pool halls—and judging by his clothes didn't make much money at it—mumbled, "Rawlings. . . . You that sonofabitch cost Sutherland his shutout?"

I shrugged. Yeah, I cost him his shutout, but I wasn't a sonofabitch.

The man rose from his chair and slid his hand on the cue until he was gripping it like a club. "You got some nerve coming in here. Goddamn Giant bastard . . ."

I had an impulse to grab a ball from the table, to throw it at him if I had to. I held back though. Ruining the game would only get everybody mad.

Stengel warned him, "If you want to start something, you'll be taking on the both of us."

Another man, who'd been seated next to Ewing's opponent, stood up. He looked like a bonebreaker, at least six foot four and more powerfully built than Virgil Ewing. He crossed his thick arms across his chest; his face was expressionless. If he was going to make it two on two, Casey and I were in trouble. I glanced back over my shoulder. It was a long way to the door, and we'd have to make it past a lot of Brooklyn pool players. Might as well stay and fight.

"Hell, boys," Ewing said with a smile on his face. "Let's

not have us no trouble here." He spoke like a tantalizing slow curveball; you wanted to either finish his sentence for him or answer before he stopped speaking. He shifted his tobacco from his left cheek to his right. "Now there ain't no reason to be mad at Rawlings here. He was just doing what McGraw told him to. Ain't that right, boy?"

I nodded. Although I didn't like the way he called me "boy."

"See?" Ewing said to his opponent. "What I tell you, Spike? It weren't his fault." Spike? I don't want to fight a guy named Spike. Ewing added, "Besides, it don't matter none to me if Sloppy Sutherland gets himself a shutout or not. So you just set yourself back down and take it easy."

Spike didn't. He took a step forward, grumbling, "Still ain't got no business coming here like—" The big fellow next to him unfolded his arms, grabbed Spike by the scruff of his neck, and pulled him down into his seat.

"C'mon now, Spike," Ewing said. "I remember when you didn't like having Southern boys coming in here. But once you got to know me and Billy there, you changed your mind, didn't you?" Ewing had nodded toward the big man, so I took it he was Billy.

Ewing continued, "Hell, least we can do is be hospitable to somebody from just across the river." Turning to me, he said, "You come to play, Rawlings?"

"No, I came to talk."

*"Talk.* Hell . . . what you want to talk about?"

"Alone. It's kind of personal."

"Ain't no need to be secret. You can see we're all friendly here. Anything you want to say to me you can say in front of my pals."

"It's about Florence Hampton," I said loudly. I thought it might convince him that our talk should be private. It didn't.

At the mention of her name, Ewing's friends started to make grunting sounds and vulgar comments. They sounded like ten-year-old boys snickering over a French postcard. The batboy giggled at their quips.

Ewing bent over the table, lining up another shot. "What you want to know? If she was any good?" His friends started hooting and the batboy almost fell off his chair.

I leaned over the table from the other side, putting my face inches from his. "Miss Hampton was a friend of Margie Turner," I said through gritted teeth. "Miss Turner is a friend of *mine*. Either you show some respect for the lady, or I will feed you the eight ball."

"Oooo . . . scary," taunted Spike.

Billy elbowed him quiet.

Ewing stood back up. We both knew my threat was empty. He could have ground me up in one fist if he wanted to. He looked annoyed but not angry. It was the look of someone who knows he's in the wrong but doesn't like having it pointed out. "What do you want?" he said.

"At the party, on Coney Island, you asked Miss Hampton to go swimming with you afterward. Did she?"

"Uh-uh. She turned me down." He added with a leer, "But she didn't say no often."

I glared at him. He stared back for a moment, then took up his cue and deftly sunk the seven ball with a bank shot.

"You didn't see her at all after she left the party?"

He paused to make another shot. "Nope."

"Where did you go after the party?"

The four ball was frozen against the rail, and he was aiming to put it in the corner pocket. I knew it was a tough shot—to make it, the cue ball would have to hit the four and the rail at exactly the same time. "I came here," he said. Then he stroked the cue smoothly and sent the four ball running swiftly along the rail, a streak of purple that was swallowed by the corner pocket with a gulp. He stood up with a smile. "Didn't I, boys?"

His friends grunted agreement.

He bent back over and ran off three more shots. "Look," he said, "I'm real sorry she got herself drowned. After all, there was some things about her that I liked real well. But I don't know nothing about how it happened."

"Did you come here straight from the party?"

"Yep."

"What time?"

"Hell, that's almost a week ago. But if I recall correctly, I believe it was about eleven. Weren't it, boys?"

Spike and Billy both said, "Yup." The batboy nodded.

"Okay," I said. "Thanks."

"No problem," Ewing said. Then he squirted a stream of tobacco juice at a spittoon only four feet away—and missed it by more than a foot. His friends looked stricken. I don't think he missed often.

Stengel and I left, and we found a saloon where the lights were low and the beer was cold.

I was poor company for Casey. While he launched into a story about a one-legged pitcher in Akron—or maybe it was about a bowlegged shortstop—my thoughts stayed on Florence Hampton.

The encounter in the pool hall bothered me. I didn't see how Ewing and his friends could talk about Miss Hampton the way they did. I guess they didn't have any more respect for a dead lady than they did for a live one.

It wasn't just the general tone of the talk that gnawed at me though. There was one phrase in specific: the way Virgil Ewing had said *she got herself drowned*—as if it was her fault somehow. It was like blaming the victim for the crime.

Oh, jeez. What if she did do it to herself? What if it was suicide?

Margie said Miss Hampton had changed after her husband died. How did she change? What thoughts were going through her mind? Did she think there was nothing left to live for? That would explain the circumstances of her death: a woman who can't swim ends up in the water, drowned, with no bruises.

But why naked? Why would she want to be found that way? Wouldn't she have some modesty left? Or was shedding her clothes symbolic, like casting off all her problems, all earthly concerns?

I was doubtful. Suicide would fit with what happened but not with what I saw of the living Florence Hampton. She seemed too much of a fighter.

One thing I was sure of: I was no judge of what would go through a woman's mind.

Fortunately, I knew somebody who was.

*Chapter Ten*

**O**n Saturday, I worked. It wasn't a day for *playing* baseball; it was a day for laboring at it. And I had to put in overtime. Because of the rainout the day before, a double-header was scheduled to make up the canceled game.

The Friday downpour had turned the Polo Grounds' infield into a treacherous mud pit. It was there that I toiled, the muck pulling at my cleats, as I worked every inning of both games at second base.

And labor I did. With the ball wet and heavy, the pitchers naturally threw a lot of sinkers, resulting in an inordinate number of ground balls. The St. Louis batters drove grounders at me as regularly as if they were hitting me infield practice. Every one was an adventure; some would strike a clod and bounce high, others would stick on a wet spot and skid with no bounce at all. It was futile to try to field them with my glove. I had to use my body, moving in front of the ball to block it and trying to keep from slipping and falling down.

By the end of the twin bill, my uniform was spotted with mud and my shins were covered with bruises. But not one ball had got past me.

There was satisfaction in my efforts because they weren't wasted. We took both games from the Cardinals. It boosted our lead in the standings to three games and gave us a bigger lift in morale.

Even John McGraw was in a good mood. In the locker room he congratulated me, "Helluva good game, Rawlings. Looked like they were using you for target practice out there." Then he punched me playfully on the shoulder, striking me harder than any of the ground balls had. With McGraw, any punch he didn't aim at your nose was considered playful.

•   •   •

The Sunday box scores showed I had a total of 21 assists in the doubleheader and no errors. I went only 1 for 9 at bat, so I avoided looking at the hits column in the stats.

I spent all of Sunday at home, bathing my sore legs and worrying about a couple of conversations I was going to have to face.

One was with Karl Landfors, to find out why he'd lied to me about James Bartlett.

The other was with Margie. How was I going to ask her if Florence Hampton could have committed suicide? And even more worrisome: would she be angry that I hadn't called her on Saturday? She might have been expecting that we'd be going out. I was never very good at guessing what women wanted.

I finally telephoned Margie Sunday evening. She didn't sound at all annoyed that I hadn't called earlier, so of course it bothered me that she wasn't bothered. Then, as my sitting room grew dark and we kept chatting, effortlessly and to no purpose, I discovered the delightful intimacy of a phone call at night. We voiced whatever thoughts were in our heads, transmitting them through lines that connected only us.

I never got around to asking her about Miss Hampton. In fact, I couldn't remember much of what we did talk about, except that her favorite color was yellow, we both liked ragtime, and we both thought that the Anti-Saloon League was a bunch of meddling radicals who would never succeed in prohibiting liquor.

And before we hung up, we made plans for the next day. Plans that I couldn't believe I'd agreed to.

• • •

Margie's parlor had the precise look of a place that had just been tidied up. The end tables on either side of her sofa glistened with fresh polish, and there was a small vase of violets perfectly centered on each one. The fringes of the throw rugs looked as if they had been combed.

The photos on the wall had all been straightened, too. I was being stared at by a dozen pairs of critical eyes. Having few relatives of my own, I didn't know what it would be like to belong to such a large family. I wondered if I was someday going to have to meet them all.

I was as painstakingly dressed as if I had come to meet a girl's family for the first time. I even went to a barber for a shave and haircut, though I wasn't due for a haircut for another week and a shave wouldn't have been necessary until some time after that.

Margie was all done up, too. Her hair was piled neatly, with just enough locks out of place that I knew it was still her. She was dressed in a trim black satin skirt and a long-sleeved white blouse. The blouse had diamond-shaped black buttons running up the front and a deep neckline covered by white lace with a lot of open spaces between the thread. A silver locket hung around her throat; when I looked closely, I saw it was a baseball pendant. The only color on her was the warm bronze flush of her skin. She looked awfully healthy considering she called in sick at the studio to take the day off.

With no game scheduled for the Giants, we were going to Washington Park to see the Brooklyn Tip-Tops take on the Indianapolis Hoosiers. A Federal League game. Somehow she'd talked me into it last night. I think it was the way she'd said *Please.*

We had some time before the game, so we sat in her parlor sipping iced tea with too much lemon and not enough sugar.

It was funny, but I couldn't think of much to say. The sweet way we'd talked the night before seemed silly in the light of day and face to face. I hated to think that we could only talk intimately in the dark and from a distance. Actually, it wasn't funny at all—it was damn awkward.

Margie chatted too much and too fast, as if to make up for my silences.

Finally, I abandoned any efforts at small talk and announced, "I talked to Virgil Ewing."

"You did?"

"Uh-huh. Friday night. Casey Stengel took me to a pool hall where he was playing."

"But we agreed to do this together." She sounded disappointed.

"Well, yeah, we did. That's why I'm telling you what I found out."

The look in her eyes told me she had a different definition of "together." "I thought we would *both* talk to him," she said.

"Oh. But . . . it was at a *pool hall*. It really wasn't the kind of place to bring a lady."

She rolled her eyes. I think she was used to going wherever she pleased. "Well, what did he say?" she asked.

"That he didn't go swimming with Miss Ham—uh . . . with Florence. He said he didn't see her after the party and that he went to the pool hall afterward."

"Do you believe him?"

"His friends backed him up, but I'm not sure." Ewing's friends didn't look like the most trustworthy bunch. I remembered the batboy nodding—he had an honest face. "I *think* it was true," I added. Then I remembered Ewing missing the spittoon. "Or maybe not."

Margie frowned.

I was having less success telling her about Virgil Ewing than I'd had at chit-chat. I pulled out my watch. "It's almost three. Should we go early and watch batting practice?" I felt a need to get out to a ballpark, in the sunshine and the open air.

"Sure," she said. Then she gave me a smile that told me our misunderstanding was forgiven . . . as long as it didn't happen again.

•  •  •

Washington Park hadn't changed much since I was a kid. The new owners had done some refurbishing—concrete replaced the old wooden stands and a new scoreboard was in center field—but it was basically the same.

Except for the attendance. This park used to be packed when the Dodgers played here, but not many people came out to see the Tip-Tops of the Federal League. Maybe the name was the problem; the Ward brothers had christened their club in honor of one of their bakery products. How can you root for a team named after a loaf of bread?

The crowd was so sparse that for two bucks I was able to get us a pair of box seats only four rows behind the third base dugout.

One similarity between the Dodgers' old and new homes was the tone of the advertising. Ebbets Field had its Tanglefoot flypaper sign. Here, to the right of the scoreboard, was a billboard that urged:

> *For Comfort Sake*
> *Demand Loose-Fitting Underwear*
> *BVD*

I wondered what the Ward brothers would have named their team if they'd owned an underwear factory.

Margie and I settled into our seats supplied with enough hot dogs and crackerjack to feed both teams.

While we watched the ball players go through their warm-ups, I noticed that we were being watched by a portly man of about forty standing near an adjacent box. More specifically, *I* was being watched.

He stared at me unabashedly while his hands mechanically fed a stream of peanuts to his flabby mouth. He was in a light brown suit with broad green stripes. A shabby black derby with a large nick in the brim was jammed low on his head. He wore a crooked blue bow tie that looked as if it was showing ten minutes to five. I never quite trusted a man in a bow tie; it was the sort of accessory worn by smarmy salesmen and petty bureaucrats.

Or maybe by a reporter for the *Public Examiner?* That would explain his seedy arrogance.

I tilted my hat down over my eyes and tried to ignore him. No use. He came over to me and made a show of bending over to look up under the brim of my hat. If he turned out to be William Murray, I was going to give him a shot in the mouth. "Mickey Rawlings, isn't it?" he asked. When he spoke, I noticed he had no front teeth—okay, so I'll aim for his nose instead.

"Yes," I answered guardedly.

"Say, you're a helluva second baseman."

"Oh, well, thanks," I said with some relief. This guy's a fan!

"Think you could sign my scorecard for me?"

"Sure. Be glad to." It was nice to be asked in front of Margie.

He handed me a Tip-Tops scorecard and a pen. I scrawled my name with a flourish and handed it back.

"Thanks." He folded the scorecard, stuffed it in an inside pocket of his coat, and walked away.

A cold wave suddenly washed through my body. There was another occupation that would fit the man's appearance and actions: private detective. I'd heard that the American and National Leagues were employing spies to see if any of their players went to Federal League games. I should have known better than to sign a Fed program. That could be hard evidence against me. Jeez.

I tried with limited success to forget the man once the Tip-Tops took the field and the first pitch was thrown.

As the game settled into its rhythm, I finally brought up the subject of Miss Hampton's death. I thought it might be easier to talk about her here; what had happened to her was so remote from the activity in the ballpark that maybe we could be more detached about it. I remembered Karl Landfors bringing his autopsy report to a game and winced at the similarity between us.

"I had a question about Florence Hampton," I began.

Margie kept her eyes fixed on the Hoosier at bat. "Yes?"

"Do you think she . . . could she have. . . . You said she changed after her husband died. Do think she could have been so upset that she killed herself?"

Margie didn't answer for a moment. Then she said calmly, "I wondered about that. She did change after William died, but she wasn't despondent. She was upset, but she seemed *determined* somehow, not depressed. No, it wasn't in her to commit suicide."

"I only knew her one day, but I didn't think so, either. She didn't seem like the type to give up on anything."

"She wasn't." Margie turned to look in my eyes and added, "Neither am I. I want to find out what happened to her."

"We will," I promised.

That topic over, we relaxed and spoke only of the game unfolding before us.

After the sixth inning, I had to visit the men's room. When I came out, my way was blocked by the man with the derby and the crooked bow tie. "McGraw know you're here?" he asked.

I tried to step past him.

He put his hand on my arm. "If you give me a minute of your time, you'll find it to be well worth it."

"Why's that?" I said, shaking off his hand.

"I'd like to make you an offer."

"For what?"

"To play baseball."

"I already play baseball."

"Not often, you don't." He smiled, but I didn't find him funny. "Now, if you were to sign with another team . . ."

"What team?"

"Brooklyn. The Tip-Tops."

"No thanks."

"You haven't heard my offer."

"I play for John McGraw. For the New York *Giants*. I'm going to be in the World Series."

"Uh-huh. Well, that sounds pretty good, if it happens. But you think McGraw's gonna play you in the Series? You hardly play as it is. Now if you come over to the Tip-Tops, you'll be our starting second baseman. We'll pay you four thousand bucks a year. Don't tell me you're making that much with McGraw."

No, I couldn't tell him that.

He dug into his vest pocket and pulled out a creased business card. Handing it to me, he said, "Think about it. Give me a call if you're interested." I looked at the card; it read *Peter Kurtz, Agent.* "You'll be in good company coming over to the Federal League. There's a lot of big-name players signing with us for next year. Like I said, think about it." He patted his jacket pocket and added with a smile, "Meanwhile I got your autograph to remember you by."

Kurtz walked away and I went back to my seat.

Jim Delahanty was at second base for the Tip-Tops. He was thirty-five, one of the last of the five Delahanty brothers who played big-league ball. I used to watch his brother Big Ed play for the Phillies. I couldn't take a job away from Jim Delahanty. But I was glad in a way that the League had finally tried to recruit me.

I told Margie about Kurtz's offer, omitting mention of the salary. Even $4,000 a year was probably a lot less than she earned for making movies.

"Why don't you consider it?" she asked.

"It's not the big leagues. Maybe someday it will be but not yet. Look at Benny Kauff out there." Kauff was the Hoosiers'—and the Feds'—biggest star. "The 'Ty Cobb of the Federal League,' they call him. If he was so good, they wouldn't say 'of the Federal League.' It's like being most valuable player in the Paterson Industrial League." Which I once was, so I knew it didn't amount to much.

"Besides," I said. "I owe John McGraw. He took me from nowhere and put me on a world champion team."

"Where was nowhere?"

"Beaumont, in the Texas League. That's where I played all last year. After the season was over, I stayed and played winter ball until spring, when the Giants came down. They have their spring training in Texas—in Marlin, outside of Waco. So I went for a tryout. And McGraw signed me."

"He must have been impressed with you."

I laughed. "Not especially, but he didn't have a lot to choose from." Normally I would have let the misconception stand, but with Margie Turner I felt compelled to tell her the unremarkable truth. "McGraw was on Daley's world tour, managing the National League all-stars. When he got back to the States, he found that the Giants' owners sold off half his infield. And the players who were left were threatening to jump to the Feds. So McGraw went to spring training without an infield. That's why he signed me. You got to have nine players on the field come opening day." I sighed, remembering that McGraw had then signed a few more infielders and I was once again relegated to a utility role.

"Strange how things work out," Margie said wistfully. "That damned world tour helped you get a job and it cost Libby her husband."

There was no blame in her voice, but the observation

made me uncomfortable. "Why 'Libby'?" I asked. "I can see how you get 'Margie' from 'Marguerite,' but how do you get 'Libby' from 'Florence'?"

"I don't know . . . . she never told me her real name, I don't think."

"Her real name?"

"Sure. 'Florence Hampton' was probably her stage name. Like 'Mary Pickford.' "

"Gladys Smith," I said.

"That's right." Margie laughed. "You really are a movie fan. Bet you don't know my name though."

"It's not Marguerite Turner?"

"Nope. Margaret Groot."

"Why'd you change it?"

She laughed again. "I just told you. Because my real name's Margaret Groot. The fan magazines would choke on that one. I grew up near Turners Falls, in Massachusetts, so I took Turner for a last name. Then Margaret Turner sounded a little too plain, so I made my first name more exotic: Marguerite. But I still prefer 'Margie.' "

Yeah, she was definitely more of a Margie than a Marguerite. Margie Groot from Turners Falls. The different name made *her* seem different. It made her even more of a regular person to me.

Maybe Florence Hampton was really a different person, too.

The Hoosiers ended up winning the game 1–0 on a pinch hit double by young Edd Roush.

I looked around before we left the park, giving one last thought to Peter Kurtz's offer. Although it might not have been an offer as much as a threat.

That's a good way to recruit players: get them banned

from organized baseball and then they have no choice but to sign with an outlaw team.

I might end up playing here after all if that scorecard ends up in John McGraw's hands.

# *Chapter Eleven*

I was at the Municipal Building at 8:30 Tuesday morning and waited until it opened at nine. This time I wasn't looking for the district attorney's office. I wanted a marriage license.

The Marriage License Bureau was on the third floor. The only person in the office was a young man standing behind a counter with a glass front; it was like a bank teller's, with a hole in the glass to talk through and a small gap between the glass and the countertop to exchange papers. The clerk's slicked back red hair was parted perfectly in the middle and he wore a massive green bow tie with vertical gold stripes. He had an expectant smirk on his face as I approached his window.

"I'd like to see a marriage license," I asked through the hole in the glass. "From June 1913. The groom's name was William Daley."

The smirk vanished. "You want to *see* a license. Somebody else's license."

I thought it a straightforward request, but he didn't seem to understand. "Yes." How much more could I elaborate?

"Most people want one of their own," he said.

"I don't. Can't I see his? Isn't it a public record?"

"Of course it is."

"Then what do I have to do to see it?"

Here I was, his first customer of the day, and already I was throwing his routine out of whack. He tilted his head to look around the rest of the office and appeared disappointed. I think he would have liked to tell me to keep the line moving, but there was no line. "All right," he said with a sigh. He stepped away to a set of oak file cabinets behind him. "June of last year, you said, right?"

"Yes."

He ran his fingers down a row of drawers, checking the labels on the front, then pulled a drawer halfway out. "Do you know the date?"

"No. Sorry."

"How do you spell 'Daley'?"

Everything was a challenge for this guy. "D-a-l-e-y."

He flipped through all the documents in the drawer. "Nope. Nothing here for a Daley," he reported gleefully.

Jeez. I thought for sure . . . "Oh! The wedding was in June. Maybe he got the license earlier."

"That's usually the way it works," he sniffed.

I started to suspect that the glass above the counter was to keep people from smacking him. "Could you look?"

"Of course," he said sourly. He pulled out the drawer above the one he'd just gone through and flipped through its contents while muttering to himself, "I am a civil servant. It is my pleasure to serve the public."

He withdrew a pale green paper from the drawer and brought it to the counter. Instead of sliding it through the gap, he held it up against the glass. "This is an official document. You can see it, but you can't touch it."

I didn't need to touch it. Having read the name of Daley's bride, I'd seen enough.

• • •

From the Municipal Building, it was three blocks to Spruce Street and the offices of the *New York Press*.

The *Press* city room was just as I remembered: loud. It was noisier than a game at Ebbets Field. There was a ceaseless din of typewriters clattering, telephones ringing, and people shouting. Apparently no one got up from their desks to talk to anyone, they just yelled across the room in a raucous crossfire of conversations.

Karl Landfors's desk was in the same distant corner of the room where I'd first gone to see him two years ago.

Since then, he'd turned it into something like a private office. He used the back of his rolltop desk as one wall, an overflowing bookcase made another, and a row of battered file cabinets a third. Actually, it was more like a nest: the furniture was all old, chipped, and mismatched. I could picture Landfors going around collecting pieces that had been abandoned by other reporters to build his "office."

Landfors had his back to me. He was seated at his desk, typing rapidly with all his fingers—I didn't know men could do that. His jacket hung on the corner of the bookcase and his derby was hooked over an unplugged gooseneck lamp clamped to the edge of a shelf. The desk top was stained with spilled ink and scarred with carved names like a schoolboy's. A large map of Europe was tacked to the wall next to him.

I rapped on the side of a file cabinet to get his attention.

"Ah, Mickey!" he said in a startled tone.

"Hi, Karl."

He pointed to a straight-back chair that still had most of its legs. As I slowly took off my hat and coat, Landfors's eyes swept back and forth over me, curious to know why I was there. By the time I sat down, I had his full attention.

I came right to the point. "There's no James Bartlett in the Manhattan District Attorney's office, Karl. You lied to me." I said it matter-of-factly, not as an accusation.

"Well . . . of course not. He's with the Brooklyn office, not Manhattan. I told you it was Brooklyn. You must have—" He didn't have much conviction in his voice.

"No, Karl. You told me Manhattan, and there's no James Bartlett."

Landfors slumped his shoulders in surrender.

I went on, "There's something else, Karl. I went to the Marriage License Bureau this morning." His eyebrows rose above the rim of his glasses. "Florence Hampton had to use her real name on her marriage certificate: Elizabeth Emily Landfors."

Karl took off his spectacles and laid them on the desk. Leaning back, he closed his eyes, and with his thumb and forefinger rubbed the red indentations on the bridge of his nose. "Libby," he sighed. "My sister."

I couldn't be mad at Landfors for lying to me. His sister was dead. "Why didn't you tell me?" I asked. Not that I blamed him. The way we went at each other, I'd never given him a reason to count on me for much support.

Landfors shrugged and his jaw started flexing, but no words came out. Then he spread his hands. "I'm not sure exactly. When I first heard about her drowning, I knew something was wrong—she never would have gone into the water of her own free will. So I tried to focus on finding out what happened to her instead of grieving for her. I don't know . . . maybe it was just easier for me to think of Florence

Hampton being dead instead of my sister Libby. If I thought of her as my sister, there would have been too much for me to think about. We'd had some . . . uh, disagreements."

"Why didn't you go to the police? There wasn't any political scandal to worry about."

"Libby's name was dragged through the mud often enough. Even as Florence Hampton, she was still my sister. I didn't want to stir up any more gossip."

"You knew she was afraid of the water."

Landfors nodded. "When we were kids—she was six, I was nine—we were ice skating on a pond near our home. Our mother told us not to, said the ice was too thin. I talked Libby into going anyway. Sure enough, she fell through. I tried to go out to her, and I fell through, too. I kept pounding on the ice in front of me, breaking it up, and slowly swimming out to her." Landfors's eyes were wide open and staring, as if the event was happening right in front of him. "Took forever. She kept going under, and every time I thought it would be the last, but eventually she'd come up shrieking again. You can't believe how loud a six-year-old girl can shriek. Anyway, I got her, and we managed to get on firm ice and back to shore. She never would go near any water outside of a bathtub after that. Said she imagined being pulled under and solid ice closing up over her head."

He reached into his pocket and pulled out a scuffed sepia photograph. He held it out to me. "This was taken just before I went to college."

I looked at the two young people in the photo: Karl Landfors, smiling broadly with his arm around his sister Libby. She already showed the features that would make her a movie favorite. "I guess she got the beauty and you got the brains," I said.

"She had *both,*" he snapped.

"Sorry, I didn't mean anything . . ." My mouth sure liked to shoot itself off at the worst times.

"No, I'm sorry," he said after a pause. "Libby *was* smart. I thought she should have used her brains . . . for women's suffrage, for political change. She could have been another Jane Addams or Margaret Sanger. Instead, she decided to become another pretty face in Ziegfeld's chorus line. We haven't—hadn't spoken for more than three years." He sighed. "You know what bothers me most?"

I shook my head no.

"I realized a while ago that it was *her* choice to make. Not mine. And I never told her that. I was too stubborn to tell her I was wrong."

Now he couldn't tell her anything. He'd waited too long. "Did you go to any of her movies?" I asked.

"Just about all of them . . . except the last one." His face suddenly brightened. "And you know what? She kept up with my career, too." He pried open the bottom drawer of his desk. "I was given all her effects." He pulled out a copy of *Savagery in the Sweatshop.* "This was hers," he said with a smile. "She read my book."

I kept my mouth reined in and didn't point out that the fact that she had it didn't necessarily mean that she'd read it.

"But what's really interesting," he said, "is what I found inside." He flipped open the front cover and some folded papers fell out. Landfors opened them up and laid them flat on the desk, rubbing the creases out with his palm.

There was the passenger list of the *Lusitania* and William Daley's death certificate, as well as the ship physician's notes. Another page, in a lady's handwriting, was headed "Arsenic." What did this mean?

"She was investigating her husband's death," Landfors said proudly.

# Chapter Twelve

**B**efore talking to Karl Landfors, I thought the Hampton investigation—we both continued to call her by her stage name—was finally taking shape. I'd managed to narrow the focus by eliminating the political angle.

Now I saw that all it really did was change shape, like a squeezed balloon. It became narrower, yes, but longer, stretching back in time to encompass the death of William Daley.

With the assumption that Daley was murdered, Landfors and I came up with two possible motives for Florence Hampton to be killed.

Landfors suggested that if Daley's murderer found out that Miss Hampton was looking into the death, he might kill her to stop her from finding him out.

I came up with another possibility: what if somebody wanted both Daley and his wife dead from the start. Was there somebody who would benefit from their deaths—inherit maybe? Karl said he was the beneficiary, but the look on his face showed it was no benefit.

This was a hell of a thing for Landfors. I was sorry for him, and I felt badly that he didn't feel he could tell me the truth from the start. The differences between us were so pronounced that sometimes they were all we saw in each other. I knew he thought playing baseball for a living was no kind of career, and I secretly worried that maybe he was right. There were more important things a man could do with his life. But there were similarities between us, too: we had the same basic ideas about right and wrong . . . and justice.

Before I left him, Landfors typed up copies of his sister's documents for me. He confirmed that the arsenic notes were in her handwriting; they read like something copied from a textbook and generally jibed with the description of Daley's symptoms written by the ship's doctor.

But it was the passenger list that I found really interesting. Among its names were Virgil Ewing, Sloppy Sutherland, and Tom Kelly.

• • •

Just as I was about to leave my apartment for the Polo Grounds, the phone rang. It didn't ring often enough for me to let a call go unanswered, so I picked up the receiver.

"Mickey! I think I have some information which might be of interest to you. Of course, then again, it might not be either, in which case no harm done. But in the event that it is—" He didn't give his name and didn't have to.

"Hi, Casey. What's up?"

"Well, like I told you before, Sloppy Sutherland, he doesn't run much with the rest of the guys on the club. But I did find out where he's going to be tonight . . . in case you want to go see him."

"Sure I do! Where's he gonna be?"

"Kitty's. In Harlem, on 131st Street, between Lenox and Seventh, I think."

"Kitty's?" The name sounded like a brothel. "What's Kitty's?"

"A gambling joint. For high-rolling society types."

"Oh, okay. What time do you want to go?"

"Well, he's going to be there around ten." Stengel hesitated, then he added in a sober tone, "Thing is, I really don't want to go there myself. Now, I like a little cards and dice as much as the next fellah, but that's just having fun and killing time. Kitty's is for the serious stuff. This place is run by the kind of people you don't want to know. And it can hurt a career to be seen there. Come to think of it, you might want to skip it yourself, and maybe see him some other time."

I didn't want to wait. This was Thursday. After a three-game series against the Cubs, we would be leaving for Boston on Sunday. "That's all right, Casey. I appreciate you telling me. I'll go myself."

"Hope it goes all right."

"Thanks."

I clicked off the phone, then immediately placed a call to the Vitagraph studio.

I was kept waiting fifteen minutes. Good thing I always showed up at the ballpark an hour before anyone else. Today I'd barely make it in time for batting practice.

Margie finally picked up. "Hello?"

"Hi, Margie. It's Mickey. Sorry to call you at the studio, but something just came up."

"It's okay. I was between scenes anyway. I'm supposed to be attacked by a lion, but the poor old thing is sleeping and they can't wake him."

"Oh." A *lion?* "Well, I found out where Sloppy Sutherland

is going to be tonight. I thought if you like, the two of us could go talk to him together." Eventually I learn.

"Of course I would. Where and when?"

"In Harlem, about ten o'clock. I can come down after the game and pick you up."

"That's silly. Why come all the way here just to turn around again? I can find it."

I gave her what I knew about Kitty's location and wished her luck with the lion.

• • •

The food, music, and fashion of half a dozen cultures all mingled together on 131st Street. A few blocks to the south, the neighborhood was predominantly German and Jewish; to the north was a growing black population. On this street, the shops, restaurants, and apartments represented a little bit of everything in a relaxed colorful mix.

There was only one problem: the only "Kitty's" on the street was a tiny coffee shop, not a casino. It advertised "Open All Night" but looked closed.

I walked up and down the street, from Fifth Avenue to Seventh, looking for another "Kitty's." There wasn't any other. How was I going to explain this to Margie? How did Casey make such a mistake?

Margie came up behind me as I was pacing and pondering in front of the coffee shop. "Is this the place?" she asked eagerly.

"Well . . . I don't know. It doesn't look like it."

"Let's go in and see."

I opened the unlocked door. One bare light bulb on the back wall dimly lit the inside. There were three small tables with chairs hooked upside down over them. Five wooden stools were lined up before the counter; the one farthest from the front door was the only one occupied.

The bulky man whose generous bottom spread over the stool had a steaming coffee mug in front of him and a *Daily Racing Form* in his hand. He gave us a token glance and said curtly, "We're all outa coffee."

"We're not here for coffee," I said.

"This is a coffee shop. What else would ya be here for?"

"Sloppy Sutherland asked us to meet him here," I bluffed. "He said we could find a game."

"Yeah? What's yer name?"

"Mickey Rawlings. I play for the Giants."

"Uh-huh. And who's she?" He jerked his head at Margie.

She answered for herself. "Marguerite Turner. Who are you?"

He made a noise that was part laugh and part cough. "I'm Joe." He took a closer look at Margie. "You look familiar," he said. "You been here before?"

"Once or twice," she answered.

"Hell, I know where I seen you! You're the girl that does them jungle movies."

"Yup, that's me," she said.

"I love them pictures," he said. "You can go on up." He pointed to a back door. "Next time use the door off the alley. It ain't good for appearances to have people coming through the front."

We walked past him. Just before stepping out the door he'd indicated, I looked back and saw a shotgun under the counter.

As we climbed a narrow staircase that led upstairs, I said to Margie, "You didn't tell me you've been here before."

"I haven't," she said. "But I figured he might let us in if

he thought I had. I've heard of places like this—the coffee shop is called a 'front.' "

I had the feeling that Margie knew many other such bits of information.

Upstairs, we were met at a closed door by a man in white tie and tails. He could have been the maitre d' of a fancy French restaurant, except he had a bulge under his left arm that I was sure wasn't a menu. "Good evening," he said with a toothy smile. "Welcome to Kitty's. What will it be tonight? Baccarat perhaps? Or would you like to try black jack? It's the latest thing, very exciting game, and we're the only establishment in New York where you can find it."

"We're looking for Sloppy Sutherland," I said. "He asked us to join him."

"Ah, very well. I believe Mr. Sutherland is at the roulette table. Go right in."

Kitty's interior looked like the set for one of Vitagraph's society pictures. The wide open room was covered with plush red carpeting, and floor-to-ceiling velvet drapes hung along the walls. Polished mahogany tables held roulette wheels, card games, and slot machines. Most of the men were dressed in tuxedos, the women in gowns. Waitresses and cigarette girls moved about the room carrying trays loaded with food, drinks, and cigars. Soft background music came from a grand piano.

Nobody seemed to be having much fun though. They all seemed too restrained. It seemed a waste to me. What was the fun of being upper class if you had to work so hard at appearing bored?

I spotted Sloppy Sutherland at a roulette table on the far side of the room. With a nudge, I said to Margie, "He's over there."

"Why don't you go talk to him by yourself," she suggested.

That took me by surprise. "Are you sure?"

"He'll probably open up more if I'm not there. Men talk differently when there's a woman around." That was true, but I wondered how she knew it. Then I wondered if women were the same way. "I think I'll just walk around," she said.

"Okay."

I walked over to the roulette table and took a spot next to Sutherland. His dark hair was perfectly coiffed, the color and sheen almost a perfect match for the black satin lapels of his tuxedo jacket. His narrow face was shaved so closely that it looked plucked, and his finely chiseled features were so delicate they seemed almost feminine. I knew he was a lot more than just a pretty boy though. I knew what that right arm of his could do when he was on the pitcher's mound.

"Hey, Sloppy," I said in my friendliest tone. "How are you doing?"

He gave me a sharp glance and reprimanded me, "It's *Walter* in here."

It never occurred to me that he would object to his nickname. Perhaps this wasn't the sort of place to admit to being a ball player at all. Maybe that was to my advantage, maybe he'd overlook that debt he owed me for spoiling his shutout.

"Of course. Sorry, Walter. Are you winning?" Piles of blue chips in front of him suggested he was.

"I'm doing all right." He had a tight, controlled voice, as if he were speaking carefully and watching his diction.

I wasn't sure how to launch into the questioning. Sometimes the direct approach was best—it could catch somebody off guard. I didn't think that would work with Sloppy Sutherland. He seemed too much in control of himself.

"This is my first time here," I said.

"Really." He placed a stack of chips on the line between the 19 and the 20 on the numbered layout in front of the roulette wheel.

"Don't you have to put it on a number?" I asked.

"It's a split bet," Sloppy explained. "I can win on either number."

The croupier spun the wheel in one direction and sent a silver ball spinning around the rim in the opposite direction. We said nothing until the ball rattled into a pocket, and the croupier announced, "Twelve! No winners."

As he raked in Sutherland's chips, I murmured, "Hey, that's too bad."

"There's more where that came from." He carefully put another stack of chips directly on the 6.

"Actually," I said, "it was Marguerite Turner who wanted to come here. She's a little more for this kind of thing than me. So what could I do? Women, you know."

A hint of a smile crossed his face. "Yes, I know."

"Oh, did you meet Marguerite? We were at that party in the Sea Dip Hotel . . . where you and Virgil Ewing were dancing with Florence Hampton."

"No, I didn't meet her. I saw her though—very attractive young lady."

"Yeah, she is. Thanks." I had a sudden idea. "Say, I ran into Ewing the other night. You know, I would have sworn that you were getting the better of it with Miss Hampton that night. But he said *he* ended up leaving with her."

"The hell he did," Sutherland snapped. Yes! A crack in his stiff facade.

"Oh, so did you end up with her?"

"Twenty!" the croupier announced. "No winners."

Sutherland watched his chips swept away again, this time

with some sorrow in his eyes. "No," he said. "No, I came here after the party. Lost two hundred bucks that night."

"Then how do you know Ewing didn't get her?"

Sutherland bit his lip. "Because the lady had taste," he finally said.

That was the last thing he was willing to say to me. I watched him lose a few more spins of the wheel, then excused myself and wandered away.

I found Margie at the craps table. She was the shooter, shaking the dice in her fist, muttering, "Come on. Eight the hard way." With a flick of her wrist she flung them on the table.

"Box cars," said the stickman when the dice landed with two sixes showing. "You lose. Next shooter." He pushed the dice to a man standing at her left.

"Aw hell!" Margie cursed the results. When she saw me, her frown was replaced by a smile, and she left the table.

"How did it go?" she asked when she was next to me.

"I'm not sure. Not badly, I don't think. The problem is I can never tell if people are lying to me or not." Margie took my arm and we started to walk slowly toward the door.

"Did he say where he went after the party?" she asked.

"He said he came here."

"Then he lied."

"How do you know?"

"I talked to a couple of the waitresses. The place was raided that night. It happens a lot this time of year—elections coming up and all."

Oh yeah, the elections that didn't have any James Bartlett running for anything. Either Sloppy hadn't heard about the raid or, more likely, he just didn't think I was capable of discovering the truth. Although it was Margie who did that. I was amazed that she broke his alibi before she even knew what it was. "That's pretty good," I complimented her.

She said beaming, "I just thought I would ask around before he had a chance to get people to back him up . . . like Virgil Ewing did."

Jeez, that was clever of her. And I suddenly found cleverness to have a most powerful allure. "I noticed there's a lot of clubs around here," I said. "Maybe we could go dancing?"

"I'd love to."

We left by the back door and stepped out into the alley. As the door closed behind, a flash of light blazed in front of us. Before I could move or my eyes could recover, a squeaky voice said, "Thanks for the picture, Rawlings. It'll look great in tomorrow's paper." Then I heard footsteps hustling away.

McGraw is going to kill me. No, worse, he'll send me down to Beaumont.

Margie could tell I was no longer in the mood for dancing. "Maybe I should just go home," she said. "It's getting late."

I agreed but insisted on escorting her home, and we went together to catch the Lenox Avenue subway.

Once we got to her flat, she insisted there was no reason for me to go all the way back to my place. With a soft goodnight kiss—on the cheek—she left me to sleep on her sofa. The gallery of grim-faced relatives on her wall served as diligent chaperones.

# Chapter Thirteen

"**M**ickey . . . Mickey . . ." The sound was dim; it barely penetrated the shroud of slumber that covered my ears. The smell of coffee woke my nose before my ears could respond to words.

My eyelids cracked open. Margie stood over me, already dressed in her yellow frock, a steaming cup in her hands. The way the sun reflected from her dress, she looked like an angel.

"G'morning," I croaked in my morning voice.

"Would you like some coffee?" she asked with a smile.

"Oh, yes. Thanks." I started to lift myself up, then remembered that I had no shirt on. Only a thin cotton blanket covered me.

Margie noticed my predicament. "I'll leave this here," she said, putting the cup on an end table near my head. "I need to do my hair."

After she left the room I hopped up and quickly put on my shirt and collar. Then I folded the blanket neatly and put it on one end of the couch. I sat back down and took a sip of the coffee. It tasted better than any I'd had before.

I could hear Margie humming in her bedroom and the click of hairpins on her dresser.

This was so . . . domestic. Delightfully so. Even the photos on the wall seemed to look at me a little more kindly. I could get used to this, I thought.

A burst of yelling broke out in the apartment next door and then the sound of breaking glass. Not everyone in this building was in a state of domestic bliss.

Her hair done, Margie and I left her apartment. We didn't worry about nosy neighbors—this wasn't the sort of place where eyebrows would be raised over a man spending the night in the home of an unmarried woman.

On our way to the trolley station, we had to step around a drunk sleeping it off on her front steps. It was probably rude, but I couldn't help observing, "This doesn't seem like the best neighborhood. I thought movie stars all lived in mansions or fancy hotels."

"But it's a lot cheaper to live in a dump," she said with a laugh. "I'm saving my money for when the movies go out of business."

"You think they will?"

"Sure. It's like the bicycle craze. Ten years ago absolutely *everyone* was riding around on bicycles—old people, young people, couples on bicycles built for two. Now only delivery boys use them."

"Huh." The passing of the bicycle fad was no great loss, as far as I was concerned. But I didn't at all like the idea of no more movies.

On the trolley ride to Flatbush, I said to Margie, "You remember that friend I have who works for a newspaper?"

She nodded.

I leaned toward her until my nose was almost touching her ear. I caught a whiff of perfume. "He thinks maybe

William Daley didn't die from food poisoning. He thinks maybe he was poisoned intentionally." I felt Margie flinch. "And maybe Florence was killed by the same person," I added.

"But *why?*"

"I don't know. That's what I wanted to ask you. Can you think of any reason why somebody would want to kill them both?"

She shook her head, her eyes wide with a mixture of bewilderment and fear.

I didn't tell her about Hampton being Landfors's sister. I figured that was private. "What do you know about William Daley?" I asked.

"Not too much. Libby didn't tell me anything personal about him. I just know what everybody else does: he was a producer, although I'm not exactly sure what that means. He was involved in theater, but he wasn't an actor or a writer. He just organized things, I think. Raised money for the shows, promoted them. Things like that."

"Do you know where he lived? Before they got married, I mean. Or anything about his family or background?"

"Not about his family, no . . . . I don't know about his background either. I think he was in the theater business for quite a few years though. I'm not sure where he lived either. It might have been at the Lambs Club. Libby did tell me that he spent a lot of time there."

"The Lambs Club?" It rang a bell. "I've heard of that before. What kind of club is it?"

"Theatrical. All the bigwigs in the theater belong to it. It's the kind of club men join to feel important."

I remembered now. John McGraw and Arthur V. Carlyle were members. But why would John McGraw be in a theatrical club?

And what made Margie think she was such an authority on men?

• • •

As Margie and I walked through the front gate of the Vitagraph complex, security guard Joe Gannon gave us a friendly salute and a broad wink.

When we entered Studio B, Elmer Garvin's greeting was far less friendly. He stood just inside the studio door, rocking on the balls of his feet. Both hands were in his pockets, stirring coins to a jingling crescendo. A folded newspaper was tucked between his left arm and his hip.

"Miss Turner," he said through gritted teeth. "We need to have a little talk." Completely ignoring me, he pulled a hand from his pocket and led her twenty feet away to where a group of unused spotlights were clustered.

Because of construction noise, I couldn't hear what he said, but he was clearly upset. He unfolded the newspaper and waved it in front of Margie's face. Then he flailed his arms the way he had when he'd tried to talk McGraw into giving him a player for *Florence at the Ballpark.* Margie didn't say anything; her head was lowered and she nodded every so often.

After a final warning wag of his forefinger at Margie's nose, Garvin walked off toward one of the sets. Margie came back to me looking chastened.

"What's wrong?" I asked.

"Mr. Garvin isn't very happy with me," she answered softly.

That much I'd already gathered. "But why?"

She raised her head. "There's a picture of us, you and me, on the front page of the *Public Examiner,* coming out of

Kitty's last night. Mr. Garvin says he doesn't want that kind of publicity for Vitagraph. And he says I'll be looking for another job if it happens again."

I took her hand and gave it a reassuring squeeze. "I'll talk to him," I said. But while I was trying to comfort her, I was thinking that Garvin's reaction was nothing compared to what I'd be getting from John McGraw.

"It's okay," Margie said. "I have to get into costume." She suddenly threw her arms around my neck and hugged me. Then she walked off to the ladies' dressing room.

I followed her with my eyes for a minute, then pulled them off and looked around for Arthur V. Carlyle. Not seeing him, I shifted my gaze to Elmer Garvin. He was positioning some sleepy-looking cowboys in a Western barroom set.

I walked over to him and interrupted, "Mr. Garvin?"

He turned around. "Yeah?"

"I want to apologize. About Miss Turner being at Kitty's. That was entirely my fault. It won't happen again."

"Yeah . . . . well, she should have known better anyway." He sounded somewhat mollified. "You gotta watch what you do in this business. The press'll murder you if they can get a scandal on you."

"I'll keep Miss Turner out of trouble," I promised.

"Hell, if you can do that, you're a better man than me. She's a wild one."

She was indeed. And I liked her that way.

"Oh, by the way, is Mr. Carlyle here today?" I asked.

"He damn well better be."

"Do you know where I can find him?"

Garvin was ready to get on with his scene. "Look for sideburns and a mustache," he said.

"Huh?"

"He's doing a Civil War picture today," Garvin explained.

"That's his standard Union officer look. Oh, he's a Confederate today. He'll be wearing a goatee, too." Then he turned his back to me and moved a yawning cowboy to a bar stool in front of a jug marked *Redeye*.

When Carlyle came out of the men's dressing room, he was sure enough wearing a white goatee with matching sideburns and mustache. A saber dangled from a scarlet sash on his gray uniform. He carried himself with the bearing of a real general.

I was admiring his outfit when he spotted me. "Well if isn't young Mr. Rawlings," he said. "How is the world treating you, my boy?"

"Fine, thanks. Good to see you again, Mr. Carlyle."

With a confidential voice he inquired, "And how is Miss Turner?"

"She's okay." Then I got to the point. "Uh, Mr. Carlyle, I was hoping you could do me a favor."

"And what might that be?"

"You're in the Lambs Club, right?"

"Of course I am. It is *the* club for men of my profession."

"Well, I was interested in William Daley. For a friend of mine. I hear he was involved in the club, and I was wondering if you could introduce me to people who might have known him."

Carlyle let his eyes drift heavenward. "Yes, Mr. Daley was one of our most active members. A fine man. The Fold isn't the same without him."

I didn't know what a "fold" was. "You knew him?" I asked.

"Everyone knew Mr. Daley." He stressed the "everyone" so it implied everyone who was anyone. "I'll tell you what I'll do," he said. "I will bring you to the club and introduce you to a few of the fellows."

"That would be great. Thanks."

"Tomorrow night?" he suggested.

I was planning to see Margie—not that we really had any plans, but it *would* be Saturday night. "Could I bring Margie?" I asked. "The Giants are leaving for Boston on Sunday, so it's my last chance to see her."

Carlyle looked as if I'd asked to bring a kangaroo. "My boy," he thundered. "No female shall ever cross the threshold of the Lambs Club. *Never!*" His hand moved to the hilt of his saber as if he would personally skewer any woman who tried.

So I agreed to go alone and thanked Carlyle for his help.

I was worried this plan might not fit with Margie's definition of investigating together though. I was also looking forward to my first visit to a gentlemen's club, no matter that she didn't seem to approve of them.

When Margie came out of the dressing room in her khaki jungle costume, I told her of Carlyle's offer. "I asked if you could come," I added, "but he said it's for men only."

She gave me permission to go by myself. "That's fine," she said. "I should probably go to the Vitagraph party Saturday anyway. Mr. Garvin would like that."

"Does he go to the parties?" I didn't remember seeing him at the Sea Dip Hotel.

"No, they're supposed to be for us to have fun without him watching. But he finds out everything that goes on. I think the weekly parties are really to keep us all together on Saturday nights and out of trouble."

I thought if that was the goal, it wasn't much of a success.

After exchanging another hug—a tighter and longer one—I left the studio and headed to the Polo Grounds to face McGraw's wrath.

• • •

McGraw said nothing at all to me. He never even mentioned my name, omitting me when he read out the lineup before the game and ignoring me again when he called three pinch hitters and one pinch runner off the bench in the late innings.

Reading the sports page of the *New York Press* on Saturday morning, I saw the long list of Giant names in the box score; everybody but me and a few pitchers had been used. I also saw that the Boston Braves hopped over the Cubs and Cards in the standings; the Braves were in second place now, two and half games behind us. Margie would be happy about that; it was almost a relief that I'd be with Arthur Carlyle tonight instead of her—I wouldn't have to listen to her gloat. No, that wasn't true. I'd much rather be with her, talking and dancing . . .

I picked out the latest issue of *Photoplay* from my book case. There were ads in the back of it for everything from bust enlargers to watch fobs. And dance lessons. I clipped an ad for the Herschelman Dance Studio in Milwaukee:

> *Be Popular! Learn the Latest Dances!*
> *The Turkey Trot and the Bunny Hug*
> *taught in the privacy of your own home . . .*

My thoughts of dancing with Margie Turner were interrupted by a timid knock at the door.

It was Arlie Latham, a 55-year-old former player whose wiry body was still in good enough shape that he'd gotten into a game at age fifty. McGraw kept him around officially as a coach and in reality as an assistant and team jester.

Latham's usually smiling face was somber and I knew something was wrong.

"Hi, Arlie," I said. "Come in."

He nodded and stepped in. An equipment bag was in his hand. "McGraw asked me to stop by," he said. "I have . . . uh . . ." He held out the bag.

I grabbed it and looked inside. This was my stuff! It should be going on the train tomorrow. What the hell?

"I'm sorry," Latham said.

McGraw's not taking me on the road trip? Oh, jeez. Am I—

Latham said quietly, "McGraw says he'll send you the release papers Monday."

Yes, I'm fired.

"Would you like coffee?" I offered, trying to keep my composure.

He answered something that sounded affirmative, and the next thing I knew I was bringing him a ginger ale.

"What about today's game?" I asked.

Latham shook his head.

Damn.

He then grew talkative and tried to cheer me. "You know," he said. "I'm more surprised than anybody about this. I know McGraw really liked you. Said you had a good head, that you play the way we did in the old days." Like McGraw, Latham had been a third baseman—Latham a star with the St. Louis Browns in the 1880s and McGraw the ringleader of the fabled Baltimore Orioles a decade later.

Latham leaned forward and said with reverence, "McGraw once told me that you could have been an *old Oriole.*" This was the highest praise that could be given to a player, and I did take some comfort from it. They invented strategies that are now considered fundamentals: the bunt, the hit-and-run, the Baltimore chop.

Latham then launched into a few stories about the old Orioles, all ones that I'd heard many times before. The ones about planting extra baseballs in the long outfield grass, tripping base runners when the umpire wasn't looking, using mirrors flashed from the bench into the eyes of opposing fielders, substituting softer baseballs when the other team was at bat.

Latham settled back on the couch. "You see," he said. "McGraw's used to doing anything—stretching the rules, sometimes breaking them. And he does it until he gets caught."

I stared at him blankly.

"You know, I umpired for a couple of years," he said going off on a different course. "When Bill Klem first broke in as an umpire, he had a run-in with John McGraw. And McGraw said he'd have Klem's job before the year was out. Bill Klem, he didn't blink an eye. He just told McGraw that if he could get his job, it wasn't worth having. And then he made sure McGraw didn't get it. Stood his ground and McGraw had to back down."

An *umpire* got McGraw to back down. I pictured Tom Kelly in his umpire outfit with Florence Hampton on his arm. No way was I going to be outdone by an umpire again.

Latham stood up. "Well, I got to be heading back to the clubhouse. Got to pack up all the gear and uniforms and—"

"What time's the train leaving, Arlie?"

He smiled. "Eight in the morning. Track twelve."

After he left, I thought McGraw did have some good qualities keeping a guy like Arlie Latham around. He had a real soft spot for old ball players. Hell, the gatekeepers and watchmen now working at the Polo Grounds could have been an all-star team from the 1890s. There was Dan Brouthers, the slugger of the old Orioles; Amos Rusie, the Hoosier Thunderbolt; and Smiling Mickey Welch, the old Giants pitcher I was named after. Some of the current players were rude to the old-timers. I respected the former stars, though, and tried to learn from them. There's a lot to learn from guys like Arlie Latham.

•  •  •

I picked up Arthur Carlyle at the Vitagraph Studio at six o'clock. Margie was still filming, so I didn't see her. And I made no effort to. I didn't want to tell her I'd been dropped from the Giants.

Carlyle insisted that we take a cab to the Lambs Club. I thought it extravagant, but he said going by trolley wasn't stylish.

Joe Gannon at the gate called us a taxi. When it arrived, we settled in the back of the green Chandler. "To the Lambs Club, my good man," Carlyle ordered the driver in his finest *thea-tuh* voice.

The driver pulled an unlit cigar from his mouth. "Gimme an address, pops."

"Forty-fourth Street. Number 134," Carlyle directed him in a seething voice.

The driver clamped the cigar back between his jaws, where it remained for the rest of the journey.

As we left Flatbush, I tried to make up for the driver's rudeness. "I really appreciate you taking me to the club," I said.

"My pleasure," Carlyle said. "Not many young people have respect for the traditional things anymore."

"How long have you been a member?"

"Almost fifteen years now."

"I thought the club was for actors. Why is John McGraw a member?"

"Oh, Mr. McGraw likes to hobnob with the luminaries of the theater. Wouldn't everyone?" I think I was supposed to be honored to be in Carlyle's presence. "A number of prominent men are members who aren't actors," he said. "Robert Ingersoll was a member. Victor Herbert. And Stanford White—he designed the Fold."

Stanford White was the only one I'd heard of. "What's the 'fold'?" I asked.

"Our home. The club building."

"Are you the only movie actor?" I asked, hoping he could name some people I'd heard of.

"I am *not* a movie actor," Carlyle roared. "I am appearing in motion pictures for only one reason: to have my Hamlet preserved on film."

"Like Sarah Bernhardt?" I asked. Two years earlier she'd made a film of *Queen Elizabeth,* a poor movie but one that she said gave her immortality.

"Yes, all the best actors are filming their most important roles. James O'Neill in *The Count of Monte Cristo.* James K. Hackett in *The Prisoner of Zenda.*" Those, too, I thought to be poor movies, but maybe I just didn't appreciate plays. "So I will film *Hamlet.*" He added with pride, "Sir Henry Irving himself told me I was the best Hamlet since Edwin Booth."

"Vitagraph is going to make it?"

"Yes, if they ever come to their senses. I will finance the film myself. I've already been acquiring the costumes and sets. It will be the definitive *Hamlet.*"

"How well did you know William Daley?" I asked, trying to move off of the subject.

"Fairly well. Fine man, he was. A bit of a rogue in his earlier days, I believe. But a good producer. In fact, I had some business with him myself. Invested in some of his shows, made me a decent sum of money."

"Were you in on the World Baseball Tour?"

"No, no. I wouldn't invest in *baseball.* When that tour was going on, I was appearing in *Hamlet,* keeping myself in practice for the movie. Little theater in Somerville, Massachusetts. Went over quite well, if I do say so myself." I didn't think Carlyle had any inhibitions about saying so himself.

For the rest of the journey, he proceeded to do just that.

When we arrived at the Lambs Club, Carlyle announced, "Here we are, my boy." Then he gracefully exited the cab, and conveniently became absorbed in staring at the six-story brownstone while I paid the driver the $1.30 fare.

Carlyle led me in to the lobby where there was a sign that read *Floreant Agni.* I asked Carlyle what it meant, and he translated *May the Lambs Flourish.*

I had to sign a guest book. I wrote my name big and bold, to thumb my nose at John McGraw if he were to see it.

"Let's go into The Grill," Carlyle said.

It was on the second floor, but he insisted on taking an elevator. Stairs probably weren't stylish.

The Grill was dark paneled with black beams supporting the ceiling. A long polished bar ran along one wall with a plethora of drawings and paintings above it. Carlyle pointed to one in a place of honor. "That is Charles Lamb," he said, "for whom the club is named."

The rest of the room was filled with tables like a restaurant, and a number of men were dining. Most were just drinking. Carlyle suggested we stop at the bar first, where he ordered us both brandies.

The room had an aura to it, a feel of comradeship and

good cheer. Margie was wrong—this wasn't for men to come and feel important, it was for men to come and be convivial. A place where you could swap yarns that you knew would stay within these walls, where they would remain and reverberate through the years. The very walls and tables had a warmth and hospitality to them.

It reminded me of my uncle's general store in Raritan, New Jersey. In winter, men would gather around the shop's pot-bellied stove to talk baseball for long hours while I would keep the stove filled with wood and absorb their stories. It wasn't fancy like this club, but it had the same friendly feel.

A great circular table in the center of the room was the center of attention. The men there talked louder and laughed harder.

Carlyle subtly pointed to it and said with reverence, "That's the Round Table. Only the elders of the Flock may sit there except by invitation."

"Are you one of the elders?" I asked. Carlyle looked as old as any other man there, so I thought he might be.

His face fell a little and I knew he wasn't. But he took it as a challenge. "My boy, do you see that fellow with the meerschaum?"

I nodded. It was impossible to miss him. The man's enormous white pipe was carved in the shape of an animal—a lamb, no doubt. He was dressed nattily and his silver whiskers looked better groomed than those of the European kings whose pictures had been appearing in the papers. They swooped down from his sideburns and curved up to meet his mustache. His chin was bare, as was the top of his head.

"That is Otis Haines," Carlyle said. "The Shepherd." It sounded like the equivalent of Pope. "And I will introduce you."

Carlyle went over to him by himself first. I could see

Haines shaking his head no. Then Carlyle said something else, and Haines nodded.

Carlyle returned to me. "Bring your drink," he said. I'd have rather left it at the bar. Or traded it in for a beer.

When Carlyle made the introductions, Otis Haines gave me a hearty handshake. "So you're one of John McGraw's boys," he gushed. "I didn't recognize you at first. I'm quite a Giants fan." I decided not to tell him that I was no longer one of McGraw's boys.

"Very good to meet you," I said.

One of the men got up and gave me his seat next to Haines. Nobody moved for Arthur Carlyle. He excused himself to go back to the bar.

"So what brings you to the Lambs Club?" Haines asked.

I'd almost forgotten why I came. "I was told William Daley used to be a member," I said. "I have a friend, a young lady—"

"Ah, to the ladies," Haines said loudly, holding up his glass in a toast. Everyone at the table drank from their glasses, and I followed suit, grimacing at the taste. The others then went back to their stories.

"Anyway," I went on, "she wanted me to find out whatever I could about him. Did you know him?"

"Yes, I did. He lived here, in the rooms upstairs. This young lady, she wasn't one of his paramours, by any chance?"

"His what?"

"Mr. Daley fancied himself quite a man with the ladies. And from what I understand the ladies fancied him."

"Oh no. She wasn't . . . no. Just a friend. Just acquaintances, really. Did he have any particular friends here?"

Haines looked grave. "I do not wish to speak unkindly of any Lamb. Especially one who has gone to the final pasture.

Mr. Daley, however, was not held in high regard by the Flock."

"So he was disliked?"

"I wouldn't say disliked. He was a most friendly fellow and very good company. It was his professional ethics that were objectionable."

"What was wrong?"

"He didn't treat his investors very well. Mr. Daley perfected the art of creative bookkeeping."

"Did you invest in his shows?"

"Good heavens, no. I'm no sucker. His investors always lost their money, even if the show was a smash."

"Did any Lambs invest with him?" I asked, though I already knew one had.

Haines chuckled. "No. His reputation was well known. I don't know anyone who was foolish enough to enter into a business venture with him."

I looked at Arthur Carlyle at the bar. He was engaged in telling a story with a lot of arm motions, but I could see him glancing at us.

"Well, thank you, Mr. Haines. I should probably get back over to Mr. Carlyle."

"Good meeting you, son. Give my best to Mr. McGraw."

Before going home, I remained with Carlyle at the bar for a while. I bought him a few drinks and tried not to let on that he was now a suspect in William Daley's murder.

# Chapter Fourteen

John McGraw was in a window seat that swayed like a rocking chair from the jostling of the train. He looked to be half dozing, with a stubby black pipe clamped loosely in his teeth and a copy of *The Sporting News* folded carelessly on his lap.

"Mr. McGraw," I said in the deepest voice I could muster. I stood in the aisle, holding the top of the empty seat next to him for support.

He looked up at me, startled. "Rawlings," he sputtered, "you—didn't Latham tell you—"

"That I'm off the team, yes."

"Then what the hell are you doing here?" He was fully awake now.

"I bought my own ticket. I wanted to talk to you."

"I don't see what the hell good that's gonna do. What's done is—"

"Didn't I play hard enough? I know my batting average isn't real high, but I thought I was doing okay."

McGraw paused. "Yeah, kid," he conceded. "You did play hard . . . and used your head too, I'll give you that."

I knew it wasn't my play on the field that got me fired, but I wanted him to concede that first. I figured what I did between the foul lines was the most important thing.

"Then why did you give me the boot?"

He aimed his blue Irish eyes at me, and in his best Little Napoleon style said, "Because you didn't do what I told you, and I don't put up with that from nobody."

I didn't have an answer for that.

McGraw then settled back in his seat and said in a more relaxed voice, "You know, we had a fellow named Sammy Strang a few years ago. And there was a game at the Polo Grounds—the old Polo Grounds, before it burned down. Anyway, it's a big game, against the Cubs, middle of September, both of us neck and neck for the pennant. We're down by one run in the bottom of the ninth, but we got runners on first and second and nobody out. Sammy Strang comes up to bat and I give him the bunt sign. Hell, everybody in the goddamn ballpark knows that you bunt in a situation like that. So what does that sonofabitch Strang do? He swings away at the first pitch and knocks it over the left field fence. Home run. Game's over and we win 4 to 2.

"In the locker room after, Strang's celebrating, thinks he's a big hero. I ask him, 'What happened? You miss the sign?' He says, 'Nah, I seen the sign, but he put the pitch right in my gut.' I tell him, 'Yeah? Well that's a hundred dollar fine for ignoring the bunt sign. Stick *that* in your gut.'

"See? I don't put up with somebody not doing what they're told."

"But you didn't kick him off the team."

McGraw took the dead pipe out of his mouth. "No. No, I didn't," he admitted.

"I'd have bunted," I said.

McGraw smiled. "Yeah, I believe you would have." He

put his thumb in the pipe bowl and tamped down the ashes. "Sit down," he ordered.

I quickly did so, eager to demonstrate how obedient I could be.

"Look," he said, "I told you to keep away from them movie people. And what do you do? You get your picture in the paper coming out of a gambling joint with one of them. You didn't listen to me." He shook his head. "I ain't gonna put up with that."

"It won't happen again," I promised. "I mean the gambling won't happen again. And I don't want to be in the movies. But I still want to see Margie—Marguerite Turner. She's a nice girl."

"I don't want another Tom Kelly on my hands."

"Like I said, I don't want to be a movie actor. I want to be—I *am* a ball player."

"It wasn't just him going into the pictures," McGraw said, dropping his Little Napoleon manner and adopting the tone of a beleaguered boss. "It was his goddamn head. It blew up bigger than one of them airships. Sonofabitch thought he could do whatever he wanted, as much as he wanted to. Boozing, women, the works. He figured that's what a movie star was supposed to do." McGraw shook his head. "He got a nice little wife, and he treats her rotten. I've paid bills for hotel rooms he wrecked and had to calm his wife down when he went whoring around."

"I won't—"

"Okay, okay. You're back on the team. Now, I don't mind a little gambling—I like to play the ponies, myself. And a drink now and then is okay. But don't do nothing that will distract you from the game or look bad in the press. If you want to keep company with that movie actress, that's your business. But keep it out of the papers, and leave it behind you when you're on the field."

"I will, Mr. McGraw. Thanks." I stood up to leave, then reached over to shake his hand.

He took it and added, "Same as Sammy Strang though. It's a hundred out of your next paycheck."

As far as I was concerned, he could keep the whole check. I just wanted to play baseball again.

I walked through the train, looking for Arlie Latham.

I found him in the club car, sitting alone. I told Latham I was back on the Giants and he looked pleased by the news. Then I sat down and asked him to tell me about when he played for the old Browns, and he looked even happier.

•  •  •

While a brass band on the pitcher's mound blasted its way through "The Star Spangled Banner," I stood near third base holding my cap over my heart. Even though I wouldn't be starting today, I was grateful just to be back on the team and standing among a line of Giants.

The atmosphere in the park had the stirring feel of opening day or the Fourth of July. Red, white, and blue bunting was draped around the fence, and spirited Boston partisans crammed the park to standing room only.

On the real Fourth of July, the Boston Braves had been in the National League cellar. Now, a month later, they were just two games out of first place and the city was aglow with pennant fever. Braves manager George Stallings was already being hailed as a local hero, and the papers were calling him the Miracle Man. If they could sweep this series from New York, Boston would be at the top of the standings.

There was one peculiar aspect to this series, brought

about by the Braves' recent successes. We were in Fenway Park, an American League ballpark, home field of the Red Sox. More Boston fans now wanted to see their National League team play than the South End Grounds could hold. So a week before, the Braves abandoned their old park and arranged to use spacious new Fenway for the rest of their home games.

The Braves also claimed they'd be playing World Series games in Fenway. But the New York Giants would have something to say about that.

As far as I could tell, the Braves didn't have a team that could win. In fact, they didn't have a complete team at all. Other than their doubleplay combination—elfin shortstop Rabbit Maranville and ex-Cub Johnny Evers—and a solid hitting catcher in Hank Gowdy, the Braves had nothing but pitching. And a young pitching staff it was, untested in the pressure of a pennant drive and sure to fold when faced by Giants veterans Mathewson, Marquard, and Tesreau.

It was little right-hander Dick Rudolph pitching for the Braves this day, against Rube Marquard. And by the sixth inning, my theory about Boston folding was looking pretty good. Marquard held the Braves scoreless while Rudolph faltered, and we were up 5–0. I could almost hear Margie's voice whispering in my ear, *They have the pitching. That's ninety percent of the game.* Hah! She should see this game.

Although John McGraw was winning his tactical match with George Stallings, he was losing one he considered equally important—the bench jockeying duel. Like the Philadelphia Athletics' Connie Mack, Stallings managed in a suit and tie rather than a uniform. Unlike the gentlemanly Mack, Stallings spewed out a constant stream of cusses—most of them aimed at John McGraw. McGraw dipped into his own repertoire of profanity in response but couldn't match Stallings's blue streak.

While he cussed, Stallings paced in front of the Braves' dugout, picking up every scrap of paper. No other manager would perform such groundskeeping duties, but Stallings was one of the most superstitious men in baseball, and litter in front of the dugout was considered bad luck—almost as serious as stepping on a foul line.

I didn't suffer from any such superstitions myself. Unless you count the fact that I never let other players use my bats. But it's well-known that each bat has only a certain number of base hits in its wood—meaning if somebody else gets a hit with my bat, that's one less hit that I'll get. So that's science, really, not superstition.

McGraw and Stallings continued to curse each other, and the Giants continued to chalk up runs.

We were ahead 8–0 by the time we batted in the top of the ninth. After our first two batters went down on strikes, McGraw put me in as a pinch hitter for Larry Doyle. I thought maybe he was putting me in the game to show he wasn't mad at me anymore.

As I approached the plate, umpire Bill Klem announced the substitution to the crowd. At my name, a chorus of boos rolled through the stadium. They remembered me! Nothing gets boos like coming back to a city where you once played.

I stepped into the box, giving a cursory glance at McGraw. With nobody on, there shouldn't be any signs, no play should be on. So why was he signaling for a sacrifice bunt? I stepped back out of the box and stooped down to pick up a handful of dirt. Rolling the gravel between my palms, I took another look at McGraw. He was repeating the sign: bunt.

So that's what this was: not a show of forgiveness but a

test. He wanted to see that I'd follow his orders even if I looked like a fool. Lay down a sacrifice with nobody on? I'll be laughed out of the stadium.

But that's what I did. On Rudolph's first offering, I squared around and dropped a bunt back at him. And I made sure it didn't look like I was trying to drag it for a base hit.

Then I ran like hell for first base. I must have caught Rudolph by surprise because I beat the throw. The boos were deafening now. I hoped McGraw was satisfied.

He wasn't. The next sign was for a steal. With us eight runs ahead, he wants me to steal. The Braves will kill me for showing them up.

I stole anyway. Rabbit Maranville took the throw at second too late, then applied a hard tag to my head as I was getting up. I let it pass; I would have done the same.

I guessed what was coming next, and sure enough McGraw gave me another steal sign. I didn't care if I was out or safe, I just ran for third on the next pitch and slid safely under the third baseman's tag. He then "accidentally" spiked my left calf as I lay on the ground. Blood spread in my sock, but I made no move to fight him, and I didn't rub my leg.

I stood up. As the third baseman tossed the ball back to Rudolph, McGraw vocally ordered, "Steal home."

"Just what I had in mind," I growled.

Dick Rudolph looked at me nervously. He didn't know what crazy thing I would do next. The crowd was issuing one loud roar of disapproval at my actions. A few bottles came out of the stands. Stallings rushed out of the dugout to collect them.

Rudolph went into his stretch, and I broke for home, dreading the collision with Gowdy. Then Klem threw his arms up and yelled, "Balk!"

I trotted home to score, looking back at Rudolph. I wanted to apologize to him. He was suffering for the punishment McGraw was meting out to me. Gowdy stood over home plate with his arms crossed. I stepped around him to touch the plate, then trotted back to the dugout. I glared at McGraw, who refused to catch my eye.

In the clubhouse afterward, I sat on the wooden stool in front of my locker, peeling the bloodied sock off my leg. It stuck to the wound and hurt like hell. My eyes burned at the pain.

McGraw came up to me. "See what you can accomplish when you do what you're told?"

"Yeah," I grunted. I couldn't see that I'd learned anything from his lesson.

"When you're told what to do, and you obey, it makes it easy for you. You don't have to decide anything. Instead of *thinking,* you just gotta worry about *doing.*"

Maybe he had a point, but I preferred thinking for myself.

• • •

That's what I was doing later that night. Thinking.

I was in my hotel room, laying on the paper thin mattress of my bed. My left leg was propped up with a pillow, and I'd taken the bandage off to let air get at the wound.

While I rested my leg, I exercised my mind with the materials Karl Landfors had given me. I scanned the passenger list again and the report of the ship's doctor.

Landfors had also provided me with a schedule for the World Tour. The tour had begun last October after the World Series, with a series of exhibition games across the country. The teams worked their way west, until they arrived in Seattle, their last stop in this country. They left Seattle for Vancouver, where they boarded *The Empress of China* for Asia. After a voyage of twenty-three days they arrived in Yokohama, Japan. By January 8, they were in Australia. Then a swing through Europe, culminating with a game before the king of England in London on February 26, after which the teams left for the United States from Liverpool. And William Daley died aboard ship on March 2, four days before the *Lusitania* docked in New York.

I picked up the passenger list again. Two hundred and forty-seven passengers were on board. Was I going to check into every one? Of course not. But there was one who did not appear on the list, who might have had a motive to murder Daley: Arthur V. Carlyle, who lied about making money on one of Daley's shows.

What if he used an assumed name? Then he wouldn't be on the passenger list, even if he was on the ship. I didn't think his ego would allow it, but it was possible. Ego. . . . Maybe that was why he lied about Daley—his ego wouldn't allow him to admit that he had been suckered.

Wait a minute. . . . Carlyle said he was in a play during the world tour. If he was, then he couldn't have killed William Daley.

• • •

Tuesday morning, I limped to the Somerville Theater in Davis Square, near the Cambridge border.

The ticket booth was closed, as were the front doors. No performances were scheduled until the afternoon. I went into the alley next to the theater and knocked on a side door.

After a few minutes, the door was answered by a man looking like a sultan who'd been interrupted from a date with his harem. A gold turban was wrapped around his head and decorated on the front with a huge ruby. He had a small pointed black beard and enormous mustaches with the ends twisted up. His round beaming face was a deep unnatural bronze color, and he had dark green makeup around his eyes. He was only half dressed, with an unbuttoned undershirt and loose trousers that he held up with one hand.

"Yes?" he said.

I stared at him. His throat was pinkish white, and I looked for the stitches to show where the head had been attached to the neck. I mumbled, "My name's Mickey Rawlings." Too late, I realized there was no need to give my real name. He didn't recognize it anyway. "I . . . uh, I'm a reporter for the *New York Press.*"

"A New York paper!" He sounded delighted and not at all foreign. "Well I suppose word is getting around about our little theater here."

"Oh, yes," I agreed. "In fact, I was having dinner at the Lambs Club the other night and several people were talking about it." I laid it on thick, and he went for it.

"Well, come on in. Let me show you around. We're doing *Kismet* now, you know." He stroked his little beard with his fingers.

"Yes, I saw the posters outside." They showed somebody wearing an outfit like the one I saw before me.

He led me past a backstage that made the Vitagraph studio look neat in comparison. Then he took me on a tour of the dressing rooms and the auditorium. He talked proudly, as if he had personally laid every brick in the wall and put every seat in the auditorium. It was clean and attractive, and I could see reason for his pride, but an empty theater wasn't something I could get excited about. But then an empty baseball stadium probably wouldn't look like much to an actor.

"You're an actor, I take it," I said, interrupting his tale of the theater's construction.

"I am indeed. And the owner and the manager. Harry Gardiner's the name." He stuck out his hand, and as we shook he added, "That's with an 'i' between the 'd' and the 'n.' Aren't you going to write this down?"

I had no paper or pencil; I'd have to remember to bring those the next time I impersonated a reporter. "No need," I said. "I have a good memory."

"Ah, very well."

"That's your makeup for the show?" I asked.

He chuckled. "Oh no. I am a *bit* player." He said "bit" with a pride I wished I could match when I told people I was a utility player. "Actually," Gardiner went on, "the only reason I even get bit parts is because I own the place."

"But if you own it, why not take the starring role?"

He laughed loudly, then bent forward as if sharing a confidence. "Because I would soon find myself with no audience at all." He slapped his thigh and laughed again. "Truth be known—and I'm afraid it is—I'm not much of an actor. But I love it. The theater's in my blood. So I opened my own place where I can always have a role. But I try to bring in big names for the featured parts." He patted the turban on his head. "Although I do on occasion allow myself the pleasure of *dressing* for the main role."

I suspected the occasions were many. And I decided that actors were even more eccentric than baseball players.

"Arthur V. Carlyle was one of the big names, wasn't he?" I asked. "I understand he performed in *Hamlet* here."

"Yes he did. He's the biggest star we've had here. I was lucky to get him."

"Last winter, wasn't it? When did it open?"

"January first, New Year's Day. I have the poster in my office, if you'd like to see."

"Certainly," I said, although it didn't matter now. On New Year's Day, the world baseball tour was in Japan, halfway around the world.

As Gardiner led the way to the office, I said, "I hear Carlyle is planning a movie version of *Hamlet,* so I was curious to know how his last stage performance was."

"Well . . ." Gardiner hesitated. "He did draw crowds. People remembered him from his younger days. Especially the ladies—they threw flowers at him on the stage. Of course they were old ladies—they had to be to have seen Carlyle when he was in his prime—but he loved the attention."

We arrived in a small office that had photos and posters taped to the walls. Gardiner pointed to a poster that showed a young Arthur V. Carlyle in a black costume holding a skull; Carlyle appeared to be talking to it.

"How did he do?" I prodded. I didn't really care, but Gardiner's evasiveness piqued my interest.

He looked uneasy. "Let's say that his memory is not quite what would be desired in an actor. Dropped a lot of lines. And ad libbed horribly when he forgot them. It got worse every week. Usually if a fellow's rusty with his lines, he'll get better as he goes. But he spoke in very good voice . . . until the laryngitis."

"Laryngitis?"

"Yes, it forced him to end the engagement early. Actually, maybe a film version is a good idea. You don't need to remember lines, and of course you don't need any voice at all. It was terrible for me though. He was playing to packed houses."

To maintain the reporter ruse, I asked Gardiner a few more questions, and he did a lot more talking.

Before I left, Gardiner said, "If you see Arthur Carlyle when you get back to New York, tell him I'd love to have him again. His fans are still asking for him. I don't care if he reads the telephone directory up there. If he brings in an audience, I'll hire him."

"I'll tell him," I promised, with no intention of keeping it.

# Chapter Fifteen

**A** jangling bell shattered my sleep. In reflex, my right hand shot out and slammed down on the alarm clock. The harsh sound stopped. I grabbed hold of the clock and looked at its face: a quarter after seven. When the ringing started again, I realized it wasn't the alarm, it was my telephone.

I hopped out of bed and winced when my left leg hit the floor. After hobbling to the parlor, I answered the phone with a groggy, "Hello."

"Hi, Mickey," a cheerful female voice greeted me. "It's Margie. I saw in the paper about you being spiked. Are you okay?"

"Oh, that was nothing. Happens all the time." As I spoke, I looked down at my bare legs. My left calf was swollen and red and had bled through the bandage during the night. I gently poked it with my forefinger; it was hard as a Louisville Slugger, and I wasn't so sure about it being "nothing."

"Thanks for the flowers," Margie said.

I'd almost forgotten that I'd sent her flowers before leaving for Boston. "Oh, you're welcome. Did you like them?"

"They're lovely." Margie must have noticed the sleepiness in my voice because she added, "Did I wake you?"

"Mmm . . . a little bit. We got in late last night." Actually, our train from Boston didn't get into Grand Central until two in the morning.

"I'm sorry to call so early, but I'm at the studio and we're going out on location in a few minutes. We're filming at Coney Island today—Steeplechase Park. I thought you might want to come along. You don't have a game today. I checked the schedule."

I was tempted, but a few hours of additional sleep was even more appealing.

Before I could answer, she went on, "I packed a picnic basket. I thought we could have lunch on the beach."

A picnic with Margie on Coney Island. . . . Suddenly I felt awake, and I agreed to go. I didn't even mind that she was so sure of herself that she'd already packed the lunch.

•  •  •

A motley fleet of Vitagraph vehicles was parked along Surf Avenue in front of the toothy Funny Face that marked the entrance to Steeplechase Park. Everything but a stagecoach had been used to transport cameras, props, costumes, and about a hundred studio employees to the site.

The weather was clear and dry, and a warm sun shone above. Thousands of vacationers were taking advantage of one of the last perfect days of summer by visiting the Pavilion of Fun. A throng of them gathered on the sidewalk to watch the doings of the movie people.

Tom Kelly stood on the front seat of a fire engine, waving to the crowd and basking in their attention. As usual, he ignored his wife, who sat on the back of the hand-pumper, with her legs hanging down and waving in the air. She was dressed in a girlish frock of soft pink and looked frightened by the commotion. I didn't remember seeing Esther Kelly at the studio before, only at the party. The party. . . . I looked up at Tom Kelly again. I had yet to talk to him about Florence Hampton; maybe I would get a chance today.

Arthur V. Carlyle stood near the Kellys, rummaging through his makeup kit perched on the back of an ice truck. I felt guilty at the sight of him because I had falsely suspected him in William Daley's death. And I felt sorry for him, too, having seen at the Lambs Club that he wasn't the big shot he thought himself to be. Maybe the poor guy needed his huge ego to make up for being slighted by reality. I'd decided not to tell Margie anything that I'd found out about Carlyle. Leave him in peace, I figured.

Margie was dressed in a red skirt and white shirtwaist. As she adjusted a flowered pink bonnet on her head, it struck me that the outfit looked familiar, though I couldn't remember when I'd seen her in it before.

Elmer Garvin passed by us, pacing the sidewalk, and the onlookers parted before him. His hands were deep in his pockets, and I could hear the metallic rattle of coins over the noise of the crowd. Garvin was barking orders to the cameramen and assistants as if he was planning a great battle.

"How has Garvin been?" I asked Margie. "Is he still mad at you?"

"No, I don't think so. I asked him if you could come today, and I think he liked that. He treats us like children, so he likes to be asked permission for things. Besides, he's short of actors for the picture, so he might ask you to do a few scenes."

Oh, yeah, McGraw would love that. I'd have to stay away

from Elmer Garvin. "How can he be short of actors with all these people here?"

"We're going to be shooting scenes all over the park, so he's using some of the actors to fill in as directors. So he needs other people to fill in as actors . . . like you!" Margie tapped me playfully on the chest. "Even Esther Kelly is going to be in the picture," she added. "She's never been in a picture before. Hasn't even been on the stage for the last few years."

That would explain her frightened look, I thought. "Is *everybody* going to be in this movie?"

"Everybody from Studio B. This is going to be feature length. Mack Sennett is making a six-reel comedy called *Tillie's Punctured Romance* with Charlie Chaplin. Mr. Garvin's trying to get this picture shot and released ahead of him. It would be the first feature comedy ever. And a feather in Mr. Garvin's cap, of course."

"What's it going to be about?"

"Mr. Garvin is calling it *Coney Island Capers.* I think that's about the whole story. We're just going to film a lot of scenes and then he'll edit them together. Maybe they'll come up with a plot when they do the titles. You can turn almost anything into a decent movie with the title cards."

I hadn't had breakfast and started to give some thought to grabbing a Coney Island red hot. I asked, "When's lunch time?"

Margie laughed. "Twelve noon. Maybe earlier if we're between scenes." She led me to a pie truck. I was relieved to see there were no pies in it, just box lunches for the crew. And one wicker picnic basket. She pointed to the basket and asked, "Do you think you can wait?" The basket was large enough to hold a feast for ten people. I could wait.

Garvin climbed atop the fire engine with a megaphone,

and all the Vitagraph personnel gathered around him. He split them up into smaller companies, each with its own director and cameraman. Garvin sent a crew with Tom Kelly as its director to shoot scenes at the Human Roulette Wheel; Arthur Carlyle was to direct filming at the Funny Stairway; other crews were sent to the Earthquake Float, the Falling Statue, and the Eccentric Fountain.

He then led the largest Vitagraph contingent, including Margie, with me tagging along behind her, to the Steeple-chase ride itself.

The Steeplechase was an eight-horse racetrack that ran for half a mile around the park. The horses weren't real, but painted metal miniatures that rode on iron rails. Each one held two people, usually a man in back and a woman in front. Propelled only by gravity, there was no talent involved in winning, and it didn't matter who won because the main purpose of the ride was simply for a man to hug the young lady seated in front of him.

When we got to the platform at the top of the course, Elmer Garvin asked me, "Mr. Rawlings, would you be so good as to join Miss Turner for a ride?"

"Sure," I said. Then I remembered John McGraw. Then I thought of the excuse it would give me to wrap my arms around Margie. I decided to hell with McGraw—I was going on the Steeplechase.

Garvin had a camera set up at the bottom of the track. Margie straddled a horse, and I got on behind her. I wrapped my arms around her waist, hugging her firmly.

A lever was pulled and the race was on. As we bobbed along the hills and drops, I maintained a tight protective grip around her. Halfway down, I suddenly thought of a way to protect myself from McGraw; I leaned forward, burying my face in her hair, effectively hiding it from the camera.

At the end of the five-minute ride—far too brief I thought—the cameraman ordered, "Go back up! We're going to set up for another shot."

After five or six more trips, none of which we won and all of which we enjoyed, Garvin said, "Okay, go out the exit and stick around. We'll take the blowhole shots in a little while."

Margie and I left with the rest of the crowd to run the gauntlet of the Blowhole Theatre. While a seated audience howled with laughter, a cackling dwarf and an evil clown scurried about tormenting the steeplechasers as they tried to leave. The dwarf would charge at a woman until she was positioned over a hole in the platform floor; a blast of air would then shoot upward, billowing her skirt and exposing her underclothes. Meanwhile the clown chased the men around, shocking them with an electric cattle prod. I was lucky to get through with only one jolt.

Margie fared better. When the dwarf made a run at her, she calmly lowered her head and charged at him until he backed off. Then she stepped directly on the blowhole to block the air and walked off the platform.

Suddenly I thought of Florence Hampton. I could picture her doing the same thing. And I remembered where I had seen Margie's outfit before—it was just like the one Miss Hampton had worn at Ebbets Field.

I thought maybe it was time to find Tom Kelly and have a little talk with him. Besides, getting zapped by a cattle prod wasn't something I wanted to repeat for the camera. Elmer Garvin would just have to do without me.

I said to Margie, "I think I'm going to walk around for a while."

"Okay," she said. "But be back for lunch."

"I will."

I sought out the Human Roulette Wheel where Tom Kelly

had been assigned, and that's where I found him. He wasn't directing though. He was leaving that to the cameraman. Kelly apparently preferred to stay in front of the lens, where his face could be captured on celluloid and later projected on a movie screen for the benefit of his adoring fans.

The cameraman was up in a rafter, taking an overhead shot of the action below. The wheel was a large disk about fifty feet across. A dozen or so people would cluster in the center of the wheel before it started turning. When it began to spin, some would be propelled out to the rim. As the wheel picked up speed, others would be flung out, skidding ignominiously on their bottoms, and cheerfully whooping their lungs out.

I couldn't help noticing that the humans in the Human Roulette Wheel were having a lot more fun than those who'd been playing the real roulette wheels at Kitty's.

Even Tom Kelly looked like a boy at play. As the wheel spun again and people struggled to stay near its center, Kelly slid out on his back, his arms spread and his legs kicking in the air. Only one person remained; it was Esther Kelly, who sat dead center on the wheel, her arms clasped around her knees, smiling broadly at her victory.

The cameraman kept taking more shots and moving his equipment to new locations, so I never did have a chance to talk to Tom Kelly.

At a quarter to twelve, I went back to the Blowhole Theatre. Garvin greeted me angrily, "Where the hell you been?"

"Around," I said evasively. John McGraw was enough to answer to. I didn't work for Elmer Garvin.

"I had to use somebody else for your close-ups," he said. I shrugged. "Sorry."

He glowered at me, then shook his head and pulled out his watch. "Lunch everybody!"

We all went out to the cars and trucks. While the others got their box lunches, Margie pulled out the picnic basket. She handed it to me and I hooked it over my arm. "Let's eat on the beach," she suggested.

I agreed and we walked away. Garvin hollered after us, "Be back here by one sharp!"

We found a spot on the beach far back from the water, where the bathers were somewhat sparser. Margie pulled a red plaid blanket out of the basket; we stretched it out on the sand and sat down with the basket between us.

While my stomach growled with anticipation, Margie started to unpack the food, announcing each item: ham sandwiches, hard-boiled eggs, dill pickles, cherry pie. A bottle of ginger ale and a couple of glasses were next to emerge. Then she dug in once more. "Oooh . . . . look what we have here," she cooed. And she pulled out a bottle of champagne. Oh no.

I'd sworn to myself that I would never drink the stuff again. But it was meant to be a treat, so I'd have to suffer through it. "Would you like me to open it?" I offered. I figured that was supposed to be my job. She nodded and handed me the bottle.

Margie unwrapped the sandwiches and laid them out on top of the closed basket drawers as if it was a dining room table. I struggled to peel the foil from the neck of the bottle, then twisted off the wire around the head of the cork. The cork shot off with a blast, and champagne bubbled over onto my trousers. I must have swung the basket too hard on the walk over.

"Sorry," I said as I tried to brush the puddles off my pants.

Then I checked the bottle; it was still two-thirds full. Maybe I should have shaken it harder.

I filled one of the glasses and held it out to Margie.

"No, I better not," she said. "Mr. Garvin said he might want me to do some stunts this afternoon. You go ahead though."

Gee, thanks. "Let's save it," I said. I hopped up and walked over to retrieve the cork. It had landed on the blanket of a dozing man who was tanning his abundant belly; he was also risking arrest—going barechested on a public beach could cost him a weekend in jail.

After returning to Margie, I sat down and tried to put the cork back in the bottle, but it wouldn't go. So I slipped the cork in my jacket pocket and resigned myself to drinking the champagne.

We nibbled at the sandwiches, Margie drank her ginger ale, and I sipped my champagne. It tasted as good as I remembered, but its aftereffect was vivid enough in my memory that I drank very little of it.

Staring at the waves rolling onto the beach, Margie said softly, "I wonder what the beaches are like in California."

I had no idea, which didn't inhibit me from giving an opinion. "They're about the same," I said. "Except they face the other way."

Margie chuckled. "Some picture companies are moving there."

"To California?" I didn't see why anyone would want to go to the West Coast. There wasn't any big-league baseball beyond St. Louis.

"Uh-huh. There's plenty of sunshine, and they can shoot pictures all year round. We have to shut down in the winter."

While reaching for an egg, I successfully knocked the champagne bottle onto the ground. It was as accidental as the spiking I'd taken in Boston. The liquid vanished into the sand, allowing me to switch to ginger ale.

"Mr. Garvin is thinking about going to California for the winter," Margie continued. "And bringing the whole studio out there."

"This winter?"

She nodded.

So that's what she was getting at. "Oh," I said. Well, baseball season would be over, maybe she'd want some company. Maybe we could both see what California beaches looked like. As I thought about it, I found myself developing a powerful curiosity about them.

After we polished off most of the pie, I pulled out my pocket watch. "Ten to one," I said. "Should we go back?" The sun had dried my pants, so there would be no problem facing the rest of the movie company.

"Oh, I suppose," Margie sighed. "I'd rather go swimming, but I guess it's work time." Too bad—I'd have liked to see her in a bathing dress.

We packed up the basket and went back to the pie truck. I was so stuffed, walking was a major effort.

Elmer Garvin stood with one foot on the running board of the fire engine, and a watch in his hand. When he saw us, he checked the time, then gave us an approving nod. "This afternoon," he said, "we're going to change things around. You two will go on the Human Roulette Wheel."

Spinning around didn't seem such a good idea on a full stomach, and my head was starting to hum from the champagne. But we obediently followed Tom Kelly to film some more shots.

It turned out I was right. After the second spin, my stomach was cramping and my head throbbing. After the third, I was doubled over with pain and looking for a place to throw up.

Margie came over to me. "What's wrong?" she asked in a concerned voice.

"Don't know," I answered brusquely. I hated being sick this way. Especially in front of her. This wasn't an honorable malady, like a broken bone or a gaping bloody wound. It was embarrassing.

She put a hand to my forehead. I don't know exactly what she detected, but she concluded, "You don't feel right. I'm taking you home."

I nodded okay.

Margie checked with Tom Kelly, who didn't care if we stayed or left.

Outside the park, she commandeered the milk truck and a driver to take us to Red Hook.

• • •

By the time we were dropped off at Margie's apartment, I could barely straighten up enough to walk to the door. I walked bent, hugging my belly to stifle the pain that clawed at my gut.

Inside, I ran to the bathroom and dropped to my knees in front of the commode. Expelling the lunch made me feel no better. I didn't know what was wrong with me. I vaguely wondered if the ham sandwiches were bad.

Margie knocked at the door. "Are you all right?" she called.

Between heaves, I weakly replied, "I'll be okay in a while."

"I'm going to call a doctor," she said.

"No!" I yelled with all the strength I could put into it. I

never let doctors near me. A doctor might find something really wrong with me, something that would mean I couldn't play baseball. I sure wasn't going to let a doctor poke around at me just for a bellyache.

We argued back and forth, Margie giving sensible reasons why I should be seen by a physician and me repeating "No" to every argument. She finally gave in.

When I finished with the bathroom, I felt weak, and chills started to shake my body.

Margie took me to the bedroom. I mumbled that the couch would be fine. She insisted I take the bed and she'd take the couch. It was my turn to give in. I even agreed to drink a cup of milk that she'd heated.

I immediately fell into a dark oblivion that muffled all thought and feeling.

It was dark when I woke with a shiver. In a moment, I realized it wasn't internal this time. Margie was brushing my forehead with a damp cloth. Nothing in my life ever felt so soothing. I was almost surprised that this girl who fought lions could have a touch so tender. I reached up and grabbed her hand. I brought it to my lips and softly kissed it. Then I plopped my head back on the pillow and slipped into an easy comfortable sleep.

•  •  •

It was light when I woke again, the daylight of early morning. My head was groggy, and my stomach felt emptier than it ever had before. I was feeling stronger, but disoriented. Since I wasn't in my own bedroom, I first thought I was on a road trip, in a strange hotel. The furniture was what one would typically find in a hotel—plain, sturdy, sparse.

It took a minute for me to remember that I was in Margie's

apartment. I lay still, listening, and could hear her moving quietly in the kitchen and humming to herself.

I pulled off the blanket and saw that I was down to my underwear. I was pretty sure I hadn't undressed myself. As I swung my legs out of bed, I also noticed that the bandage on my left calf had been changed.

I quickly dressed. The kitchen sounds were now accompanied by the smell of fresh-brewed coffee. After slicking down my tousled hair, I almost raced to the kitchen.

Margie was stirring a pot on the stove and humming snatches of *"The Merry Widow Waltz."* She was wearing a billowing lavender summer dress that didn't look like something to be worn around the house. Her long brown braid was carefully wrapped in fashionable pile atop her head, with tortoise-shell hairpins holding it in place.

"G'morning," I said.

She turned around. "You're up! How do you feel?"

*"Much* better, thanks."

She came over and felt my forehead. "You feel better," was her verdict. "Hungry?"

"Oh yes."

"Good! That's a good sign. I made oatmeal. It's not fancy, but I thought something plain would be better for your stomach. I know how to make other things. Do you want eggs instead?"

"No. Oatmeal sounds great. And the coffee smells wonderful." She took the hint and poured me a cup. "Aren't you going to be late for work?" I asked. "I don't want to get you in any more trouble with Garvin."

"I called in. Mr. Garvin gave everybody the day off today. He's trying to edit the film they shot yesterday."

She spooned the oatmeal into bowls and set them on a small kitchen table next to a window. It overlooked an alley that wasn't very scenic. Not that I was looking anywhere but at Margie.

The oatmeal seemed the best food I'd ever eaten. And I kept it down, all three servings of it. My stomach felt better, warm and full. I felt strong enough to play against the Phillies this afternoon.

"Thanks for . . . uh, taking care of me last night," I said. "I'm sorry about all the trouble."

"It was no trouble. It was actually . . . well . . . I liked . . ." She averted her eyes and pointed to a vase on a small shelf next to the window. "It was very sweet of you to send the roses. And you remembered my favorite color." The flowers were wilted and more brown than yellow, but I liked the fact that she saved them. "It was sweet of you to bring the champagne yesterday, too," she added. "I wish I could have had some."

The champagne. I didn't bring the champagne.

# Chapter Sixteen

At eight o'clock that night, I was home alone, seated in my chair, basking in the glow of two victories.

One was against the Phillies, a win that kept us a game up on the Braves in the standings. With my leg starting to heal, I played the entire game at third base and went two for four at the plate.

The other victory was against a killer. I knew I hadn't brought the champagne to the picnic, and if Margie didn't, then somebody else had planted it in the basket. To avoid scaring her, I'd chosen not to tell Margie that somebody had tried to poison me—or us or her. I wasn't sure about the poisoner's intent, and I figured I'd wait until I was more certain before telling her about it. My guess was that I was the target, and whoever planted the bottle simply didn't care if Margie died, too.

Right now I wasn't trying to figure out who did it or why, nor was I considering the prospect of another, possibly more successful, attempt in the future. Instead, I was celebrating our survival. I thought perhaps the fact that we were both still alive was a sign that we were meant to be together.

Actually, considering all that had happened in the last twenty-four hours, I was in a surprisingly cheerful mood. The two things that mattered most to me were baseball and Margie, and both were going well. The way Margie had taken care of me stayed in the back of my mind and comforted me throughout the day. And the two hits I'd gotten in today's game gave me 36 hits in 148 at bats for the season.

Ah! The batting average. I still had to work out my new average. I grabbed a pencil and sheet of paper from the coffee table. I never had much in the way of formal schooling, but somewhere I'd picked up enough long division to calculate a batting average: 36 into 148—no, it's 148 into 36 . . . comes to . . . 0.2432. Rounded off, that's .244, just six points shy of .250.

I slapped the pencil on the table with a satisfied thwack. The door seemed to echo the sound as somebody started knocking on it.

I hopped out of my chair and swung the door open.

My visitor was a towering young man with small black eyes deeply set above a broad squat nose. He wore no tie or jacket; just a red flannel workshirt and denim trousers that looked new and stiff. A misshapen tan crusher was perched on his head.

It was that bonebreaker friend of Virgil Ewing. The one from Marsten's Billiard Parlor. Spike—no, that was the other one. "Uh . . . Billy, isn't it?" I greeted him.

His greeting was a right hand that shot up and grabbed me around the throat, his thumb and fingers nearly meeting behind my neck.

Without a word, he took a step forward, forcing his way into my apartment. I brought my hands up and dug my fingertips into his wrist, trying to loosen his hold. Impervious to the pressure, he lifted me by the throat, swung me around, and slammed my back against the wall. My head ricocheted off the hard plaster and bounced forward. With just his one meaty paw under my jaw, Billy held me so that my head was pinned against the wall and my toes dangled loosely. We were almost eye to eye, which meant I was half a foot above the floor.

I hoped a neighbor might see us through the open door. I couldn't turn my head, but I strained to look from the corner of my eye. Then I saw Billy's left arm reach out and I heard the door slam shut.

My mind raced. What's going on? And why?

He leaned over, planting his face inches from mine. "Who you work for?" he growled in a soft drawl similar to Ewing's.

"Nnnggg," I answered. My jaw and tongue were pinned together by his fist.

He eased up a little, lowering me until my heels touched the floor and loosening his fist until it made a U around my throat. "Who you work for?" he repeated.

The question threw me. So I told him the truth, although he already knew it. "The Giants," I said. "I work for John McGraw."

That wasn't the answer he wanted to hear. His fist tightened again. "What was that business in Marsten's? How come you was asking Virg all them questions?"

"It was just like I told him," I croaked. "We were all at a party just before Florence Hampton died. Miss Hampton was a friend of the lady I was with. I was just trying to find out if Ewing knew what happened to her."

"You're trying to pin it on him."

I tried to shake my head no but I couldn't move it. "I'm not trying to pin it on anybody," I said. "I'm just trying to find out what happened."

"What you gonna do if you do find out?"

I didn't know. I guess I hadn't thought things out that far. My shoulders were free enough to shrug them. "I don't know," I admitted lamely.

I'd finally given him a satisfactory answer. He let go of my throat and took a step back. I started to reach up to rub the pain away, then dropped my hand. I wasn't going to give him the satisfaction.

Billy pulled a package of Beechnut chewing tobacco from his shirt pocket and held it out to me. "Have a chaw," he said. It sounded more like an order than an offer.

"No, thanks." It was one of the few baseball traditions I didn't follow. The one time I tried it, I got almost as sick as I had last night.

Opening the pouch, Billy shook his head. "Where I come from it ain't polite to say no. This here is from Virg. If you got nothing against him, you'll take a chaw of his tobacco."

Well, I didn't want to be rude. I reached in the pouch and pinched together a wad of the brown stuff. As I lifted it to my mouth, I could feel my mouth start to water, not with appetite but in self-defense.

Just before it passed my lips, Billy's hand shot out even faster than it had before and knocked the tobacco from my fingers. What was he mad about now?

"This stuff just killed Larry Harron," he said.

"It what?"

"The tobacco got poison in it."

"You tried to kill me!"

"Naw, I didn't. I just wanted to see if you was gonna take it."

What the hell. . . . "Who's *Larry Harron?*" I asked.

"You seen him. At Marsten's. The boy with the shoulder." Billy hunched up his right shoulder.

Jeez. The Dodger batboy. "He's dead?"

Billy nodded.

"Why? He was just a boy. Why would anybody want to kill him?"

"Hell, nobody wanted to kill Larry. He was a good kid. It was Virg Ewing they wanted dead."

"How do you know that?"

"Like I said, this is Virg's tobacco—"

"I don't get it. When—"

"Just listen, and I'll tell ya." He looked around the room.

"Let's sit down," I offered.

Billy took my chair and I sat on the sofa without objection.

"It happened this afternoon at Ebbets Field," Billy began. "Larry didn't come out to the dugout when the game started, so Virg sent me to look for him. I checked all around, but I didn't find him till the game was over. He was in the tool shed. Poor kid was puking his guts out and he looked just about dead. He gimme this tobacco, said he took it from Virg's locker and thought he was being punished for stealing. Poor kid was always trying to be just like Virg, so I guess he wanted to learn to chew. Anyway, we took him to Kings County Hospital, but he died by the time we got there. Doctors said he was poisoned—"

"By the tobacco?"

"Naw, the doctors didn't have no idea what killed him. I figgered out it was the tobacco."

"Somebody poisoned Ewing's tobacco?"

"That's the thing. This ain't really his tobacco. It was in his locker, but it wasn't his. See, Virg always mixed licorice with his tobacco." He smiled. "We used to rib him about it when we was kids—adding candy to your tobacco ain't considered real manly." He held up the Beechnut. "No licorice in this."

"So if Larry Harron took it from Ewing's locker, somebody else must have put it there," I said. "And there's poison in it." To my mind, chewing tobacco was lethal enough without adding poison.

"Yep. And they meant to kill Virg with it."

"Who do you think did it?"

"I figured it might have been you."

"No," I said firmly, as another suspect immediately sprang to mind: Sloppy Sutherland. He had the means: access to the locker room. No, that was *opportunity*. But wouldn't Sutherland know about the licorice? "Who knows that Ewing mixes licorice with his tobacco?"

Billy shook his head. "Nobody, I don't think. Like I said, it ain't manly. Virg don't want people to know about it."

Okay, what about motive? Maybe it goes back to their competition for Florence Hampton. Sutherland thinks Ewing killed Miss Hampton, so he tries to kill Ewing to get revenge. Or Sutherland killed Miss Hampton and thought Ewing was on to him, so he tries to kill Ewing to shut him up. Or maybe it had nothing to do with Miss Hampton's death. Maybe their general hatred of each other had just boiled over.

While I thought over the possibilities, I asked Billy, "You and Ewing grew up together?"

"Yep. In Gatlinburg, Tennessee."

"You're related?"

"Probably, but not close."

"How come you're trying to protect him?"

"Well, he had some trouble when he first come up to the city. You folks do things different than we do back home. Just 'cause we talk a little slow, you figure we think slow. So you try to take advantage of us. That happened to Virg a lot his first year. Then his ma asked me to come up here with him."

"To protect him."

"Naw. To protect other people. Virg don't take it kindly when people try to take advantage of him. He got a temper."

"Seems like you do, too."

"Yeah, well, sorry 'bout that." Billy looked a little ashamed. "You know," he said, "when you was asking Virg about where he went after that party . . . and he said he went to Marsten's . . ."

"Yeah?"

"Well, he didn't come to the pool hall."

"No?"

"Uh-uh. You think maybe he got into something that night that made somebody want to kill him?"

"Hard to tell. Do you know where he did go?"

"Naw. I asked him about it after you came to Marsten's. He wouldn't tell me." Billy cleared his throat noisily. "So, do you or don't you think it's tied in to what you was asking about?"

I thought for a moment, only to find that I didn't have an answer. So I picked one at random. "Probably," I said.

"Good."

"Why good?"

"Then you can help me find out for sure." It sounded as much like a request as a bunt sign from John McGraw. I was not expected to decline.

"First you almost strangle me, and then you ask for my help? Why the hell should I?"

"I expect whoever tried to kill Virg is gonna try again," Billy said calmly. "And I ain't sure what I can do about it. Leastways not by myself. I liked what I saw of you in Marsten's: you woulda fought us if it come to it, but you was smart enough to avoid it."

Lucky, was more like it.

"You're asking questions 'bout Virg anyway," Billy continued. "So you can do a little more poking around for me."

Actually, I could see some advantages to joining up with him. If Ewing wasn't at the pool hall the night Florence Hampton drowned, I still had to find out where he was—and why he'd lied about it. Having Billy on my side could come in handy.

I also saw a possible disadvantage. "If it turns out that Ewing did something," I said warily. "That he hurt somebody maybe. Would you still try to protect him? I mean, if I found out he did something wrong, are you going to come after me?"

"If Virg did something, he had good reason for it."

"That doesn't answer the question."

"You find out the truth and that'll do me jest fine."

"Okay. You got to help though."

"How?"

"Keep an eye on him. If you see him doing anything strange, going someplace unusual, meeting with somebody you don't know, let me know. Especially if you see him with Sloppy Sutherland."

Billy frowned. "You think it was him?"

"I don't think anything yet. Just watch and let me know."

"And what if he does get together with Sutherland?"

I wasn't sure. "Call me," I said. Maybe by then I'd know.

# Chapter Seventeen

The morning papers all carried the story of Larry Harron's death. Most gave it prominent space on their front pages, eclipsing their coverage of the war in Europe. They all gave the official cause of death as accidental arsenic poisoning. Since he was found in the ballpark's tool shed, the police concluded that he'd gotten into some of the groundskeeper's chemicals.

There was variation in the papers' descriptions of the boy. His reported age ranged from twelve to sixteen. Some papers omitted any mention of his physical disability, while others suggested he was mentally retarded and didn't know what he was eating. None mentioned any family.

The newspapers were unanimous in describing Larry Harron's popularity among Dodger fans; most echoed the *Brooklyn Eagle,* which called him "a favorite of the Ebbets Field faithful."

The *Public Examiner* took its usual hysterical approach to the story. Instead of stopping with a report on Harron's death, it had a column written by William Murray headlined *Does Death Stalk the Dodgers?* Murray suggested that Florence

Hampton, as part-owner, and now the batboy Harron had been killed in some plot to hurt the Brooklyn team. "How long until a Dodger player is murdered?" he wrote. Little did Murray know that it almost *was* a ballplayer who was killed.

At least I wasn't mentioned in Murray's article. He was pursuing a new scenario now. Instead of actresses who knew Mickey Rawlings being potential murder victims, it was people associated with the Dodger team.

I allowed myself a moment of relief that William Murray was off my back. Then I realized he had the right approach—there was some sense behind the sensationalism. Murray was looking for patterns in the tragedies of the last three weeks to see how they connected. I needed to do the same and see where the murder of Larry Harron—or attempted murder of Virgil Ewing—fit into the pattern.

I thought about calling Margie and decided against it. She'd be at the studio, and I didn't want to cause her any more trouble with Elmer Garvin.

Besides, I didn't know how much I should share with her. I still hadn't told her that I wasn't the one who put the champagne in the picnic basket. At first I held back to avoid scaring her, to keep her from worrying. Then I realized she would probably do a lot more than worry. She'd likely go after whoever tried to poison us and possibly put herself in danger in the process. I wasn't sure if I should say anything about it now.

I wasn't sure if I should tell her about Ewing and the batboy, either. Not until I found out more about it.

I called Casey Stengel's number to ask him about Larry Harron. No answer.

Next I went to the ice box and pulled out a small tissue-wrapped bundle from the bottom shelf. Before Ewing's friend Billy had left, I'd asked him to leave the tobacco with me, but he wouldn't. I guess he didn't trust me completely. He forgot about the wad he'd knocked to the floor, though, so I wrapped it up and saved it. In a case that was mostly conjecture, it was the first hard evidence I had.

I laid the tobacco on the coffee table and sat back in my chair, staring at the leafy shreds of Beechnut. Yes, it was evidence, but it was telling me nothing.

Perhaps there wasn't much to tell. It could be a mistake to try to draw complex conclusions from simple facts. Like the death of William Daley, the simple solution being that he really died from tainted oysters. The only evidence to the contrary was the material left by Florence Hampton—the notes from the ship's physician and the description of arsenic that she had written. Maybe she just couldn't accept his death as being from natural causes.

Aloud I cursed the speculative diversion about William Daley and the baseball tour. Reality was what mattered. Reality was the dead blue body of Florence Hampton, the intense pain I'd suffered a couple of nights ago, a wad of poisoned tobacco, and a dead batboy who had never harmed anyone.

Means, motive, and opportunity. I'd learned a couple of years ago that a murderer would have to meet all three criteria. They ran through my mind yesterday, but I hadn't yet applied them to each death and each attempt.

I picked up a pencil and the scratch paper with my batting average calculations. Flipping it over, I started to write.

Victim: Florence Hampton. Suspects: Ewing, Sutherland, Kelly. They all met the means, motive, opportunity criteria. They were all with her the night she died, they each had a romantic interest in her, and all were strong enough to drown her.

Next case, an attempted murder. Intended victims: Mickey Rawlings and/or Marguerite Turner. Suspects: I put down a question mark. Motive: another question mark, but I thought maybe somebody didn't like us asking questions about the night Miss Hampton died. Means: poisoned champagne. I added a question mark there, too. I couldn't *prove* that it was poisoned. Opportunity: Tom Kelly was the only one there. No, that's not true. Opportunity was wide open. The picnic basket had been left in the truck all morning. Anybody could have slipped the bottle in. Even Ewing or Sutherland; they were playing in Ebbets Field that afternoon so could have easily been on Coney Island in the morning.

Finally, Larry Harron. Motive: somebody wanted to kill Virgil Ewing. Means: poisoned chewing tobacco. Opportunity: Sloppy Sutherland. Tom Kelly would have been at the studio. No, he wasn't! Margie said they all had Friday off. He could have gone to Ebbets Field and got into the locker room somehow.

Okay, I'll go back to William Daley. Motive: question mark. Opportunity: Ewing, Sutherland, and Kelly were all on the cruise. Means: poisoned oysters.

Jeez, poison again.

Daley dead, officially of food poisoning but with symptoms that match arsenic. Florence Hampton dead by drowning. Me nearly poisoned, probably, and with symptoms matching those in Florence Hampton's arsenic notes. The Dodger batboy poisoned by arsenic. There was almost a pattern here: Arsenic, drowning, arsenic, arsenic.

Why the change-up? A pitcher will vary his pitches, but would a murderer? Wouldn't he stick to the method that worked? Damned if I knew.

Looking over everything I'd just scribbled, I realized that I didn't *know* very much at all.

I called Karl Landfors and filled him in on everything.

"That's curious," he said. "There could be several reasons why somebody would change methods. One would be to confuse the trail, to keep a pattern from becoming obvious. Or it could be desperation. If he thought he was about to get caught, he might try anything. Or perhaps convenience. Something presented itself and he took advantage of it."

"Couldn't the answer be that there's more than one killer?" I suggested. "Say Virgil Ewing drowned Florence Hampton and then Sloppy Sutherland tried to poison Ewing to get revenge."

"Hmm. It's possible, of course. Let me give it some thought."

"Okay." I didn't say so, but I felt better having Landfors think about it.

# Chapter Eighteen

Landfors did more than think about it.

Three days later he called back. The first words out of his mouth were, "Florence Hampton was poisoned."

"She was drowned," I argued. "You showed me the autopsy report. There was water in her lungs."

"That's true, there was." In a flat, tired voice he explained, "The poison wasn't enough to kill her. She was probably weakened by the poison, thrown in the water, and then she drowned."

"Huh. How do you know about the poison?"

"I had her exhumed."

"You dug her up?"

There was silence, then he said wearily, "Yes, that's what exhumed means. I had Libby dug up and reautopsied."

Libby. Sometimes I forgot this was his sister we were talking about. "Do the police know?" I asked.

"No, there was no need for that. I simply went to Greenwood Cemetery in Brooklyn; she was buried in the Daley family plot. I told the cemetery administrator that our family wanted her body moved back to Ohio, and he had her disinterred. I hired a private coroner to do the examination, then I told the administrator that we changed our minds and decided to let her rest next to her husband. So he had her buried again." Landfors wasn't gloating at the success of the ruse; he sounded exhausted, as tired as if he'd done the digging himself. "Only you and I know she was poisoned . . . and the coroner, of course." He paused, then added, "It was arsenic."

"Is this autopsy right?" I asked. "If she had arsenic in her, why wasn't it found the first time?"

"Nobody expected to find it. The assumption was that she drowned, and when her lungs were found to be full of water nobody bothered to do a chemical analysis. The second autopsy is correct. Arsenic is easy to detect if you look for it."

"It is?"

"Yes, certainly. Arsenic is an element—it doesn't break down, it stays in the body. Even a tiny amount can be detected."

I had an idea. "Are you in your office?"

"Yes, why?"

"I'll be there in half an hour."

• • •

I put the champagne cork on Landfors's desk; it had still been in the pocket of the jacket I'd worn to Steeplechase Park. Then I took the wrapped wad of chewing tobacco from my pocket and placed it next to the cork.

"Can you get these tested?" I asked.

"For poison?"

I nodded. "The tobacco is from Virgil Ewing's locker. It's the stuff Larry Harron, the Dodger batboy, got hold of."

"My understanding," Landfors said, "is that you don't ingest the tobacco though. You chew it and spit, right?"

"Doesn't always work that way." Grimacing at the memory of my own early experience with the odious substance, I explained, "When you first try it, you usually end up swallowing some."

Landfors's face developed the same sour expression that it had when he'd tasted my coffee.

"And the cork," I said, "is from the champagne Margie and I had on the beach. I thought maybe some of it could have soaked into the cork."

"Could be. . . . I'll have it tested if you want. But it sounded to me like you just had a stomach ache. If it was poison, why didn't Miss Turner have the same symptoms?"

"She didn't drink. She had stunts to do in the afternoon."

Landfors's eyebrows rose and fell. "You drank it and she didn't?"

"Yeah, why?"

"I don't know. Maybe you better tell me the whole story again. What you ate, where you were . . . everything."

I filled him in on every detail I could remember of our picnic lunch and concluded with the opinion, "I'm sure somebody tried to kill me. Or us."

"Damn," he exhaled. "I'm sorry, Mickey. I didn't mean for you to get this involved. I don't want anything happening to you. Libby was *my* sister; it's *my* responsibility to find out who killed her." He peered at me through the thick lenses of his spectacles and said stiffly, "I am hereby withdrawing my request for your help. I think you should forget about investigating my sister's death and concentrate on baseball." It sounded like something John McGraw would say, but it was more polite than McGraw would word it.

"Hell no," was my answer. "I've been in worse scrapes. Besides, now I have a personal reason to stick it out."

Landfors paused then nodded. "Very well. Thank you." He started to toy with the cork, trying to stand it upright on the big head. He muttered, almost to himself, "Arsenic . . . poison . . ." The cork kept falling down and he kept trying to stand it up. I didn't think it was such a good idea for him to be playing with it, and I wondered if poison could work its way through human skin.

"Something's bothering me," he finally said.

Yeah, I could tell. "What?" I prompted.

His eyes stayed down, staring at the cork. "Poison. Why poison? That's a woman's murder weapon."

A *woman's* murder weapon? They had their own murder weapon?

"The business with Virgil Ewing bothers me, too," he continued. "That's awfully convenient, the batboy getting killed instead of him. How about this: what if Ewing put the poisoned tobacco in the locker himself, and then left it for somebody else to take. Everybody assumes it was meant for him, and he's eliminated as a suspect. Very convenient."

Landfors drummed his fingers on the desktop. There was more on his mind, but it didn't pass his lips.

I had one more idea. "We're still guessing about William Daley," I said. "Can you have him dug up—exhumed—too? And checked for poison?"

"Well, it's possible, of course. But I couldn't make the request on my own. I'm just his brother-in-law, not immediate family. There would have to be a court order. That would mean getting the police involved and publicity." He thought for a moment. "Later, maybe, if we have to. Let's see how things work out."

"Okay. Hey, I got to get to the ballpark."

"All right, I'll let you know as soon as I have the test results on these things." As I stood to go, he stopped me with a hand on my arm. "Take care of yourself, Mickey. Be careful . . . really careful."

• • •

I had nine innings on the bench, while Grover Cleveland Alexander and the Phillies beat Jeff Tesreau 3–2 for a split of the four-game series. Nine innings, an hour and a half, to mull over my conversation with Karl Landfors.

Watching big husky guys like Alexander and Gavvy Cravath of Philadelphia, and our own Tesreau and Fred Merkle, I became skeptical about a ballplayer using poison. Fists maybe, or a bat—something straightforward, where you can feel the impact on your target. Not poison.

I thought of the game's craftiest players—Ty Cobb and Johnny Evers—and of the most crooked—Hal Chase and Heinie Zimmerman, who were known to throw games for gamblers. Not even these men would resort to such a cowardly weapon as poison.

Nor would somebody who had once been a player— Tom Kelly.

A woman's murder weapon. I never thought of a woman as a killer.

But by the time the game was over, there were some questions I wanted to ask Margie Turner.

• • •

At eight o'clock, that's what I was doing, in her parlor, in her apartment in Red Hook. She'd settled herself on the sofa in a way that suggested I was to sit next to her. Instead, I'd taken an armchair across from her, so as to keep her in full view, to see her reactions to my questions.

"When we were at the Sea Dip Hotel," I said, "I asked you who Florence Hampton was with, and you didn't want to say. It's time to tell me now. I can't find out how she died if I don't know what she was doing when she was alive."

Margie's eyes dropped. "What did you want to know?" she asked quietly. It didn't sound like she was eager to tell me anything.

"Tom Kelly. I want to know about Kelly. He was chasing Florence Hampton at the party, and she didn't like him at all. I saw that. What was going on? His wife was there watching, and he didn't even care."

Margie said softly, "No, he doesn't care much about Esther at all." She looked away, seeming to scan the photos that populated her wall.

"Did he care about Florence Hampton?"

"Not really, no. I don't think he cares about anybody but Tom Kelly."

"If he didn't care for her and she didn't like him, why was he trying to romance her? And why was he so jealous— angry—when she danced with Sloppy Sutherland and Virgil Ewing?"

"Well . . . no offense, but he thought baseball players were beneath Libby. He thought it looked bad for an actress, especially his own leading lady, to be associating with athletes. See, being a movie actor went to Tom Kelly's head. He believed every word the fan magazines wrote about him. And he believed that all women adored him. He made passes at a lot of them . . . even me once. As far as I could tell, he usually got turned down, including by me."

"Did he think Florence Hampton adored him?"

"No, I don't think he had that strong an imagination. But

he thought a leading lady should have a romantic interest in her leading man. The fan magazines and the studios always try to pair actors and actresses romantically."

"How did his wife feel about that?"

"Esther Kelly is a sweet lady. She never complained, never seemed bitter. She did get upset sometimes though."

"Like she did at the party."

Margie nodded. Then she looked me straight in the eye and said, "I would leave a man who ever treated me the way Tom Kelly treats Esther. I'd slap him silly, then I'd leave him."

I thought she would probably use her knee on him, too. "Why doesn't Esther leave Kelly? Doesn't she have an acting career of her own?"

"I don't know why she doesn't leave. But she hasn't acted for a few years. Not until the other day at Coney Island. She said she liked doing the picture because there weren't any lines to memorize." Margie suddenly waved a finger in the air and blurted, "She gave up her career for that man! She gave up her own career and devoted herself to getting him started in the business. And this is how he repays her. The son of a—" Then she collected herself.

If Margie could get this agitated about it, I could imagine how his wife might have felt.

I said, "Do you think—I'm just wondering if it's possible—could a woman kill another woman if she thought her husband was interested in the other woman?"

*"Esther Kelly?"* Margie said incredulously. "No, she's too . . . too sweet, I suppose. Harmless." Margie sounded sure, but I wasn't. Esther Kelly had been sitting alone with Florence Hampton at a table in the Sea Dip dining room. Opportunity.

"No, not necessarily Esther Kelly," I said. "Just in general. Could a woman do that?"

*"I* couldn't," Margie said. "Or *wouldn't* anyway. Not over a man. Besides, if anybody should be killed, it's the man."

I was starting to feel uneasy.

Margie started to talk on about the battle of the sexes, not very coherently. She mingled complaints about women not being allowed to vote with assertions that women could be just as good killers as men if they wanted to.

Now and then I nodded, as if in agreement with her points. I was only half listening, though, as another scenario took form in my mind.

If a man is chasing other women, his wife would have cause to kill him . . .

William Daley ran around. "Quite a man with the ladies," Otis Haines had said. "A bit of a rogue," Arthur Carlyle had said. Could *his* wife have killed him? Could Florence Hampton have had Daley murdered while he was on the world tour? And then somebody found out and killed her to get revenge?

I said nothing about this possibility to Margie. I didn't know how to suggest that her friend might have been a murderess. And with the way she had just been talking, Margie might have said she approved of Florence Hampton killing her philandering husband. I wouldn't have wanted to hear that.

There was too much going unsaid lately, and it started to gnaw at me. Karl Landfors and Margie Turner were both keeping things from me, and I was keeping my thoughts from them.

I made an excuse to leave early. Margie looked troubled by my departure, but I felt that I had to get away from her and think things out on my own. I wasn't in the mood for togetherness.

I went back to Manhattan thinking maybe part of the

solution was falling into place. Florence Hampton falls in love with a man, they marry, he cheats on her, so she has somebody kill him while he's out of the country. A friend of William Daley finds out about it and kills her to avenge Daley's death.

Then the pieces stopped fitting. Why kill the batboy? And why try to kill Margie and me?

That question was coming up a lot lately: Why me?

Then another bothersome question came to mind: What did Margie mean, *Not over a man?*

# Chapter Nineteen

**M**argie phoned me early the next morning. She offered to call in sick so that the two of us could visit Esther Kelly at home while Tom was at the studio. I wasn't crazy about her getting into more hot water with Elmer Garvin, but I agreed.

Two hours later, we were strolling east along Lafayette Avenue toward Clinton Hill, Brooklyn's most fashionable residential area, near Fort Greene.

Although Margie said nothing about my early departure the night before, she spoke with an urgent cheerfulness as if trying to effect a reconciliation. I didn't know how to tell her that there really was no rift. I hadn't been angry at her, merely confused. So I tried to show her, taking her hand and interlocking her fingers with mine. She immediately got the message and relaxed.

We walked on, absorbing the gentle sunshine of a waning summer. August was nearly over, and the weather would soon be getting cooler.

The Kelly house was a vintage three-story brownstone on Clinton Avenue between Willoughby and Myrtle. Its spacious, carefully tended front lawn was bordered by perky daffodils and delicate white lilies. On any other street, the home would have been the jewel of the block, but here it was dwarfed by the newer, palatial mansions of its neighbors.

I rapped the brass knocker on the front door. It was promptly pulled open by a stout thirtyish young lady in an ill-fitting black and white maid's uniform. She had frizzy red hair, and bold brown freckles mottled her fair face.

"Is Esther Kelly in?" Margie asked.

"And who might you be?" the maid demanded in a voice that had more of Ireland than Brooklyn in it. From her tone, she wasn't asking for the information to convey it to Esther but to decide whether she herself approved of us.

"My name is Marguerite Turner," Margie answered politely. "And this is Mickey Rawlings."

I tipped my boater.

"Mickey Rawlings the baseball player?" the maid gushed with sudden warmth.

With all due modesty—none—I admitted I was.

"I'm a Giants fan!" she bellowed. In a loud voice, as if challenging the neighbors, she added, "I know I'm in Brooklyn now, and maybe I shouldn't say so, but with Mr. Kelly having been a Giant, I root for John McGraw's boys."

Good as it was to find a Giant fan on this side of the East River, I'd have rather she just let us in.

But she went on, like Casey Stengel in a talkative mood, "You know, I was at that game where you broke up Sloppy Sutherland's shutout. Tuesday being my day off, I always go to a ballgame, even if it's only the Yankees playing. Too bad you boys couldn't win that game against Sutherland. *You* did wonderful, laying down that bunt like you did. You know, most people like the big sluggers; me, I like you little infielders—you have to play so much harder."

"Well . . . uh, thank you," I said. Not that it was much of a compliment, but it gave me a chance to interrupt. "Actually, do you think you could tell Mrs. Kelly we're here? I have to get back for a game this afternoon."

"And here I am talking your ear off," she said with a friendly slap on my shoulder. It fell as heavily as a blow from John McGraw. "Come on in and I'll tell her you're here."

She led us into a foyer that was as big as a dining hall, then went to get Esther.

"I think you have an admirer," Margie said in a teasing voice. She sounded more amused than jealous.

"Nice house," I said, ignoring the comment. And it was. It also felt as if I'd been here before, though I knew I hadn't.

While Margie's place didn't fit the "Homes of the Stars" pictorials that appeared in the movie magazines, the Kelly house looked like a prime candidate for such a photo spread.

Off the west side of the foyer was a parlor with white wicker furniture, a matching white grand piano, deep green carpeting, gold chintz curtains. . . . That was it! I *had* seen the room before, in a *Photoplay* pictorial on Mary Pickford's home. Opposite the parlor was a formal dining room; its maple furniture and colorful tapestries were arranged in the same way as Clara Kimball Young's. The Kellys must have used the fan magazines as decorating guides. I was sure that somewhere in the house Tom Kelly had a den and wondered if it was modeled after William Farnum's or Francis X. Bushman's.

The maid brought Esther in, leading her by the hand like a child. Next to the chunky maid, Esther looked like a little girl, tiny and frail. Her clothes reinforced the impression of youth: a frilly pink dress that came just below her knees, scarlet ribbons tied into her blond hair, and white satin shoes laced on her dainty feet. Her skin was as pale and smooth as porcelain. Except for large blue eyes, her facial features were on the same diminutive scale as her overall size—a button nose, ears with no lobes, and small pouty red lips.

Margie gave her an affectionate hug. "Esther, dear," she said. "I hope we didn't come at a bad time. We should have called first."

"Oh, that's all right," Esther answered. "This is a very good time." I couldn't imagine how her high weak voice could have ever been heard in a theater. "I'm glad you're here," she said. And she did look happy at having company, though there seemed to be a touch of fear in her wide eyes. "Tom isn't here though. He's at the studio. Shouldn't you be there, too?"

"No, not today," Margie said.

"Why don't you folks come into the parlor, and I'll fetch some lemonade," the maid offered.

"Yes, Bridget," Esther Kelly said. "Thank you." She obediently followed the maid into the Mary Pickford parlor, and we followed behind. Bridget helped Esther climb into an oversized rocking chair, then left the room. Margie and I chose a settee with pastel green cushions so thin that I could feel the weave of the wicker through them. The Kellys apparently considered style a higher priority than comfort.

After we settled into the squeaking couch, Margie and I looked at each other, silently asking which one of us was going to start the questioning. We probably should have planned ahead.

Esther showed no sign of starting a conversation. She was absorbed in getting the rocking chair to rock. Since her feet didn't reach the floor, she had to do it by clutching the arms of the chair and shifting her weight back and forth.

"This is a lovely home," Margie began. She had the same

approach to interrogation that I did—start innocuously, then hit them with the tough questions.

"Thank you," Esther said. "We're very happy here. This house has been in my family since I was a girl. Tom had things redone after we got married, but I still like it. Sometimes I almost get lost though. It's not like it used to be . . ." Pointing to a painting above the white marble fireplace, she said, "That is my father." The portrait was of a man with severe eyes and black chin whiskers; he wore a naval uniform so old-fashioned that he might have sailed with John Paul Jones. "He built this house," she added. "Tom let me keep the painting when he redecorated."

Margie rolled her eyes at Tom Kelly's generosity.

"How long have you and Tom been married?" I asked.

"We were married on May second, nineteen hundred and eleven." She recited the sentence as if she had carefully memorized it.

Bridget brought in the lemonade on a tray. She handed glasses of the yellow drink to each of us, giving me a wink as she handed me mine. I heard Margie try to stifle a giggle.

After the maid left, Margie asked Esther, "How did you like working in the picture the other day?" We were taking forever to get to the questions about Florence Hampton.

With a blank look, Esther answered after a pause, "It was very nice."

"That was your first picture, wasn't it?" I said.

Esther hesitated. Then she said slowly, "The first show I was in was *Uncle Tom's Cabin*. At the Century Theatre on West Forty-seventh Street. I was six years old. I played Little Eva. The footlights burned very hot and they scared me, but I liked being in front of an audience. The show was a big hit. It ran for three and a half years."

Margie and I exchanged bewildered glances. I didn't

know what to think. I had enough trouble determining if somebody was telling the truth or lying. With Esther Kelly, I wasn't sure if she was telling us anything at all. She seemed so lost.

Margie gave it another try. "Florence Hampton used to be on the stage, too. Were you in any plays together?"

Esther answered flatly, "Florence Hampton was very nice. She wasn't in *Uncle Tom's Cabin.* Maude Adams was. She was my understudy. And there was a very nice girl who played Topsy . . ." She went on to give us a full cast list, as well as descriptions of the sets and costumes.

Bridget came in again. "I have some lovely little cucumber sandwiches," she announced.

*Cucumber? Yech!* A vegetable sandwich was about as appetizing to me as a chaw of tobacco.

As the maid stood in front of me holding out a tray of sandwiches, an idea popped into my head. I said to Esther, "I've heard Tom has a remarkable den. Do you think I could see it?"

"Yes," she answered, and she started to pull herself off her chair.

"No, you two stay here and chat. Maybe Bridget could show me to the den."

"I'd be happy to," said Bridget.

Margie gave me a quizzical look.

"Well, okay," Esther said, as she settled back in her seat.

After serving sandwiches to the ladies, Bridget said, "Come along now." She then led me to a room on the second floor.

Tom Kelly's den was worse than I expected. It went beyond masculine all the way into the realm of the barbaric. Weapons and dead animals were the motif. A pair of crossed sabers was above the mantel of the flagstone fireplace;

above them was the head of a grizzly bear with its mouth agape. There were flintlock rifles, dueling pistols, a blunderbuss, daggers, and halberds around the walls. Tacked alongside the weapons were the hides of zebras, leopards, and tigers. On the floor in front of the fireplace was a lion skin with a massive maned head. A leather armchair and a foot stool were the room's only furniture.

Bridget turned to leave. Trying to keep her, I asked, "Did Tom Kelly shoot all these?"

She laughed. "No, sir. Mr. Kelly bought everything in here. I don't think he knows how to hunt."

"Well, he looks like an outdoorsman. I'll bet he's still in good enough shape to play baseball if he wanted to."

"Yes sir, he certainly is. He did play baseball this winter. On that world tour, you know."

"I heard about that. I didn't know he played."

"It was a *wonderful* trip," Bridget said. "I'd never been on a ship before. Well, when I was a little girl, my family and I came over from Ireland. But not since then."

"You were on the tour?"

"Of course! The missus wouldn't go without me. I take care of her."

I said confidentially, "Well, I'm glad to hear that. Just between you and me, I don't think Tom Kelly takes care of her quite the way he should." I tried to be subtle in my criticism of him.

"Hah! He treats her *awful,* he does."

I guess there was no need for subtlety. "You know," I said, "I suppose you're right. In fact, the first time I saw him was at a Vitagraph party on Coney Island. The whole time he was trying to dance with Florence Hampton. Left poor Esther in tears. I heard she was so upset, she spent the night in the hotel."

Bridget furrowed her brow. "That was the night Miss Hampton died?"

"Yes."

"No, she didn't stay in any hotel. It was *Mister* Kelly who didn't come home. The missus came in. I remember because—" Then her face flushed and she clamped her mouth shut.

"What's the matter?" I asked.

She kept her lips sealed tight and shook her head.

"It's just between us," I promised gently. "What do you remember?"

Bridget gave in. "The old fellah brought her home that night . . . almost morning, it was."

"What old fellow?"

"Oh, I don't know his name. He's an old gentleman, with a bit of a limp." Bridget then warned me, "Now don't you go to thinking anything improper about the missus. That fellah left her at the door. I expect the way her husband treats her, she just needs somebody nice to talk to sometimes. That's all there is to it."

"I'm sure you're right," I said. "Have you seen her gentleman friend before?"

"Well. . . . There's been a few other times he's brought her home."

"Huh. And you say Tom Kelly didn't come home at all that night?"

"No, not until morning." Bridget didn't sound like she wanted to say any more.

"I like Esther," I said. "I'm glad it's you who takes care of her. She's in good hands."

Bridget smiled.

"You said Tuesday's your day off?"

She nodded.

"The next time the Giants are at the Polo Grounds on a Tuesday, you give me a call, and I'll make sure there's a couple of passes for you."

With effusive thanks, she promised to take me up on the offer, and we went back downstairs.

From Margie's dazed expression, I could tell she wasn't getting very far with Esther. So after an excuse about having to get ready for the ballgame, we said goodbye and left.

We walked west on Myrtle Avenue. In the distance ahead of us were the church spires and treetops of Brooklyn Heights.

Soon I'd have to hop a trolley for Manhattan. "How about coming to the game?" I suggested.

"No, I should go back to my apartment. Mr. Garvin will phone to see if I'm really sick—not that he's worried about my health but to check that I'm not at a ballgame. I'd better be home when he calls."

"Oh, okay. Uh . . . about me leaving you alone with Esther. For the life of me, I couldn't understand what she was talking about. So I figured it might be better to let you talk to her by yourself and see if you could get anywhere."

"I don't think I did," she said. "I tried, but . . . well, Esther seems so forgetful."

"She had a good memory about that play she was in."

"True, but she's vague on anything that's happened recently."

"Did you ask Esther where she went after the party?"

"She said she came right home."

"Huh."

Then Margie said, "I made a few phone calls last night. After you left." Her tone tacked on the word "early," though she left it unspoken.

"About what?"

"About Esther. The standard story in the fan magazines is that she abandoned her career to help her husband get into acting. But what I was told by some theater people was that she couldn't get a part anymore. She couldn't remember lines, wasn't reliable. They said she drank too much."

"She doesn't seem like a boozer."

"No, no she doesn't. So, are you going to tell me what you found out from *Bridget?*"

I thought I was being teased. So I was happy to report that I'd had more success than she had. *"Bridget* told me that Esther did *not* come right home after the party. She didn't get in until almost morning. And Tom didn't come home at all."

"Ooh. You did good."

"Not only that, but a man brought her home that night. Bridget didn't know who he was though."

"You did *very* good."

Hell, I'd learned it from her. I just did the same as she had when she talked to the waitress at Kitty's casino. I was starting to figure out what "together" meant—not necessarily being in the same place at the same time but cooperating.

I was feeling good about Margie Turner again. Good enough to ask her to dinner on Friday night. A candlelight dinner for two was what I was thinking. Her thinking was that it sounded like a great idea.

•   •   •

The game against the Cubs was one of those tormenting matches which neither team seems to want to win. The problem was, we *needed* a win to keep pace with the Boston Braves. We squandered half a dozen scoring chances, until the Cubs booted a couple of ground balls in the ninth to give us the victory 2–1.

While changing after the game, McGraw stuck his head in the locker room. "Dodgers just beat the Braves four nothing," he announced. "Stengel hit two homers."

Strangely enough, there were cheers for the Dodgers in the Giants' locker room. We now had a one game lead on the Braves.

McGraw's announcement also reminded me that I still hadn't gotten through to Stengel about the Dodgers' batboy.

From a wall phone next to the locker room door, I called Ebbets Field. After some explaining and convincing, I was put through to the Dodgers' clubhouse, and Stengel got on the line.

I almost had my lips touching the mouthpiece as I spoke so my teammates wouldn't hear me calling Ebbets Field. The Dodgers were still The Enemy no matter that they did us a favor today. "Casey," I said. "Mickey Rawlings. Hear you had a good game."

"Yeah, I was seeing the ball real good today. Rudolph threw me change-ups that looked fat as grapefruits. Kind of like this knuckleball pitch that—"

"Casey, what I want to talk to you about is Larry Harron."

There was an abrupt silence at the other end.

"The batboy," I prodded. "He got poisoned last week."

"Yeah, I know. He was a good kid. It's a damn shame about him. We're all taking it kind of hard."

"I read it was an accident. I don't suppose there was anybody who had something against him?"

"Nah, everybody liked Larry. Damn good kid."

"He was at the pool hall when we went to see Virgil Ewing."

"Yeah, that's right."

"He was an honest kid?"

"I think so . . . why?"

"He wouldn't lie about anything?"

"Nah, not Larry."

"What if it was for Virgil Ewing? If Ewing said he did something and asked Harron to swear to it, would he lie to protect Ewing?"

"For Ewing, huh. Maybe. The kid worshipped Ewing. Wanted to be just like him. Why?"

"Oh, no reason. Just wondering."

"You ask some strange questions."

"Yeah, I know. Thanks, Casey."

*Chapter Twenty*

**T**hanks to Elmer Garvin, we had to make a slight change of plans Friday night. Instead of a quiet candlelight dinner for two, we were in noisy Luna Park on Coney Island with a million light bulbs blazing all around us.

Luna, on the inland side of Surf Avenue, didn't specialize in wild mechanical rides the way Steeplechase Park did. Instead, Luna Park had more of a circus atmosphere, complete with clowns, acrobats, and animal attractions. Animals of the oddest species were engaged in all kinds of occupations. Men and women took rides on African elephants; children were pulled around the park by billy goats hitched to little carts. There were pools of water with lethargic sea lions basking on their edges and skittish donkeys plunging into the pools from diving boards.

Vitagraph crews had again spent the entire day shooting reels of film, taking advantage of Luna Park's attractions. Only one scene remained to be shot: a night scene for the latest episode of Margie's *Dangers of the Dark Continent* serial.

The entire company was gathered around a large pool

that wasn't currently in use by diving donkeys. Garvin was trying to have it made into a jungle pond, complete with a menagerie borrowed from the park.

Margie, dressed in her khaki shirt and brown jodhpurs, stood patiently next to the camera. The other actors were less patient, fidgeting on the side as they waited for the filming to be over so they could all go home.

Garvin shouted instructions to the workmen setting up the set. They tried to arrange bushes and sand to make it look a little less like a swimming pool in Brooklyn and more like a lagoon in Africa. They moved spotlights and herded uncooperative monkeys who darted among the actors and spectators. One animal handler had a python coiled around his arm. The snake started to whip its tail against a parrot tethered to a perch. The parrot screeched, and other birds joined him in a shrill chorus. It was a chaotic scene that looked hopeless.

I stayed on the fringes, careful not to knock anything over or get in the way.

Tom Kelly stood not far from me with his shoulders drawn up and his hands clasped behind his back. The electric lights of Luna showed his strong handsome profile to great advantage, but no one was noticing. All eyes were on Margie and the activities at the pool.

I sidled my way through the onlookers until I was standing next to him. "Hi, Tom," I said. "How you doing?"

He shrugged. Kelly didn't look to be in a mood for conversation, so we watched the animals for a few minutes while I tried to think of the best approach to get him to talk.

I decided to go for his ego. "I was wondering if you could give me some advice," I said.

He looked puzzled but interested. "About what?"

"Well, to tell you the truth, I'm getting tired of sitting on a bench for John McGraw. I thought maybe I'd try doing moving pictures for a living. Like you did. Not that I could be a leading man like you, but I could probably do comedy."

Kelly laughed. "From what I saw in that movie with Florence Hampton, you'd be good at it."

"Hey, thanks." I was sure he hadn't meant it as a compliment, but I wanted to be agreeable.

"The movies are pretty good," said Kelly, nodding thoughtfully. "There's nothing like seeing your name in lights. And the fans . . . they're better than baseball fans. With baseball, it's kids and men bothering you for autographs. When you're in the movies, it's the ladies that go after you." He nudged me with his elbow and chuckled. "That's real nice."

"Sounds good," I said, with a guilty glance at Margie.

"And another thing about the pictures," he continued, "is you don't have to worry about your arm going dead or losing your hitting eye. You can last for years as an actor. Hell, look at old Carlyle there. He's been acting since the Civil War."

"You gave the game another go this winter, though, didn't you?"

"On the world tour, yeah. Daley didn't take me along to play ball, but I got into a few of the games."

"Why *did* he want you?"

"For publicity. See, he thought nobody would know baseball players in Asia and Europe and them places. But they'd know a famous movie actor like me." Kelly drew himself up a little taller. "The pictures are big all over the world."

"So how'd you end up playing?"

"Because McGraw kept losing his players. Mathewson and Doyle decided not to go at all. Fred Merkle stayed with the team until we got to San Francisco, then he left. You know, a cruise sounds like fun, but not many people really want to spend four months traipsing around the world. When *The Empress of China* set sail from Seattle, there weren't enough players left to field two teams. So McGraw had to play me. Sonofabitch almost choked asking me to play for him again.''

"How'd you like it?"

Kelly smiled. "It felt good." He paused as a far-off look glazed his eyes. "It felt really good." After another moment he said, "You know how it feels when you hit the ball with the sweet spot of the bat?"

I nodded.

"Nothing like it, is there?"

"Sure isn't," I agreed. "Except maybe snagging a line drive. A low line drive that you have to dive for. And it almost pops out of your glove when you hit the ground, but you hang on to it."

"Yeah, or stealing home! You ever steal home?"

"Yup. My first year, I stole home on Christy Mathewson."

Kelly slapped my shoulder. "On Mathewson! That's great! I love to see them college boys get shown up." He chuckled, then said almost wistfully, "Yeah, it was good to play again."

We watched as Garvin had some black sheets stretched out to block some of the electric lights of Luna Park. Then he had a spotlight moved closer to the pool.

"You think you might go back to baseball?" I asked Kelly. I was starting to think I might like him for a teammate.

"Nah. Sometimes I think about it. . . . As much as I try, and as much fun as it is sometimes, I can't really get the hang of being a movie star. It just ain't a natural thing for a fellow to do. I might like to play again, but McGraw would never take me back."

"Maybe somebody else will."

"McGraw would ruin it for me. He'd bad mouth me."

"You know anybody he doesn't bad mouth?"

Kelly laughed. "Yeah, well. You know, on the way back from the world tour, I *was* thinking of maybe playing again. But then we come in to New York harbor and there's Federal League agents scrambling to sign up the players that were on the tour—"

"I remember that. The papers called it 'The Battle of the Docks.' "

"Just about *was* a battle. Some players had recruiters pulling on each arm—"

I saw my opening. "Sounds like the way Sutherland and Ewing were fighting over Florence Hampton at the Sea Dip Hotel."

Kelly's voice dropped. "Yeah, well, the point is that none of the Feds went after me. Hell, if the Feds don't want me, nobody else will."

I pretended I didn't hear. "Say, Tom, after that party, did you see which one of them ended up with her?"

"The party," Kelly repeated in a flat voice.

"Yeah, I left early. I'm a beer man, myself—couldn't stand that champagne they were serving. So I didn't get to see how it ended up. Did you?"

"No."

"They leave before you did or after?"

Kelly gave me a cold stare and walked off. I had the feeling I still needed to work on my interrogation technique.

Before I could determine if I'd learned anything useful from Tom Kelly, the action started for Margie's scene.

Garvin first had her fend off an attack by baboons. The gibbering animals didn't appear particularly frightening. In fact, they were more interested in playing with each other than in attacking Margie. She used all of her acting ability to pretend that she was trying to escape from them.

"Stop camera!" Garvin yelled. "Okay, that wasn't bad. Now they chase you into the pool—the lagoon." Even he wasn't fooled by the makeshift set. "You dive in to get away from them. Start camera!"

To the thorough disinterest of the baboons, Margie obediently dove into the pool with a loud splash.

"We need more light to see her in the water," the cameraman said.

Garvin yelled, "Turn on the moonlight!" The big spotlight near the pool flashed on.

"Still ain't enough," the cameraman complained. "The other lights are interfering."

"Stop camera! Move the light closer."

"Can't," came the answer from a workman. "Cord ain't long enough."

"Son of a bitch! Nothing works right around here." To the cameraman, Garvin said, "Just do the best you can." He began pacing along the side of the pool, his hands plunged in his pockets. "We gotta come up with something for her to do. She looks like she's just swimming." That's exactly what Margie was doing, quietly treading water while Garvin tried to work out the next step of the action. He finally announced, "I got it! What we need is a crocodile. They got any crocodiles here?"

A crocodile. Was he serious? I moved closer to the pool. I wanted to talk Margie out of taking such a risk.

Then her face went suddenly dark, the "moonlight" gone. I turned my head to the spotlight. Its big bulb was swinging down toward the pool, right above Margie's head.

I blurted, "Watch out!" just before the lamp hit the water with a sizzle of steam and an explosion of glass.

With one motion and zero thought, I slipped off my coat and went into a dive. Just before I hit the water, I remembered the spotlight was electric. "Go up like a Klieg light," the workman at the Vitagraph studio had said.

I hit the water, bracing myself for a jolt of electricity that didn't come. I bobbed up for air, then dove under toward the spot where Margie had been. I groped around, grabbing hold of nothing but water. Then a piece of cloth, then a body inside the cloth. To my relief, the body fought back at me.

We both came to the surface spitting water and gulping air. "You okay?" I gasped.

"Think so," Margie answered with a cough.

"Grab hold," a man's voice said, and an arm came between us. Margie reached up and was lifted from the water. Looking up, I saw it was Tom Kelly pulling her out. He looked worried and asked if she was all right. I wasn't sure if he was really concerned or if he was using the opportunity to soften her up for a future pass.

"Somebody go down and get the goddamn light," Garvin ordered.

His first concern was for the spotlight instead of Margie? I was still in the water, so I dove under—not because I cared about the equipment but because I might have slugged Garvin if I'd gotten out of the pool at that minute.

I found the lamp and grabbed one of its legs but couldn't pull it up. Then I felt something, a piece of string tied around it, with a couple of inches dangling loose. I tugged off the string, then left the spotlight at the bottom of the pool and bobbed to the surface. I heard Elmer Garvin order the dark sheets taken down, and the area was again brightly illuminated by the lights of the park.

"Gimme your hand, Mickey." It was Tom Kelly again. He pulled me out of the water, and with a soft slap on my back pushed me next to Margie. He then walked away, leaving us alone.

Margie was shivering. Her wet thin clothes clung to her like a second skin, revealing every goose bump on the real skin underneath. No one brought her a blanket, no one came to ask her if she was hurt or needed help. Florence Hampton would have; I almost looked for her, though I knew she would never come.

I moved next to Margie and she fell into my arms.

"Are you cold?" I asked, stroking her gently.

"No," she answered through chattering teeth. Her shivering was from fear, not cold. I left her for a moment anyway to pick up my jacket from the ground. My boater was floating in the pool, and I decided to leave it there.

As I put my jacket around Margie's shoulders, Elmer Garvin was talking with a member of the crew about what happened. The workman was explaining that when the light fell over it pulled the cord out of the socket before hitting the water. Garvin was complaining about the baboons who must have tipped it over.

"The light didn't hit you?" I quietly asked Margie.

"I dove under . . . when I saw it falling . . . it hit me on the shoulder but not hard. I'm okay."

Elmer Garvin finally came over to check on his star. "You hurt?" he asked.

"No." Even if she had been, I don't expect Margie would have admitted it. Just like a ballplayer, I thought.

"You want to try another shot?" Garvin asked.

I felt her flinch. Before Margie could answer him, I spoke up. "No more tonight. I'm taking her home."

Garvin exhaled an exaggerated sigh. Then he said, "Yeah, okay, might as well. This ain't working nohow." He grudgingly offered to have somebody drive us.

I turned him down and said we'd take a cab.

Just before we left, Garvin observed, "You two sure don't have much luck around here, do you?"

Luck had nothing to do with it. Those monkeys didn't tie the string to the light stand.

•  •  •

The cab ride was wordless as we sat next to each other, the summer night slowly drying some of the water from our clothing.

And it was wordless when we got to her apartment, and Margie took my hand and led me through her parlor and into her dark bedroom.

Our moist clothes were peeled off, slowly, as I fumbled with hers and she with mine. We dropped them on the floor where we stood, then embraced and fell together into bed.

Our bodies were still damp from the pool, and at first we stuck together wherever we touched.

Our combined body heat quickly dried us.

Then we were wet again, with sweat.

•  •  •

Afterward, we lay closely together, so close we were almost occupying the exact same space. Margie's head was cradled in my right arm and our legs were intertwined. I mapped out her body with mine, memorizing the feel of every feature that pressed against me. I wondered exactly how this had happened and was very glad that it had.

My arm started to tingle, falling asleep under the pressure of her head, but I didn't want to move it. This felt so warm, so close, so good. I didn't ever want to move from this position.

The warm breaths that wafted on my neck became louder and more evenly spaced. She was asleep. And my arm was getting numb. I tried to flex my fingers but could barely feel them. If I moved my arm out from under her, I'd wake her. So I decided to remain still, even if it cost me my right arm. I'd just have to learn to throw lefty.

Then a new feeling took hold of my body: hunger. My stomach felt hungrier than it ever had before. I started to picture food. My mouth started to water and my stomach rumble. I began to hope it would growl loud enough to wake Margie. Then I could pull my arm out, and go see what was in her ice box.

I tried to fall asleep, but my stomach was raging inside. I had to get to the kitchen.

Margie moaned in her sleep and suddenly shifted her body. I tried to take advantage of the shift by disentangling myself from her. She moaned again, and this time it wasn't a sleepy sound. She nibbled my neck, then smoothly swung a leg over my waist. I think she misinterpreted my movements.

That's okay. My stomach could wait until breakfast. And it was going to have to be a really *big* breakfast.

# Chapter Twenty-One

I cranked the handle of the new Victrola that now graced my parlor. As the heavy record disk began to spin, I lowered the bamboo needle until it caught a groove. The rippling piano of Eubie Blake's *"Fizz Water"* started to sound, traveling from the vibrating needle through some hollow brass tubing and out the sound hole in the front of the walnut cabinet.

On the way home from the Polo Grounds, I'd stopped at a music store and bought the best talking machine they had, as well as half a dozen records and several packages of needles. The bamboo needles were something of an extravagance since they lasted for only one play, but they gave a softer sound than steel and didn't chew up the records. And I was in an extravagant mood.

It was Saturday afternoon after the Giants game and a couple of hours before I was to meet Margie at Vitagraph's weekly party. The festivities were to be on Coney Island again, this time at Stauch's Dance Hall next to Steeplechase Park. Margie and I had decided that we should be there, if only to show that the "accidents" we'd had weren't going to scare us away.

I'd told Margie about the string that was tied to the spotlight. There was no doubt now that she was a target, too. I wanted her to be careful, so I also told her that I suspected the champagne that had made me sick had been poisoned. She took it all pretty well, and we agreed not to let on that we knew someone was trying to kill us. So tonight we would dance, a show of defiance at whoever was trying to harm us.

I started to sway to the rhythm of Blake's syncopated music. Then I began moving my feet and brought my hands up as if holding an invisible girl. I danced in front of the Victrola, imagining Margie and me as the next Vernon and Irene Castle.

In the middle of the next record, the phone rang. I closed the cabinet doors to lower the volume of the music and picked up the receiver.

"Mickey Rawlings?" The Southern drawl was vaguely familiar.

"Yes?"

"This here's Billy Claypool."

"Who?"

"Billy. Virg Ewing's friend. You told me to call you if I seen Virg with Sloppy Sutherland."

"Yes, of course." Actually, I'd almost forgotten about him. "What's up?"

"The two of 'em just went into a bar together. You think Virg might be in trouble?"

"They look like they're fighting or arguing?"

"Nah, they look like they're best buddies. I don't know what's going on. I never seen the two of 'em like that."

This I had to see. "Where are they?"

"Nappy's. It's a little place near the Navy Yard." He quickly gave me directions.

"Wait for me. I'll meet you outside."

We hung up and I rang the Vitagraph studio. Margie wasn't available, so I asked Joe Gannon the guard to tell her that I'd probably be late to the party.

•   •   •

The ornate spires of Wallabout Market's administration building dominated the evening sky near the Brooklyn Navy Yard. The structure looked more like a cathedral than an office building, and one that would have been more appropriately situated in Paris than on the Brooklyn waterfront.

Nappy's, on the other hand, would have been a blight on any neighborhood. The tavern, just off Washington Avenue, was a dilapidated one-story shack that looked like a Western saloon in a Bronco Billy Anderson movie. Its clapboards were bare of paint, the only color on them provided by streaks of rust from a corrugated tin roof.

Billy was standing outside the door, his brawny arms folded across his chest. He gave a nod when I approached him.

"They still inside?" I asked.

"Yup."

I rubbed the grime from a window pane near the front door and looked through. Virgil Ewing and Sloppy Sutherland were hunched over a small table. With them was Peter Kurtz, agent for the Federal League.

So that's what they were up to.

"What you want to do?" Billy asked.

"Let's go in and say hello."

Billy opened the front door and let me enter first. My foot

struck an overflowing spittoon, and its fermenting contents splashed onto my shoe. The smoke that hovered in the air wasn't nearly strong enough to mask the room's more nauseating stenches. Foul as it was, this was a perfect place to meet somebody without being noticed. It was the sort of joint where no one looked at anyone else—looking at someone the wrong way here would probably end up in a knife fight. The sailors and longshoremen who made up most of the clientele stared down at their whiskeys with total absorption. There was no music and not much conversation.

We weren't noticed until I pulled a chair up and sat down between Kurtz and Ewing at their table.

"What the hell you doing here?" Ewing demanded.

"I asked him to come," Billy answered from a standing position behind me.

Ewing looked up at Billy, clearly puzzled, but he said nothing.

Nor did Sloppy Sutherland, who eyed the door as if he urgently wanted to dash out of it.

"Well, if it isn't Mickey Rawlings," Kurtz said. "Still think you're gonna be playing in the World Series?"

"This must be some catch for you," I said, ignoring his question. "Sloppy Sutherland and Virgil Ewing jumping to the Feds together."

"Don't say nothing," Ewing warned.

Kurtz spread his hands. "I don't see there's any reason to talk to *you* about this. If there *was* a negotiation in progress, you could do us some serious harm." He added with a humorless smile, "Come to think of it, maybe we should make sure you don't get a chance to talk at all . . . ever."

"Don't talk crazy," Sutherland hissed. He didn't care about his diction now.

"Crazy?" Ewing said. "You're not the one the owners tried to kill."

"What owners?" I asked.

"The *owners.*" Ewing's speech slowed down to the pace of a change-up. "Charlie Ebbets maybe, I dunno. I figure somebody give them the idea I was talking to the Feds about jumping, so they tried to poison me."

"The tobacco in your locker," I said.

"Yeah."

*"That* is crazy," I said. "If they kill you, you can't play for anybody."

"Yeah," said Ewing. "But it's a warning to anybody else who might be thinking of jumping."

"Don't talk to this guy," Kurtz said.

Ignoring Kurtz, I asked Ewing, "What's really going on with you and Sloppy, anyway?" I turned to Sutherland. "Or is it 'Walter' in here?"

Sutherland dropped his eyes. He'd probably rather have Charlie Ebbets know he was talking to the Feds than have his high-society friends know he was in a dive like Nappy's.

"My guess," I went on, "is that feud you guys have going is to keep people from thinking you might be making a deal together. Is that it?"

Ewing downed the rest of the whiskey in his glass. Sutherland coughed. Kurtz cracked his knuckles.

"Look," I said. "I already know enough to get you in trouble if I wanted to."

Kurtz growled, "Yeah, like I said, we should take care of that. Take you out back and do some damage to your memory."

"No you won't," Billy said firmly.

Kurtz looked up at him, then shrugged and called to the bartender, "Gimme another Brooklyn!"

"Tell you what," I said to Ewing and Sutherland. "Maybe we can make a deal and protect each other. If I can guarantee that I won't tell anybody about you jumping to the Feds, you tell me everything that's been going on."

Nobody said yes, but nobody said no.

"You got a piece of paper?" I asked Kurtz.

He ignored me.

"You got a contract?" I said. "I'll sign a contract to play with the Feds. That should solve it."

"You for real?" he asked.

"Yes."

"Good. You're finally getting smart." Kurtz pulled a folded paper from his jacket pocket. I wondered how many scorecards and contracts he kept in there.

He laid the blank contract on the table and pulled out a pen. He then filled in *$3,000* on the salary line.

"You offered four thousand before," I said.

"That was before," he explained. "This is now."

I took the contract and pen anyway, and signed my name at the bottom. Smirking, Kurtz reached over to take the paper back. I handed it to Billy instead.

"Here's the deal," I said. "Billy holds onto this. If I tell on you guys, he gives the contract to Kurtz and I play for the Feds. If I don't tell, he tears it up. I trust him to do that. Anybody doesn't trust him?"

Ewing gave in first. "Okay. You're right. The feud is just to keep people from finding out that we're partners in this deal with the Feds."

"What about the rivalry over Florence Hampton? Which one of you was really seeing her?"

Sutherland and Ewing stared at each other. Sutherland finally said glumly, "It wasn't me."

"It wasn't me neither," Ewing admitted.

Sutherland elaborated, "I thought *he* was seeing her, and he thought *I* was. We didn't find out until after she was dead that she was just leading us both on." He began running a fingertip around the rim of his empty shot glass. "The whole thing started after we got back from the world tour. At first, I thought she was really interested me. But all she wanted to talk about was her dead husband. She asked a million questions about what he did on the tour—who he saw, where he went. Daley died on the ship coming back, you know."

I nodded.

Ewing piped up, "It was the same with me. She kept asking me questions about the tour, too. It bugged the hell out of me. The papers were printing all these stories about her fooling around with the players, and I thought I was the only one not getting anywhere with her."

Sutherland said, "Anyway, it just developed that people thought Virg and I were competing with each other for her. It was Kurtz here who said it would be useful to let people think that."

Peter Kurtz nodded and explained, "Nobody would suspect they're in a deal together if they're fighting over some dame."

"After the party at the Sea Dip, the night Florence Hampton died, where did you guys go?" I asked.

Sutherland sighed. "Right here, at this very table."

Ewing nodded. "Yeah."

The bartender came to the table and filled Kurtz's glass with dark rum, omitting the lime and grenadine that usually went into a Brooklyn. He asked me, "You drinking or just talking?"

"Leaving," I answered. I'd heard everything I needed to know.

"Well *I'm* drinking," Ewing said. "Get me another bourbon and a beer to chase it."

Sutherland said in a soft voice, "The thing is, I got to really liking Florence Hampton. She was a classy lady. I wish there *had* been something between us." Then he said to the bartender, "Get me a bourbon, too. A double."

I rose and gave my seat to Billy. He promised me he'd keep the contract safe, and I believed him.

· · ·

On the way home, I hashed over what must have happened, trying to think from Florence Hampton's point of view.

She was talking to players who had been on the world baseball tour, investigating her husband's death. Then rumors about her having affairs with ballplayers start to circulate. She lets them go unanswered, maybe even fosters them, so that nobody will catch on to what she's really doing. Finding out what happened to her husband was more important to her than her reputation.

Sutherland and Ewing also let the rumors propagate and their supposed rivalry be publicized so that nobody suspects they're really in joint negotiation with the Federal League.

As far as I could tell, there was no reason for either of them to have killed Florence Hampton. And now they did have an alibi for the night she died.

This case was a strange one—false names, nonexistent politicians, affairs that never happened. If only Florence Hampton's death hadn't really happened either. But I'd seen her body, cold and bloated and blue.

Not until I was back in Manhattan did I realize I'd forgotten about the Vitagraph party.

I went to bed, certain that Margie was not going to be happy with me.

was right. She wasn't happy. Maybe I was getting better at predicting what a woman would think.

I phoned Margie at six-thirty the next morning, thinking the sooner I called, the less angry she would be. Launching into my apology, I said, "I'm sorry about missing the party. I called the studio. Did you get the message?"

"I got a message that you'd be *late,* not that you wouldn't be coming." She sounded sleepy and grumpy.

"Things happened, and I couldn't come. I'm really sorry."

"Well . . . okay," she murmured. I was amazed at the way she could tack on the warning "don't let it happen again" without uttering the words.

To show her that I hadn't missed the party for a trivial reason, I told her the full story of my encounter with Virgil Ewing and Sloppy Sutherland. "They both denied meeting with Florence Hampton after the party," I concluded. "She wasn't having an affair with either of them."

"And you believed them?"

"Yes, I did."

"But the way they fought over her . . . it seemed so *real.*

If they were just acting, they're better actors than anybody at Vitagraph.''

I thought of my bat tossing routine with Casey Stengel, when we competed for Florence Hampton in the movie. That was make believe, too, but I'd wanted to win. I tried to explain it to Margie. "Well, even if it's just pretend, when you're competing with somebody, you want to win. You just do. Nobody wants to lose."

*"Men,"* she groaned.

I was pretty sure that I was included in her general disgust with the male sex.

In the hope of bringing her around, I switched to another topic. "I thought we could go to Prospect Park this afternoon, maybe take a ride on the swan boats?"

"No, I can't today," she promptly answered. "I have something else to do."

I waited for her to tell me what the something else was, until it became clear she wasn't going to volunteer it. Well, I wasn't going to ask. "Maybe another time, then," I said.

She hesitated, then said, "There's a filming Tuesday morning. Another big picture. If you want to come, I'm sure Mr. Garvin would like to have you there."

I couldn't imagine Garvin liking that at all. Perhaps Margie was trying to tell me that she'd like it. "It's not at Coney Island, is it?" I asked.

"No," she chuckled. "At the studio."

"Sure, I'll be there. How . . . uh, how has Garvin been to you?"

She snapped, "He's more concerned about a broken spotlight than about me." After a pause, she said, "Florence Hampton was my only true friend at the studio. It's not the same without her. I don't know if I want to work there anymore . . . certainly not for Mr. Garvin."

I took some satisfaction in the fact that she now sounded angrier at Elmer Garvin than at me.

"There's plenty of other movie studios who'd love to have you," I said. "Or you can do something else. You should do whatever makes you happy."

"Well, I don't know. I don't know what I want to do."

I made one more attempt to suggest that seeing me was the thing to do. "If you're busy today, can we get together tomorrow?"

"No," she said. "Not tomorrow. Better wait until Tuesday."

I reluctantly agreed to Tuesday and we hung up.

The conversation with Margie left me feeling empty. I felt like I needed to talk to a friend. So, a couple of hours later, I called Karl Landfors, the closest thing to it that I could think of.

He wasn't at his home number, but he was at his office at the *New York Press*. It didn't seem like he ever went home.

Although what I really wanted to talk about was Margie, what came out of my mouth was, "Virgil Ewing and Sloppy Sutherland are out of it. Neither of them was with Florence Hampton when she died."

"You sure?"

"Yup. They both have alibis that checked out." I decided not to tell him what the alibi was. Landfors was still a newspaper reporter, and he might let it slip out about them going to the Feds. "And there's something else," I said. "Nobody was having affairs with Miss Hampton. She used the rumors as a cover to question the players about William Daley's death."

"I'll be damned," Landfors said, in a pleased tone. Then he asked, "You're sure Ewing and Sutherland weren't fighting over her?"

I was starting to get annoyed at the way people kept asking if I was sure when I told them things. "Yes, I'm sure. They just played along."

"Then who would want to kill Virgil Ewing if not Sutherland? Why did somebody try to poison him?"

Jeez. I didn't think of that. "Are we sure somebody did try to kill him? Did you get the results on the tobacco?"

"Not yet. Assume it was poisoned though. Who would do it?"

"Well. . . . Ewing thought it was the owners who tried to kill him."

"The *Dodger* owners?"

"Yeah, he thought they might suspect him of jumping to the Federal League. I told him he was nuts, but he thought they tried to kill him to make an example of him."

Landfors said excitedly, "You know, he may have something there. I've been checking around myself, and it turns out the other Dodger owners didn't like my sister. Besides being a woman, she was in favor of players' rights. She said publicly that baseball players should be free to work for anybody they wanted to." He sighed. "She should have been a labor organizer."

I noticed when Landfors was proud of her he referred to Florence Hampton as his sister. Maybe he was finally feeling a little closer to her.

I also remembered Charlie Ebbets throwing her friends out of the ballpark. Humiliating her, yes. But committing murder? No. That was too far-fetched. "I don't know who else would have wanted to kill Virgil Ewing," I said, "but it wasn't the owners."

"Don't be so sure. Just because they're baseball owners, they're still bosses and they play dirty. They shoot down strikers, starve their families—"

"Okay, okay, Karl." I didn't want to hear another one of his political sermons.

He calmed down. "I'm going to look into this," he said.

"If you want to. Go ahead." Landfors was fond of working out grand conspiracy schemes, and I knew I couldn't dissuade him. He once told me some convoluted theory about Tammany Hall, Allen Pinkerton, and Ulysses S. Grant all having plotted the assassination of Abraham Lincoln.

But let Landfors think about it. At least it would keep him out of trouble.

•   •   •

Monday afternoon, we opened a three-game series against the Braves at the Polo Grounds. We were tied for the league lead, so when the series was over only one team would be in first place.

Just after my teammates and I completed our pregame march from the center field clubhouse to the dugout, I heard Landfors's voice calling my name.

I stepped out to the side of the dugout. Landfors was at the rail, sunlight glinting off his spectacles. He was holding a scorecard, two boxes of Cracker Jack, and—I couldn't believe it—a New York Giants pennant. Could it be? Could Karl Landfors be turning into a baseball fan?

Before I could say anything to him, John McGraw called for the start of infield practice.

"Sorry, Karl," I said. "I can't talk right now."

"That's okay. I'm . . . uh, staying for the game." He sounded sheepish about it. "I got the results on those tests for you. How about dinner after the game and we'll talk then?"

"Sounds good." I took a few steps toward second base, then spun and added, "You rooting for the Giants today?"

"Sure, why not."

Landfors was making a lot of progress. If he kept it up, he might turn out to be a regular human being someday.

What he saw turned out to be less a baseball game than a war. And it was the generals who were the highlights.

John McGraw engaged in guerilla warfare between the dugouts with tactics intended more to torment the Braves' manager George Stallings than to defeat the team. I don't think McGraw liked the idea of Stallings usurping his throne as baseball's shrewdest manager.

McGraw had enlisted help from some local boys to take advantage of Stallings's superstitious streak. He'd given free passes to the kids in exchange for them throwing a steady stream of litter in front of the Braves' dugout. Stallings scampered about, frantically collecting every bit of rubbish that fell in front of the bench. His pockets were soon crammed with scraps of paper, and the air was blue from the profanities he hurled at McGraw.

Unfortunately for Christy Mathewson and Dick Rudolph, the antics of McGraw and Stallings overshadowed their pitching performances. Through five innings, they were both working on shutouts, Mathewson giving up one hit and Rudolph throwing a perfect game.

In the sixth inning, with Boston at bat and Braves on second and third, McGraw pulled out all stops. He signaled a boy near the visitors' dugout; the kid leaned over the railing and opened a sack, releasing a black cat onto the field, the ultimate bad luck omen, almost a death knell.

The terrified cat raced back and forth in front of the dugout. Stallings let out a bellow and chased him. Then he screamed for his players to help, and a swarm of Braves was trying to grab hold of the feline; they fell over each other as they scrambled, looking like boys trying to catch a greased pig at a county fair. The cat meowed, Stallings cussed, and I couldn't tell which was more scared. John McGraw roared with laughter at the trouble he'd caused.

But when the animal was finally captured and taken away, the Braves continued where they left off. Hank Gowdy hit a sacrifice fly to put Boston ahead 1–0.

McGraw showed another of his tricks in the eighth with the Giants at bat. He was coaching third base, his little black fielder's mitt on his left hand. Chief Meyers was on second base with a double that broke up Rudolph's no-hitter.

Fred Merkle singled up the middle and Meyers was off with the crack of the bat. Rounding third, Meyers tripped on the bag and stumbled toward home. McGraw shrieked, "Back! Back!"

The throw from center was relayed home, and Meyers scrambled to get back to third base. The catcher snapped a throw that got there ahead of him and Meyers was caught in a rundown. Merkle saw it and did just what he was supposed to, going on to second base. The Braves' shortstop Rabbit Maranville did what he shouldn't, going to second to take a throw instead of covering third.

The third baseman ran Meyers toward home, then flipped a throw to the plate. Meyers quickly did an about-face. McGraw saw Maranville hadn't yet broken to cover third, so he ran to third base from the coach's box. Pretending to be an infielder, he held his glove high and yelled, "Throw it already!" Taken in by the ruse, Gowdy snapped a toss to him; McGraw ducked and let the ball fly over his head into left field. Meyers ran home to score.

But the umpire was McGraw's old nemesis Bill Klem who would have none of McGraw's deceit. He ruled Meyers out and ejected McGraw.

The score ended 1–0, and George Stallings came out

ahead of John McGraw. The little Napoleon lost out to the Miracle Man, and for the first time this season the Boston Braves were in first place.

•   •   •

We picked an Italian restaurant with red checkered table-cloths and dripping candles stuck in empty wine bottles. It was dimly lit and romantic, a place I'd have rather come with Margie Turner than Karl Landfors.

Landfors ordered chianti and calamari marinara. To the waiter's chagrin, I opted for steak, well-done, and a beer.

After proposing a toast "to the valiant Belgians: may they soon have their country back," Landfors commenced guzzling his wine faster than I downed my beer. Shifting from the war to baseball, he said, "That McGraw is something else. The way he pretended to play third base. That was sure something."

"Yeah, McGraw likes trickery, all right."

"Why does he wear the glove?"

"I don't know. Maybe it makes him feel like a player still." I chuckled. "Or maybe he's been waiting all along for a time like today when he could use it. Can never tell with John McGraw."

I was happy that Landfors was developing such a liking for the game. It took awhile before I sensed that his enthusiasm about baseball was forced. It also became clear that his rapid drinking had more to do with nervousness than thirst. Red color was starting to creep into the black, white, and gray that usually dominated his appearance, as his face flushed from the alcohol and spatters of tomato sauce trickled from forkfuls of squid onto his shirt front.

It was time to learn what he'd found out while he was still

sober enough to speak. "You said you got the test results," I prompted him.

"Yes, yes I did." Landfors took another gulp of wine, spilling a few ruby droplets on his tie. He fumbled in his jacket pocket and pulled out two bulging small brown envelopes. "They both have arsenic in them," he said. "The tobacco *and* the cork."

"So it's arsenic for everybody!" I exclaimed. As the words left my lips, I realized it sounded as if I'd just ordered a round of beers. "Miss Hampton, me, and Virgil Ewing—somebody tried to kill us all with arsenic."

"And possibly William Daley," Landfors added. He opened one of the envelopes and dumped pieces of cork on the table. "Something else about this: there's a needle hole through it. That's how the poison got in."

"I was curious about that, how you could get poison in a sealed bottle."

"That's how. It was injected. The big question is who."

I picked up the envelope with the tobacco. "I did come up with a reason why somebody might want to kill Virgil Ewing . . . besides the owners, that is. What if somebody *thought* Ewing killed Miss Hampton. People didn't know that he *wasn't* having an affair with her. Maybe somebody thought he did kill her and wanted to get revenge for her."

Landfors lifted the chianti bottle to replenish his glass, but there was nothing more in it. He picked up the empty wine glass and absentmindedly rolled the stem in his fingertips. He said seriously, "Lately, I've been thinking more about why somebody would want to kill *you.*"

That wasn't what I wanted to think about. If I let my mind dwell on the danger I was in, I wouldn't be clearheaded enough to work out a plan for getting *out* of trouble. "I want to know who killed your sister," I said. There, I said "sister."

It was more personal. "That's the important thing." It was also the key, I was sure, to the attacks on Margie and me, and the murder of the Dodger batboy.

He leaned back in his chair. "I appreciate that," he said, nodding. Then he looked about to nod all the way off to sleep. After a minute, he blurted, "So, how's it going with Miss Turner?"

"Good! Well, I think it's going good, anyway." I was still at the stage where all I remembered was what had happened last. And what had happened last was that Margie didn't want to see me and wouldn't tell me why. I didn't want to talk to Karl Landfors about that.

"You know what bothers me about poison?" I said. "It's not visible . . . you can't see where it's coming from. A gun or a knife, those you can see, and you can try to avoid them. Poison can be in anything."

"Yes, it can," Landfors said. "You should be careful, Mickey. Careful about everything." There was something he wasn't telling me. C'mon, Landfors. Out with it. But he didn't say more and I didn't prod.

*Chapter Twenty-Three*

**T**uesday was the first of September. We were going into the last month of the regular season with twenty-eight games left to play and every one of them crucial. The hundred and twenty-six games that had come before, the thousands of pitches and the hundreds of hits and runs, had left only a one game spread between the Giants and the Braves. The pennant race was just heating up.

The only warmth I felt, though, was generated by finally seeing Margie Turner again.

Margie and I were standing together in the middle of fetid Studio B. She was garbed as a waitress in a navy blue dress with a white frilly apron; a large white ribbon was tied in a bow atop her head.

The set for today's shooting was that of a fancy restaurant with a long polished bar and a dozen cloth-covered round tables. Dessert carts placed about the room held enough pies to feed all of Flatbush.

The Vitagraph studio wasn't my preferred meeting place. As far as I was concerned, we spent too much time with the movie company, among people we didn't like, in circumstances that were often uncomfortable if not dangerous. But by now I would have been willing to meet Margie in the middle of the Hudson River without a boat.

Warily eyeing the pies, I asked her, "What's this movie going to be about?"

"Just another pie-throwing movie," she said. "Lots of pies. Four reels of them." In a whisper she added, "Mr. Garvin doesn't know how to make a long movie. The film we took at Coney Island is scattered all over the editing room, a useless mess. And the front office is pressing him to release something, *anything*. So he's going back to the old way: in the studio, lots of people, lots of pie-throwing."

"What am I supposed to do?" I didn't want to be on the receiving end of any more gooey projectiles.

"I don't know. There's Mr. Garvin. Do you want to ask him?"

Garvin was passing by, with Arthur Carlyle following and the two of them in mid-argument.

*"Everybody* is going to be in this," Garvin said to Carlyle.

"I am an *actor,"* Carlyle protested. "I do not allow my face to be struck by bakery goods."

"Then duck. Now go get into costume."

Carlyle crossed his arms and planted his legs firmly; he showed no signs of moving.

"Mr. Garvin," I interrupted, "what did you want me to do?"

He looked around. "Mmm. . . . You'll sit at the bar. Think you can handle that?"

"Gee, I might need a few rehearsals, but I think I can do that."

A hint of a smile crossed Carlyle's mouth and he nodded his head at me.

Elmer Garvin didn't notice my sarcasm. "Good. Then get

into costume. A hick maybe. Mr. Carlyle, would you help Mr. Rawlings find an appropriate costume? He'll be playing a rube at the bar."

"Of course, Mr. Garvin," Carlyle said, clicking his heels together. "Whatever you say, sir."

"Go with Mr. Carlyle," Garvin said, and I followed Carlyle as he walked away. "Damn ham," I heard Garvin mutter under his breath.

The cramped men's dressing room was exactly as I remembered: like a laundry in the aftermath of an explosion.

Arthur Carlyle rummaged through racks of suits and piles of hats, socks, shirts, and shoes. "A hick," he said. "That would mean plaid. Or perhaps . . ." He paused at a tan suit with green squares like a checkerboard. "Try this."

I shed my street clothes and donned the suit. It was a perfect fit.

"Terrible," was Carlyle's verdict. "For a rube, it should be much smaller."

While he went through another rack, I asked him, "When you were on the stage, did you ever act with Esther Kelly?"

"Hmm. . . . I don't believe so. Let's see . . . she was Esther Neilson when she was acting. You know, I thought it rather peculiar that she took Tom Kelly's name. You never give up your stage name unless you give up the stage." He pulled out another suit, a bright red plaid with wide lapels.

"So she doesn't expect to act anymore."

"No, no one will risk giving her a role. I am afraid the poor lady shall never again trod the boards."

It would be a lot easier to talk with Carlyle if he spoke English. I tried on the plaid suit. Again a perfect fit. Carlyle frowned. "The problem is that you're rather on the small side yourself. I don't know if we have anything that's going to be too small for you. Try the other one again."

Back to the green and tan, but I was sure it hadn't shrunk in the last five minutes. "Why won't people give her any parts?"

He pinned up the sleeves and trouser cuffs four inches above my wrists and ankles. "Well, what I hear at the Lambs Club is that she drinks a bit excessively. Between us gentlemen, I don't blame her. Tom Kelly is not a very good husband. She made him. Without her, he would have no career. And he repays her sacrifice by philandering." Carlyle added an oversized polka dot bow tie to my neck. "So she has taken to the bottle. Poor girl can't remember lines anymore. No one is going to hire an actress who blanks out on stage. Hmm. . . . That doesn't quite do it. You need something else."

He opened a drawer of his makeup kit, pulled out a red walrus mustache, and dabbed some glue on it. "Here we go," he said as he attached it to my upper lip. I looked in the mirror. I didn't like it, but at least I was disguised enough that John McGraw would never recognize me.

"Just a *touch* more," Carlyle said.

What more could he do to me? How much sillier could I look?

From another drawer he pulled out a set of spectacles. Oh, no. I don't want to look like Karl Landfors. They were huge goggles with thick lenses. In the mirror I couldn't tell what I looked like.

Then he topped my head with a porkpie hat. "Perfect," he said. "Now go on out and I'll get into costume."

"Okay. Thank you." I added to myself, "I think."

"My pleasure. Always glad to help an aspiring member of the craft."

I went back out to the main floor of the studio and walked up to Margie. When she realized it was me, she burst into laughter. "That's wonderful!" she exclaimed.

"I feel silly," I grumbled, as I repositioned the spectacles up on my forehead so that I could see.

"That's what acting is all about. You can act however you want to—silly or evil or coy. And it's just acting. It's like being a child playing make believe. Enjoy it!"

"I'll try . . ." It would have been easier if I didn't look so ridiculous. Although if Margie liked the way I was made up, it couldn't be too awful.

When Arthur Carlyle came out of the dressing room, in a waiter costume with a handlebar mustache and a towel draped over his forearm, I waved to him and mouthed, "Thank you." He acknowledged it with a nod.

Garvin then bellowed into his megaphone, ordering changes to the sets. People scurried about in response to his commands, moving chairs and tables "a little more this way" and "a little more that way."

After everything was moved, and then moved again back to its original position, Garvin stopped yelling and began pacing. His head was down, his lips were moving, and coins jingled in his pockets.

"He doesn't know what to do," Margie whispered.

"Okay, we'll start with the bar," Garvin finally announced, as he strode to the barroom set. "Mr. Kelly, take your place please. Mr. Rawlings, over here."

Tom Kelly moved behind the counter as a bartender. I went to the front of the bar, where Garvin put me on a stool. Then he called another actor—Mr. Carver, he called him—and put him two stools away. Carver was dressed as a dandy, an unconvincing one, like Sloppy Sutherland on a bad day.

Garvin said, "Okay. You two are going to argue." He turned to me. "Just like you did with Casey Stengel. You did that good."

"Are we fighting over a girl?"

"Argue about whatever you want." He seated himself behind the camera.

I felt stiff and self-conscious. Let yourself go, I told myself. Pretend to be the character you're dressed as, and have fun with it. It's just make believe.

Something nagged at me, though, and my inhibitions remained. I scanned the crew behind the camera, and then the actors costumed as waiters, waitresses, diners, cooks, and busboys. All of them in the business of make believe. If they could do it, I should be able to.

I didn't even have to worry about John McGraw. He would never recognize me in this costume. But still I couldn't relax and enjoy my role.

Make believe . . .

I slowly realized it was Florence Hampton who kept me from abandoning myself to acting. I could feel her presence in the studio. Her death was full of make believe: false names, nonaffairs, people being other than where they claimed . . . and there was nothing fun about it.

I looked around the room again.

And I suddenly knew who killed Florence Hampton.

My mind raced as I tried to think what to do about it. Stay calm, I told myself. Don't let on.

"Okay, gentlemen," Garvin called. "Just do as I tell you. Uh, Mr. Rawlings, lower the glasses please." Mechanically, I pulled them so that they were seated on the bridge of my nose. "Start camera!" I heard the gears of the camera turn. "Mr. Kelly, start some business—polish the bar, pour a couple of drinks." Kelly poured two drinks and slid them before each of us. "Now start talking." Carver and I started talking— he about stamp collecting and I about baseball—while Kelly polished the countertop with a bar rag. "Start arguing!" Our words grew heated, incoherent but heated. "Now go for each other. Fight!" We hopped off the stools and started grappling. "Mr. Kelly, let him have it!"

Have what?

Then my head exploded.

• • •

When my eyes opened again, I was in the dressing room, laid out on a pile of musty overcoats. Elmer Garvin and Tom Kelly were staring down at me.

Tom Kelly was the first to speak. "I'm sorry, kid. The bottles must have got mixed up."

"Should have been a sugar bottle," Garvin said. "It was supposed to crumble when it hit you, not bust your head open."

I didn't know what they were talking about, but my head felt exactly as Garvin described it, like I was missing the top of my skull.

"How does it feel?" Margie's voice asked from behind me. I raised my eyes; she was kneeling behind me, a bloody cloth clutched in her hand.

"Like I've been scalped."

Margie dabbed carefully at the back of my head with the rag. "It's still bleeding some," she said.

"We sent for the studio doctor," said Garvin. "Your lousy luck sure seems to be holding." He didn't sound particularly bothered by it.

I lifted my right hand and reached back to touch the wound.

Margie caught my wrist and put my arm back down. "Don't touch it," she said. "Wait for the doctor."

It was only a few more minutes until the doctor arrived. He looked like he'd been dressed for the role by Arthur

Carlyle: white hair with matching beard, small gold spectacles, immaculate frock coat, and black leather bag. I hoped he really was a doctor and didn't just play one in the movies.

"Well, what have we here?" he asked in a soft soothing voice. It sounded like there was nothing he hadn't seen before.

"Small accident," Garvin said. "Mr. Kelly hit him with a real bottle instead of a sugar bottle."

"You should be more careful with your props." The doctor placed his bag on the dressing table. "You can all leave now."

Garvin and Kelly exited the room without hesitation.

"May I stay?" Margie asked.

"Of course, Miss Turner. You can assist me. I've patched you up often enough that you should know how it's done."

Margie gently ran the fingertips of one hand along the back of my neck. "Dr. Campbell's a good doctor," she said.

He asked me, "Can you sit up?"

I raised myself on my elbows. "Yes."

"Let's see how bad it is," Dr. Campbell said. He pulled off his spectacles and leaned over me, peering at my head. "My, that's an ugly one." His finger started to probe my scalp, and I was barely able to suppress a scream at the pressure. "You'll need a few stitches."

The doctor next crouched down in front of me and stared into my eyes. "Pupils look okay." He pulled a fountain pen out of his pocket and held it in front of my nose. "Keep your eye on the pen." He moved the pen back and forth and I followed it with my eyes. "I think you'll be fine," he decided. "We'll just have to sew up that cut."

The doctor opened his black bag. "First let me give you something to kill the pain." Reaching into the bag, he withdrew a syringe.

"No," I said. "No needles. You can sew me up, but no needles."

"It's going to be painful," he warned.

"No needles," I insisted. I didn't want anybody putting anything into me. I had some thinking to do. Stitches were okay—my head had a hole in it, so it made sense to close the hole—but I wasn't going to let anybody do anything to me that could affect my thinking. The bottle busting over my head had interrupted it, but I was going to try to get back on track.

"Very well," he conceded. Then he took a razor from his bag. "I'll have to shave around the cut." He moved behind me and started scraping with the blade. After shaving a patch of hair, he cleaned the wound with a liquid that stung worse than a fastball on the hands.

Dr. Campbell next pulled a needle and some coarse black thread from the bag. I was tempted to ask if he had another color, one that would better match my hair. "Ready?" he asked.

I tried to nod, but it hurt, so I said, "Yes."

"Hold him still, Miss Turner."

She gripped me tightly just behind my ears. I felt the needle go in. I didn't think my head could feel any worse but this was a sharp pain. I clenched my teeth so hard and quickly that I bit into my inner lip.

While Dr. Campbell continued weaving, I focused my thoughts elsewhere. On Florence Hampton's killer. As I thought about questions like how and why, the stitching became no more than a tugging sensation.

When the doctor finished, he said, "That should do it. Now if you feel dizzy or have trouble with your eyes, let me know." After packing his bag, he left the room muttering about Elmer Garvin providing him with too many patients.

Margie squeezed my hand.

"How bad does it look?" I asked.

"It's not bad," she said, trying too hard to sound convincing. "Like a little bald spot is all. With one, two . . . nine stitches in it. Uh . . . you might want to wear a hat."

I chuckled at the number of stitches—nine, a good number for a baseball player. It felt good to laugh at something, but it brought a worried look to Margie's eyes.

"Don't worry," I said. "I'm not going crazy."

No, I wasn't going crazy. In fact, my brain was working surprisingly well. It had just generated one of the most promising ideas I'd had lately. "Could you leave me alone for a minute?" I asked her. "I want to get up and walk around a bit."

"You sure?"

"Yes. I'll be right out. I need to get out of these clothes."

She left the room, and I had a minute to collect my thoughts. I stood up and shuffled to the mirror. I couldn't see what the back of my head looked like, but after tearing the false mustache from my lip I was reassured to see that I looked as handsome as ever from the front.

I then peeled out of my hick outfit, much of which was now soaked with blood.

Fifteen minutes later, I stepped back into the studio, dressed in my street clothes, my boater set lightly on my head, and generally feeling pretty pleased with myself.

The studio had gone back into production with pies flying everywhere. Margie was the only one waiting for me outside the door.

I pulled her back in the dressing room for a long kiss and a longer hug, then took leave to go to the game.

# Chapter Twenty-Four

**W**ednesday evening was our next chance to have dinner together, and Margie and I were finally able to take advantage of it. There were no candles or tablecloths though. Since we were both tired from work, we didn't bother to look for elegance. Instead we settled for a quick supper at a Bond Street luncheonette near Loeser's department store in downtown Brooklyn.

One advantage of the informal setting was that I could leave my hat on to cover up the shaved patch on my scalp. The pain was gone by now, but the skin itched like crazy.

I'd played in yesterday's and today's games, with no ill effects from the blow to my head. In fact, it might have helped—I went five for eight with a triple as we split the last two contests of the series to leave us one game behind the Braves. Although even if I'd gone eight for eight, I had no intention of getting my head broken again.

I'd also had forty-eight hours to try to figure out what to do about Florence Hampton's killer. My first impulse was to announce it to the world and let justice take its course. Then as I thought about it, I realized I didn't really *know* all that much and could prove even less. A premature accusation would only serve to forewarn the murderer.

After a little more thought, I decided I shouldn't tell Karl Landfors, either. How would he react if I told him the identity of his sister's murderer and said there was no proof? It wouldn't surprise me if he tried to even the score on his own and get himself jailed or killed as a result.

The same with Margie. Her tie to Florence Hampton wasn't as strong as Karl's, but she was even less likely than him to let her friend's death go unavenged.

So I decided to say nothing for now and vowed that I would get enough evidence to bring to the police. Once they took over, Karl and Margie would be safe.

Over ginger ale and liverwurst sandwiches, Margie finally told me where she'd been on Sunday. "I talked with Esther Kelly again," she said.

"By yourself?" That didn't sound like "together." But considering what I was keeping from her, who was I to complain?

Margie nodded. "I asked her where she really went after the party at the Sea Dip Hotel. I told her that I knew she didn't go home until late that night—"

"But I promised her maid not to say anything. I don't want to cause trouble between them."

"Don't worry." Margie patted my arm. "I didn't tell her that we learned anything from *Bridget,*" she said with a smile. "I said that somebody from Vitagraph saw her out with a man who wasn't her husband, and I wanted to hear from Esther what it was about so I could try to stop any rumors."

"Oh." Not a bad story, I thought. "So what did she say?"

"She broke down. She felt guilty."

"Why? What did she do?"

"She didn't know. She said she couldn't remember. I've

heard people say that Esther drinks and that's what cost her her career. She told me she tries not to drink at all now, but since she couldn't remember what happened that night, she assumed she must have been drunk. That's what she felt guilty about. But she was *sure* she *hadn't* been drinking. Esther seemed torn up with herself." Margie added, "I don't think she'd do anything to hurt anyone. That's what my gut says."

"Sometimes that's the most reliable guide." I thought for a bit. "Who do you think took Esther Kelly home that night?"

"I *really* wish I knew," Margie said. "I'm sure it was innocent, but I still want to find out . . . more than ever now."

"Why's that?"

"Esther kept asking me where she was seen. She really wanted to know." Margie shook her head. "And I couldn't tell her. I wish I hadn't lied to her like that."

"She remembered things from a long time ago," I said. "My aunt was like that, could remember things in detail from years ago but could hardly remember what happened the day before. People used to kid her about it. Sometimes my aunt would show up unannounced at the house where she grew up, as if she still lived there. The people who owned it eventually got used to it, and they'd call my uncle to come and get her. Then it got worse, and nobody kidded her anymore. We just knew she was sick somehow. She died when I was fourteen."

I pulled out my watch and flipped open the back cover to reveal a picture of two people. "This is her," I said. "And my uncle. They raised me."

"They look like nice people," Margie said.

"They were."

We sat for a few moments in silence. This investigation didn't seem to be doing anyone any good, nice or not. Margie and I had almost been killed, Florence Hampton—Karl Landfors's sister—*had* been murdered, as had an innocent twelve year old boy. And we were telling lies to people, causing them grief, to get them to talk.

But as cruel as it might seem sometimes, we couldn't stop now. There was still a killer to be caught.

"It'll be all right," I finally said and picked up the check.

"Would you like to come over . . . for coffee, or something?" Margie asked in a tight voice.

"Yes."

We decided to walk and were strolling hand in hand on Pacific Street toward Third Avenue, when Margie pulled up short at a second-hand bookstore. "Could we stop a minute?" she asked.

I agreed and we went over to the bins of used books and old papers stacked outside the store. One bin was crammed with old photographs. Margie started rifling through the photos while I scanned a rack of magazines not looking for anything in particular.

Margie pulled out one of the pictures. "Ooh! This is a good one," she said.

I walked over to see the creased photo of a lean bucktoothed young lady. "Who is it?" I asked.

"I don't know. But she has a good face, an honest face. I like her! She'll look good on my wall, I think."

"With your relatives?"

"Oh, those aren't relatives. Not that I know of anyway. The only relative I have is my brother."

"Then who are they?"

"People like her," she said. "My brother and I were adopted as babies. We never knew our parents and don't know of any relatives. So I collect people who look interesting, people I might *like* to have as family." With that explanation, she paid two cents for the picture.

There certainly were some things about Margie Turner that I didn't understand. Fortunately, I didn't have to understand her to like her.

We turned south on Third Avenue and were soon in her apartment. Inside, we quickly passed her adopted relatives in the parlor and almost sprinted past the kitchen with no thought of having coffee. That could wait until morning.

• • •

I found the Century Theatre on West Forty-seventh Street between Broadway and Eighth Avenue. It was a burlesque house now, the kind that gives burlesque a bad name. In the harsh light of Thursday morning, it looked seedy and run-down.

The marquee headliners were La Petite Aimee "from Gay Paree" and comic Izzy Pickle. Also advertised were Madame Fong's Oriental Dancers and "a Bevy of Beautiful Chorines."

I was here on a long shot, a hunch. If it went nowhere, nothing was lost. But I had two reasons for hoping it would work out: one was to see if I could put Esther Kelly's mind at ease, to make up for the worry we'd caused her; the other was a test to see how my luck was running. I knew I'd need a lot of it, since I had a feeling I wasn't going to get much hard evidence against Florence Hampton's murderer.

No one was in the theater's ticket booth and no amount of hammering on the front door could arouse a response.

I went to the alley door and pounded away at it. From inside came a muffled yell, "I'm comin', I'm comin', dammit!"

The door popped open with a squeak and a scrape. The

man in the doorway was old and gaunt, with drooping skin that hung loose from his throat. "What you want?" he asked in a hoarse voice. "We don't open till two."

"I'm sorry to bother you," I said. "My name's Mickey Rawlings. I play for the Giants . . . baseball . . ."

"So?"

Okay, he's not a baseball fan. "I'm a friend of Esther Kelly."

"Who?"

"Esther Kelly, the actress. She used to be Esther Nielson."

His face warmed up. "Esther," he repeated with a smile. "You a friend of hers?"

I just said I was. Wasn't he listening? "Yes, I am. She told me she used to act here. A long time ago. I was wondering if I could take a look around."

"Yeah, sure, what the hell. Come on in."

He let me in, and I followed him through the back stage. I noticed he had a pronounced limp—an encouraging sign.

"I didn't catch your name," I said.

"Frank Roche." He offered his hand. "There ain't much to see. It ain't like when Miss Esther performed here. No more real acting at all. Goddamn hootchie-kootchie dancers and shimmy-shakers is all we got now. Almost as bad as the houses in Union Square."

"You the owner?"

"Hell no. I'd show plays if I owned this dump. Nah, I'm just the stage manager. Now I'll show you what this place used to be like."

He led me to a small office, its walls covered with more photographs than hung in Margie's parlor. Taking a scrapbook from a desk drawer, he laid it open and said, "This is what it was like when Miss Esther was performing. Here's the first show." He pointed at a cast photo. *Uncle Tom's Cabin* was lettered in white paint at the top of the photo. "There she is," he said. "Little Eva." Esther Kelly was easily recognizable, looking not much different from the way she did now.

In the bottom right corner of the picture, the white paint said 1876. That's . . . thirty-eight years ago. If Esther Kelly was six when she appeared in *Uncle Tom's Cabin,* she must be in her mid-40's now, at least ten years older than I would have guessed.

"Is this date right?" I asked.

"Sure is. That's what gave the theater its name. The U. S. of A. was a century old that year."

"Do you ever see her anymore?" I asked.

He didn't answer for a minute. "She comes around sometimes."

"Like she did a month ago?"

"Yeah. She gets a little . . . well, lost sometimes. And she comes by. This is no kind of place for a lady like her. So I take her home."

I thanked him for his time and left.

My hunch had paid off. I hoped I still had enough luck left to snare Florence Hampton's killer. If luck was a bat, I'd just used up a hit.

# Chapter Twenty-Five

I didn't want to go west. Not now.

Even though it would be a relief to get out of the line of fire, away from attempts to poison me or bash in my skull, I didn't want to leave. I wanted to stay in the city until the murder of Florence Hampton was resolved. I was so close to wrapping it up. All I needed was proof.

It was Saturday morning, eight-thirty, and I had an hour to get to Grand Central Station for the start of the road trip to Pittsburgh, Cincinnati, Chicago, and St. Louis. We would be away from New York for two weeks . . . two weeks away from Margie.

I tried to call her at the studio, to hear her voice again before I left. She was tied up and couldn't be bothered. The kind of scenes she did, "tied up" could be literal.

Then I called Karl Landfors at the *Press*. He was starting to be a good second choice when Margie wasn't available. Landfors wasn't tied up, and I got through.

"You see the *Public Examiner* today?" he asked.

A rock blossomed in my stomach. "No." In fact, I'd made a point of not looking at that paper anymore.

"Interesting headline," Landfors said wryly. *"What Does He Have Against the Dodgers?* it says."

"Is the 'he' me?"

"Yes, indeed. Another article by William Murray. Appears he found out that you were with the Dodger batboy in a pool hall 'where you went to stir up trouble just before he was killed.' "

"That was a *week* before he was killed!"

"That's not the way the story reads. Anyway, he makes an interesting connection. He 'reminds' people that you're a suspect in Florence Hampton's death and that she owned part of the Dodgers. Then he suggests you killed the batboy. And finally he predicts you're going to kill a player if you're not stopped. Says it's because you can't beat them on the field."

"I'm going to kill *Murray* if *he* isn't stopped!"

"Calm down. Nobody takes him seriously. None of the mainstream papers have picked up on this. By the way, he says Casey Stengel is your next target."

Jeez. What a load—

"Actually," Landfors said, "you won't have to worry about him much longer."

"Why not?"

"When my sister's murderer is caught, he can't continue to call you a suspect."

How did Landfors know I was on to the killer? "Uh . . . what do you mean?"

"Let's just say that you don't need to do any more investigating."

"You mean *you* know—"

"Yes, I do."

"Who was it?" I wanted to know if we'd come to the same conclusion.

"I'd prefer not to say yet. Not until I have proof."

"Tell me. We can put the information we have together."

He paused. "No," he decided. "I'm planning to take care of it myself."

Fine. You don't tell me your murderer, I won't tell you mine.

We were at an impasse, so after a little more fruitless back and forth we hung up.

Then I wondered what he meant about planning to take care of it himself. If he tried something stupid . . .

Now it wasn't just Margie that I wanted to stay in town for. I wanted to get Florence Hampton's killer behind bars before Landfors got himself in trouble.

Those quiet, harmless-looking guys. They're the ones you have to watch out for. When they get riled, they can really go berserk.

• • •

That night, as we rattled west through Pennsylvania, I struggled my way into the upper berth of a Pullman sleeper. I fidgeted in the bunk, simmering in the heat and absorbing the aromas of its previous occupants. Pullman beds were notorious, apparently designed for maximum discomfort. Now it seemed worse than usual, as I thought about having Margie next to me. I never felt so alone as I did lying sleepless in the sleeper car.

Eventually, I began to imagine the curtain-shrouded berth as a cocoon, where I was shielded from the outside world. I used the isolation to gather my thoughts on the Hampton investigation, organizing them where they fit together and mentally cataloging the missing pieces I had yet to fill in.

I already was two for four: I knew who killed Florence Hampton and who poisoned the champagne I drank.

Then there were two murders I wasn't so sure about: William Daley's and Larry Harron's. I wasn't sure in my head, anyway, although my gut was certain. I had to work backward with those deaths; instead of establishing means, motive, and opportunity to identify the killer, I had to start by knowing who the killer was and then trying to figure out how and why.

And there were those "accidents"—the spotlight that almost killed Margie in the pool and the bottle that smashed over my head. The spotlight had had a string tied to its leg. I knew that was no accident. And I wasn't sure about the switched bottles being a mistake. What bothered me about these incidents was the change in method. Although Karl Landfors said a murderer might change tactics if he was desperate. Maybe the killer knew I was getting close.

So I continued to think.

By the time the train arrived in Pittsburgh, the only conclusion I'd come to was that lying alone in a Pullman berth was torture compared to being in a bed in Brooklyn with Margie curled up next to me.

•  •  •

Monday was Labor Day. For many, it signaled the end of summer, and men would soon be discarding their straw hats. The tradition was to buy a new boater every Memorial Day and destroy it after Labor Day. I measured summer differently and had my own tradition: I put on a new hat when the opening game of the baseball season was played and continued to wear it until the last out of the World Series. Except for the ones I left floating in the Luna Park swimming pool and covering the pale dead face of Florence Hampton.

On this day, however, I wasn't thinking of death. My thoughts were solely on baseball as I sat in the visitors' dugout of Forbes Field, the only ballpark in America named after a British general. We were playing a holiday double-header against the Pittsburgh Pirates.

My teammates were anyway. Determined to keep pace with the Braves, John McGraw decided he would play only the regulars, no utility players, and was limiting the pitching rotation to three men: Mathewson, Tesreau, and Marquard. I was a spectator. And, though I would never admit it to McGraw, that was okay.

I got to sit back and watch Honus Wagner, the old Flying Dutchman, play baseball. For two games, eighteen innings, the forty-year-old Wagner put on an exhibition of how the game should be played—slashing line drive hits, stealing bases, snaring everything hit to him at shortstop. I never could understand how a man so awkward looking, so bow-legged and ham-fisted, could play the game's most elegant position so superbly. But those bowlegs carried the Dutch-man around the bases with the same dash and brilliance as Ty Cobb. And those huge hands of his would shovel up any grounder hit to the left side of the infield; he'd scoop up about a bucketful of dirt with the ball and throw most of it along toward first, but he'd nail the runner. And through it all, he had as much fun as a kid playing a sandlot game. His rough homely face—much like Casey Stengel's, only more so—was lit up with the sheer joy of playing.

With Honus Wagner leading the Pirates' attack, Pitts-burgh swept both games. We took no consolation from the fact that the man who beat us was the player McGraw himself rated as the best in baseball history. The Boston Braves had won both ends of a doubleheader at home. Their first-place lead was now three games.

At the hotel, I tried telephoning Margie again. Again she was busy at the studio. We didn't connect until later that night when I reached her at home. "How are things at the studio?" I asked her, though I didn't care about the studio.

"Crazy. I think Mr. Garvin has lost his mind."

"Why? What's he doing?"

"It's what he's not doing. You remember he couldn't do anything with the scenes we shot at Coney Island?"

"Yeah . . ."

"It's the same with the pie-throwing movie. He just doesn't know how to do longer pictures. So you know what he's going to do now?"

"Uh-uh. What?"

"He's actually going to let Mr. Carlyle film his *Hamlet* movie. Shows how desperate Mr. Garvin is. Well, it's sweet in a way, I suppose. Mr. Carlyle's a ham, but he's like a little kid having his dream come true. So, that's a long answer, but the studio's been crazy. How are you?"

"Oh, okay. I'm not playing, we're losing, and . . . and I miss you." What was in my head just slipped right out of my mouth.

After a second, she said softly, "I miss you, too."

Then we were quiet. I didn't know what else to say. I didn't want to get mushier and I couldn't go back to small talk. So I promised to call again soon.

• • •

The road trip went on. One more game in Pittsburgh, which we won, then to Cincinnati, where the last place team swept us. The Braves had a five and a half game lead over us, and we knew it was almost over.

I continued to miss Margie, despite calling her every other day. And I fretted over what Karl Landfors might be up to.

There was one advantage to being away from New York: with no chance to question people or get evidence, I made the most out of reviewing every bit of information I already had. The picture slowly became clearer to me, and my mind continued to work over the crimes, trying to answer the questions that remained.

After dropping three out of four games to the Cubs, the team gathered at the Illinois Central station on Randolph Street. We waited on the platform for the train that would take us to St. Louis, our last stop. I sat on my suitcase, feeling grateful that it was a short enough trip that we didn't need a Pullman train.

And one more piece of the puzzle slipped neatly into place.

When we arrived in St. Louis, I made two phone calls and had just about all of it figured out.

•  •  •

It was three days before we'd be back in New York, and I was worried about Landfors. I tried calling him at the *Press* to see what he was up to. I decided that if he sounded close to doing something reckless, I'd tell him all I knew.

He wasn't there. A secretary at the paper told me he hadn't been in for a week. What was that guy up to?

Landfors was forcing me to act. I wasn't going to get much more evidence. Could I get the killer to confess? Set a trap maybe? I'd have to try.

I called Margie. This time she was second choice for a phone call. She gave me the daily news: Arthur Carlyle's *Hamlet* was starting production, the Brooklyn Tip-Tops were on a six-game winning streak, and she wished I'd be back soon.

What I told Margie was far less routine. I didn't tell her everything but enough for now.

# Chapter Twenty-Six

I danced off second base, taking a long lead as Sloppy Sutherland went into his stretch. He spun, threw to the shortstop who snuck in behind me, and I dove headfirst back to the bag, my hand barely reaching it before the swiping tag came down on my wrist.

"Safe!" called the base ump.

Twenty thousand Dodger fans hooted in disagreement.

I called time, and stood up to brush myself off. The crowd continued booing and yelling. They packed Ebbets Field this Saturday morning to see the Dodgers eliminate us from the pennant race. There was no question that the Braves would win it. They had a nine game lead with only nine games left to play, and the Brooklyn fans wanted the death blow dealt to us in Flatbush.

As I stood on the bag, I was suddenly sent back to another Saturday less than two months ago. August first. Just like today, the Giants' Christy Mathewson facing Sloppy Sutherland before the screaming patrons of Ebbets Field. But then there had been Florence Hampton seated in a box seat, waving her handkerchief, cheering her Dodger team. Now she was dead. And the hunchbacked Brooklyn batboy was gone from the scene, too. Also dead.

No! My mind was drifting off the game. This had never happened to me before; between the foul lines, I never thought of anything but the game in progress.

"Time!" I called.

"You already got time," the umpire growled. "What's your problem?"

"Uh, twisted ankle. Let me walk it off."

"Go 'head," he grudgingly agreed.

To the loudening hoots of the crowd, I walked on the outfield grass, trying to clear my head. Okay, two outs, top of the ninth, tie game, and who the hell ransacked my apartment while we were out of town—no, worry about that later. Should I be pretending to limp? Did I tell the ump which ankle was twisted? Tomorrow, it will all be over. Florence Hampton's killer will be in jail. Baseball, baseball, dammit! Get your mind on the game . . .

"C'mon. Let's get this show on the road!" Bill Klem bellowed from behind the plate. I went back to the base.

The show. After the game, I'd be off to the Vitagraph studio, seeing Margie for the first time since the road trip. . . . You're going to get picked off, if you don't get your head straight.

I took only a two-step lead off the bag, almost frozen, trapped between memories of the past and plans for the future, barely aware of what was happening now.

On Sutherland's next pitch, Fred Merkle hit a shallow loop single to right field. The sound of wood on horsehide exorcised all nonbaseball thoughts from my brain and sent me racing for third. I didn't think it was hit long enough for me to score, but McGraw windmilled his arms sending me home. It was risky, but the strategy was right: play for a win on the road, a tie at home. I took a sharp turn at third, so hard that I almost skidded into the waving McGraw.

The final sprint home, and I saw Casey Stengel's throw coming into the plate. All the way on the fly, no cut-off. I was going to be out.

The throw was just off the mark, on the first base side of the plate, and Virgil Ewing had to move up the line to field it. I went into a wide hook slide away from him, as he swept across with the tag. And he missed me!

I sprung up, confident that I'd scored the go-ahead run. But as I trotted in to join my cheering teammates in the dugout, I didn't hear any call by Bill Klem. I turned my head. Klem was standing with his arms crossed behind his back, bobbing up and down on his toes. No call.

Oh, jeez. I must have missed the plate when I slid. I hustled to the farthest end of the bench and took a seat trying to look inconspicuous. If Sutherland threw the next pitch, my run would count. I just had to hope—

"He missed the plate!" Wilbert Robinson screamed from the Brooklyn dugout.

Damn!

All he had to do was step on the plate, but instead Virgil Ewing spun toward the Giants' dugout, and lumbered to the end of the bench nearest him. With the ball in his bare right hand, he started working his way up the line of players, tagging each one.

Hell, I wasn't going to just sit and wait to be tagged out. I jumped up and sprinted past him. He lunged and missed me. But I still had to touch home plate.

Sutherland broke in from the mound to cover the plate. Ewing tossed the ball to him. I skidded to a stop, and headed back toward Ewing.

Hah! It worked. I caught Sutherland off guard—instead of

stepping on the plate, he flipped the ball back to Ewing. I was now in a rundown between home plate and the dugout.

I changed direction again.

Sutherland realized his mistake and waved his glove, screaming, "Throw it! Throw it!"

Ewing yelled back, "I'll get the sonofabitch myself!" Not a smart thing to yell. Did he think I couldn't hear him?

Knowing there would be no more throws, I sprinted headlong for home, with the sound of Ewing's shin guards rattling behind me as he gave futile chase. I stepped full in the middle of the plate, and Bill Klem called, "Safe!"

I trotted triumphantly back to the Giants' dugout. A rundown between home plate and the dugout—only in Brooklyn.

From the bench, I watched contentedly as Ewing and Sutherland started quarrelling, then shoving, then throwing punches. This time they weren't faking it.

• • •

My run did hold up for the win, deferring for at least another day elimination from the pennant race. The victory did nothing to endear me to the Dodger partisans at the Vitagraph studio, and their greetings when I arrived were decidedly cool.

Except for Margie's. Her greeting was a long kiss and a tight hug. Then a few more kisses. She made it hard to keep my mind on what I had to do today.

"Are they still planning to finish the picture today?" I asked her. The studio had been set up like the inside of a castle, and the actors and actresses were all wearing the costumes of knights and ladies.

She nodded. "They only have one more scene to film. Mr.

Carlyle had them shoot it exactly like a stage play. In sequence and with every line spoken."

"But it's a movie. Nobody will be able to hear them."

"That's the way he wants it. He says nobody is going to meddle with his *Hamlet.* You'd think he wrote it instead of Shakespeare."

"Elmer Garvin is going along with him?"

"He doesn't know what else to do. I think Mr. Garvin's relieved, really. None of the long movies he was trying to make worked out. Now he just has to keep a camera rolling while Mr. Carlyle takes care of the rest."

"Where is Carlyle?"

"In the dressing room, I think."

"Okay," I sighed. "Let me talk to him."

She let me go, after another hug.

Arthur V. Carlyle was alone in the men's dressing room. He stood before a mirror, adjusting and smoothing his costume. He was dressed all in black—tights that weren't flattering to his knobby knees, a loose woolen shirt, and a velvet cape attached with a gold clasp. Gold was the only other color he wore—heavy chains hung around his neck, and a tight gold belt girded his waist. A small dagger was tucked in the front of the belt, and a dueling sword hung from its side. His hair had been dyed so that not a trace of gray showed. He looked as he had on the poster I'd seen in the Somerville Theater.

"Mr. Carlyle," I said.

He turned slowly to face me. "Ah, Mr. Rawlings."

I dug into my jacket pocket and pulled out a rolled up handkerchief. I took a step toward Carlyle as I unfolded the cloth. Then I held up the small syringe that had been wrapped in it. "This what you were looking for when you broke into my apartment?" I asked.

Carlyle chuckled. "My boy, I did no such thing. I suspect it was a Mr. William Murray of the *Public Examiner* who did that. He seems to have something of a vendetta against you, by the way. Come to think of it, I do seem to recall speaking to him on the telephone a few days ago. And I might have mentioned to him that you had something hidden in your residence that would incriminate you in Miss Hampton's death . . . and that you were out of town in the event somebody wanted to uncover this evidence." He added with a disapproving sniff, "Apparently, Mr. Murray is not a very capable burglar."

Apparently, he wasn't much of a music fan either. If Murray had cranked up my Victrola, he would have heard a strange rattling sound.

"Margie told you the deal," I said. "And you agreed to it."

"Did you expect me to concede without a fight?"

"It's over. You know it's over. Accept it. I will stick to my offer: I won't tell the police until the picture is finished. Then you turn yourself in."

In a flash, his sword was unsheathed and its tip pressed against my Adam's apple. "And if I choose not to accept your offer?" he taunted. The swiftness of his move was more shocking to me than the result.

I backed away, but he stayed with me, walking forward and keeping the pressure on my throat. The prop sword wasn't razor-sharp, but it had enough of a point that it was a hair away from puncturing my throat.

Stay calm, stay calm, I told myself. My impulse was to knock the sword aside and tackle him. But that could force his hand, and I would be impaled. The thing to do was remain composed and firm. If I showed a belief that there was no chance of him killing me, maybe he'd get that feeling, too. "Margie and I aren't the only ones who know," I mumbled, trying to speak without moving my larynx. "Look at the syringe. There's no needle on it. It's already being tested for arsenic." Actually, the needle was still stuck in the sound chamber of my Victrola where it had broken off.

Carlyle didn't remove his eyes from mine, but I saw some hesitancy in them and the pressure of the sword eased slightly.

He stood back from me, his arm holding the sword straight out. Why hadn't he gone for the dagger? It looked far more deadly than the sword.

Hah! I *was* right about him. He didn't have what it took to kill close up and personal. With growing confidence, I said, "This isn't your style, Mr. Carlyle. Leaving poison for somebody to drink or tying a string around a spotlight and pulling it or switching bottles for somebody else to hit me on the head. *That's* the way you do things."

"I didn't switch the bottles," Carlyle said quietly. "Somebody was just careless with them. *I* am not careless."

I took that as an admission to the other attempts. "No, you're not. You planned things very carefully. Especially William Daley's murder. That was nicely done."

Carlyle acknowledged the compliment with a nod and a smile. I was back on plan, using the best weapon I had against him: his own ego.

"You arranged to be in a play," I went on, "during the first part of the world baseball tour. It gave you an alibi. The problem was the theater crowds were too good, even though your performances were so bad—"

His eyes blazed. "Only because I *wanted* them to be bad. I was playing the role of a bad actor."

"Understood," I acknowledged. "So you claimed laryngitis to get out of the contract . . . because you had to get on a boat to England. In time to take the *Lusitania* back to the

United States with William Daley. You disguised yourself as a waiter?"

"A steward. And it's a ship, not a boat."

"And you poisoned William Daley because he cheated you out of your money."

"It wasn't the money. It was my dream. He almost scuttled my dream of recording *Hamlet* on film."

Carlyle's hand trembled slightly and the blade of the sword wobbled. Then he dropped his arm and lowered his head. "You're right," he admitted. "I'm not much of a murderer. I can't kill you." He tensed as if expecting me to attack him; I still held back. Then he lifted his head again. "I *am* an actor," he said with deep pride. "Allow me to perform my final scene, and I shall confess to the police."

As he moved to the door, I stopped him with a hand on his arm. "One more question. Why try to kill Virgil Ewing? That was you, too, wasn't it?"

Carlyle said matter-of-factly, "Yes, that one was rather easy. I played a locker room attendant—"

"It's called a clubhouse man."

He smiled. "Yes, well, I simply went in with a stack of towels. An old theater trick: directing the audience's attention where you want it. If you're bringing somebody something they want, they look at *it*, not at the person who's carrying it."

"Like if you bring them a bottle of champagne."

"Exactly." And another smile crossed his face.

"But why Ewing? How does he fit in?"

"The same principle: misdirection. You were getting a little too inquisitive. I thought if Mr. Ewing was to be killed, you would direct your attention to Mr. Sutherland or one of Miss Hampton's other suitors."

"An innocent twelve-year-old boy *died* just because you wanted to throw me off your track."

"Yes. So?"

The deal's off.

I swung my fist up, then held back. I had to let Carlyle go ahead with his scene. I still needed him to confess.

I opened the dressing room door and through clenched teeth said, "After you, Mr. Carlyle."

•   •   •

The actors and actresses, wearing garish makeup and elaborate costumes that were no doubt designed by Carlyle, were all in position. Elmer Garvin barked, "Start camera!" and the cameraman cranked away.

Arthur Carlyle stood center stage and began his dialogue, "Come, for the third, Laertes . . ." He spoke loudly, as if forcing the film to record his voice as well. He spoke strange words that made no sense to me, and I thought there were advantages to pictures being silent.

I stopped listening to the words and just watched the action, eager for the conclusion. Margie stood next to me, our hands locked together.

There was a sword fight between Carlyle and another character, the two of them swapped weapons, people started stabbing each other. All this to the accompaniment of the actors' loud jabbering. It looked like everyone was dead, so I figured it must be just about over.

Arthur Carlyle lifted a golden goblet to his lips and drank. "O, I die, Horatio . . ." He fell to the floor and began writhing overdramatically.

"What the hell is he doing?" I whispered to Margie.

"It's the death scene," she answered.

He was dragging it out, talking and talking as his body twitched in exaggerated convulsions. "So tell him, with the occurrents, more and less . . ."

Finally, he stopped talking and lay still.

"Is it over?" I asked.

"Yes," Margie said. "That's the end."

But the camera kept rolling, and another actor bent over Carlyle's body reciting, "Now cracks a noble . . ."

I turned to Margie. "You said—" I was taken aback by the peculiar smile on her face.

"Goodnight, sweet prince," boomed from the stage. "And flights of—Hey! He's not breathing!"

• • •

After Arthur V. Carlyle's body was carried out of the studio, and the police had gotten statements from everyone present, Margie and I ducked out into the parking lot.

I pulled her between a milk truck and a fire engine and whispered, "What did you do?"

"*I* didn't do anything," she insisted. "Mr. Carlyle probably decided there was no reason to live. His film was completed and he was facing the electric chair. So he used his death scene for a dramatic exit."

"I didn't expect that. I had no idea he would commit suicide. Now he can't confess."

"Does it matter?" she asked.

"What do you mean 'does it matter'? We don't have enough evidence to prove to the police that Carlyle killed anyone."

"But if he's dead, what difference does it make? He murdered other people, now he killed himself. Doesn't that work out even?" There was a logic there, but I wasn't sure what it was, and I wasn't sure I agreed with it.

Maybe if Margie and I both testified about what Carlyle had told us, we could still go to the police. "When you talked to him," I asked her, "what did he say? Did he admit anything to you?"

"Yes. He was very open about it. He seemed proud of what he'd done, almost gloating."

"What exactly did he say?"

Margie shook her head. "No. First you tell me how you knew about him and why you didn't tell me before."

"I didn't want to tell you until I was sure. And when I was sure, I thought it would be safer for you not to tell you everything. The less you knew, the less incentive Carlyle would have to kill you."

"Oh, okay," she said, but I could tell she disagreed with my reasoning. "So, how *did* you know he killed Libby?"

It was embarrassingly simple. "I saw him do it. I just didn't know it until that pie-throwing movie a couple of weeks ago."

"When you got kaboshed with the bottle."

"Yeah. Turned out that really was an accident. Anyway, Arthur Carlyle was dressed as a waiter, and I recognized him. He was the waiter at the Sea Dip Hotel, the one I tried to get some champagne from, he ignored me and brought it to where Florence Hampton and Esther Kelly were sitting. That's how he poisoned her. Lucky for Esther that she really *wasn't* drinking."

"But he came to the party late."

I remembered the word Carlyle used. "Misdirection. If you remember, he made a big fuss when he arrived. That way nobody would suspect he had been there earlier, in another costume."

"And he used the same costume two weeks ago?"

I nodded. "Garvin told me that he had standard disguises for each role he played. He probably *couldn't* change the way he did things. I think he took some precaution though. He put those glasses on me so I could hardly see anything through them. It was his bad luck that I had to lift them up just to find my way around. So I saw him. And I knew."

"Wow," was all Margie said.

"Okay, your turn. What happened when you talked to Carlyle?"

"Well, I told him what you said. That we knew he killed Libby and William Daley and that he tried to kill you. But if he turned himself in, we wouldn't say anything until his movie was finished. He didn't believe me at first, so I told him to check his makeup box and see if his needle was there. How did you know about the needle?"

"When we were filming at Steeplechase Park and everybody was getting ready with their costumes and everything, Carlyle was at his makeup kit on the back of a truck. But he was *directing* that day, so what did he need makeup for? I didn't remember that until I woke up in the dressing room after the bottle knocked me out. I knew that a needle had been used to put arsenic in the champagne we took to the beach, so I checked his box and there it was."

"Oh. Well, that convinced him. Mr. Carlyle admitted to me that he poisoned Libby at the party. He said he followed her when she left. She was terribly sick but still alive he said. He stripped off her clothes and dropped her off the pier to drown. He thought people would assume she'd gone swimming with Virgil Ewing."

"See, Ewing asked her to go swimming before Carlyle made his grand entrance. He had to be there earlier. Maybe we do have enough to go to the police after all. Did he say anything else?"

"No. I did mention something else to *him,* though. I told him about a rat I'd seen in the ladies' dressing room once."

*"What?"*

"It was a big gray rat, and he must have eaten some poison. He was rolling and twitching. I told Mr. Carlyle it was the most spectacular death you could imagine, much more dramatic than any actor I'd ever seen. And I told him I thought they used strychnine in rat poison." She smiled innocently. "Do you think the police would be interested in any of that?"

Probably, I thought. What I said was, "You're right. Carlyle's dead. What difference does it make?"

## Chapter Twenty-Seven

I knocked gently on the door of Karl Landfors's Greenwich Village apartment. In all the time I knew him, I'd never been here before.

"Come in, it's all ready," he yelled through the door.

What was ready? I hadn't told him I was coming. I swung my equipment bag onto my shoulder and pushed through the unlocked door.

Landfors's cramped apartment looked just like his office, with bookcases and file cabinets the principal furnishings. Books, papers, and maps overflowed the shelves and drawers; they were strewn about the rest of the furniture and spilled over onto the floor. Two spindly logs smoldered in a small brick fireplace to ward off the chill of the cool autumn morning. Landfors was seated at a desk next to it, with his back to the door.

"Karl, it's me," I said, stepping around a steamer trunk just inside the door.

He swiveled around in his chair to face me. "Mickey! I thought you were the porter."

"What porter?"

"For the trunk."

"Oh. No. I came to—I brought you something." I reached into my bag and pulled out a round metal can. I placed it on his desk. "It's Arthur Carlyle's last scene . . . where he dies. This is the only print." I pulled out another can. "And this is the negative."

Landfors looked bewildered. "How did you get these?" he asked.

"A friend got them for me."

"Who?"

"Oh, somebody who knows the layout of the Vitagraph studio and is agile enough to get in through a window at night."

"Ah. Well, that was nice of her," Landfors said.

"Anyway, I thought you might want to see it. Carlyle's death is probably the closest thing to justice that's ever going to come out of all this."

He stared down at the cans, expressionless.

"The way the police figure," I went on, "is Carlyle took the strychnine to make the scene look more dramatic. They don't know he also did it to avoid being arrested."

Landfors abruptly asked, "Didn't you wonder why Vitagraph suddenly decided to film *Hamlet?*"

"No, not really. They filmed all kinds of things."

"They have two studios at Vitagraph: one for dramas and one for comedies. Didn't it strike you as strange that Studio B, the *comedy* studio, was filming *Hamlet?*"

Until yesterday, I didn't know that *Hamlet wasn't* a comedy. "No."

"I arranged it."

*"You* did?"

With a grunt of exertion, Landfors lifted a massive red scrapbook from a shelf above his desk. "Like most show people, Libby kept a record of everything she did in her career. And it's all here—playbills, photographs, newspaper clippings . . ." He laid the leather-bound book open on the desk and slowly started turning the pages. "I couldn't bring myself to look through it until a couple of weeks ago." Stopping at a spot where two pages were sealed together, he slipped a forefinger between them. "In here I found a playbill and a news article. The interesting thing is that they weren't about her. They were about Arthur Carlyle. The program was from the play he was in during the world baseball tour, and the clipping was about him leaving the show early. Libby must have had some suspicions about Carlyle—"

"And if Carlyle caught on that she suspected him, that was his motive to kill her," I finished.

Landfors nodded. "Exactly."

"But why would you arrange to have his *Hamlet* movie made? What would that accomplish . . . except giving him what he wanted all along?"

"It was going to be released as a *comedy*. I was to write comic title cards for the picture. Carlyle would have been humiliated."

"All you wanted to do was *embarrass* him? What the hell kind of revenge is that?"

"Well, this isn't *proof* of anything. See, I thought I could get Carlyle to break down. That movie was his dream, his shot at immortality; it's what he lived for . . . and what he killed for. I thought that if he saw his dream shattered, that it was all over for him, perhaps he would give it up, tell us what happened to William Daley and how he did it."

This was a *plan?* Landfors had better never again make fun of any of my ideas.

"I know how he did it," I said. It was while waiting for the train in Chicago that I realized the world baseball tour wasn't a continuous trip. They'd left on *The Empress of China* and returned on the *Lusitania.* A couple of phone calls to Boston gave me the schedules of the shipping lines. I explained to Landfors, "Carlyle left the play in Somerville just in time to catch a ship to Liverpool. When he got there, he turned right around and came back on the *Lusitania* as a crew member. And he served Daley a poisoned dinner."

Landfors began tapping one of the cans of film. "So he thought this was going to make him immortal, huh?" He stood and twisted open the cannister. "No, I don't think I need to see it." With that, he dumped the roll of celluloid into the fire. As the film burned, shriveling and melting in the heat, he added the negative to the blaze.

"I found something else my sister saved," Landfors said as the fire died down. "Letters from William Murray. He wrote them back when he was a theater critic. Appears he was quite infatuated with Libby, and he offered to give her favorable reviews if she returned his affection. She must have declined because his later reviews of her were vicious." He handed me a bundle of letters tied together with a ribbon. "I thought I would pass these on to one of the *Public Examiner*'s rival scandal sheets. The only thing they enjoy more than smearing public figures is attacking their competition. It should get Murray off your back."

I couldn't see any reason to have Florence Hampton's name appear in yet another scandal sheet. She'd gone through enough. I tossed the bundle in the fire and the flames burned brightly for a few more minutes.

Karl and I stood and watched until the embers no longer glowed.

• • •

A month later, the World Series was over; the Miracle Boston Braves swept the Philadelphia Athletics in four games. Another season gone, another Fall Classic that I could follow only from the newspaper accounts.

Karl Landfors was in France. Just after I'd left his apartment, a porter picked up his steamer trunk, and Landfors took off for Europe to cover the war. He told me he thought it would take longer than most people were saying, years maybe. And he predicted the United States would eventually get involved in the conflict.

Marguerite Turner was gone, too. Gone from Vitagraph and from New York, on a train to California to make pictures with D. W. Griffith. She left with the promise to come back when the moving picture craze was over. Deep down, I didn't expect to see her again.

Before Margie left, she talked to Esther Kelly, to explain about the Century Theatre and reassure her about the memory lapses. I talked to her husband Tom and gave him Peter Kurtz's business card in case he wanted to give baseball another try.

With Landfors in Europe, Margie in California, and no baseball to play, I was at a loss to find something to occupy me. I thought of asking Casey Stengel to tell me a story—I figured one of his yarns could go on for months—but he was on an exhibition trip to Cuba with the rest of the Dodgers team.

I was facing a long winter alone.

In November, the Federal League announced that Sloppy Sutherland and Virgil Ewing had signed with the Brooklyn Tip-Tops for 1915. Billy Claypool, true to his word, sent me the contract I'd signed for me to destroy. The next month, I read that Tom Kelly had signed with the Feds to manage and play for their Buffalo franchise.

As the weeks went on, I followed Karl Landfors's battle reports in the *New York Press* and hoped he would come back soon and in one piece. I read in the movie magazines about Margie Turner's upcoming films with D. W. Griffith and wished she would return in any condition at all.

It seemed all I was doing was reading about people I could no longer see in person. Reading wasn't the thing for me. What I needed was the feel of the horsehide in my hand, not the smudge of news ink on my fingers.

My spirits didn't pick up until I received a contract from John McGraw to play with the New York Giants for the 1915 season. I realized I did have things to look forward to. After winter would come spring—spring training.

Then opening day in April. New grass on the infield soft and green, bunting-draped bleachers filled with cheering fans, the crack of the bat, and the feel of a leather mitt on my hand . . .

There would be the rebirth that comes with spring. All teams would be even in the standings, each with an equal shot at the pennant. All players would start the season with the same batting average. Never mind .250, I could end up hitting .400!

And at the end of season, maybe I'd be in the World Series.

I would just have to wait till next year.